KT-561-136

Contents

DICK KING-SMITH

THE BIG

PIG BOOK

Three favourite stories

THE SHEEP-PIG • ACE • DAGGIE DOGFOOT

TED SMART

HAMISH HAMILTON LTD

Published by the Penguin Group
Penguin Books Ltd, 27 Wrights Lane, London W8 5TZ, England
Penguin Putnam Inc., 375 Hudson Street, New York, New York 10014, USA
Penguin Books Australia Ltd, Ringwood, Victoria, Australia
Penguin Books Canada Ltd, 10 Alcorn Avenue, Toronto, Ontario, Canada M4V
3B2
Penguin Books (NZ) Ltd, Private Bag 102902, NSMC, Auckland, New Zealand

Penguin Books Ltd, Registered Offices: Harmondsworth, Middlesex, England

First published 1998
1 3 5 7 9 10 8 6 4 2

The Sheep-Pig first published by Victor Gollancz Ltd 1983
Published in Puffin Books 1985
Text copyright © Dick King-Smith, 1983
Illustrations copyright © Mary Rayner, 1983

Ace first published by Victor Gollancz Ltd 1990
Published in Puffin Books 1991
Text copyright © Fox Busters Ltd, 1990
Illustrations copyright © Liz Graham-Yooll, 1990

The moral right of the author and illustrator has been asserted

Daggie Dogfoot first published by Victor Gollancz Ltd 1980
Published in Puffin Books 1982
Text copyright © Dick King-Smith, 1980
Illustrations copyright © Mary Rayner, 1980

Made and printed in England by The Bath Press

Without limiting the rights under copyright reserved above, no part of this
publication may be reproduced, stored in or introduced into a retrieval system,
or transmitted, in any form or by any means (electronic, mechanical,
photocopying, recording or otherwise), without the prior written permission of
both the copyright owner and the above publisher of this book

British Library Cataloguing in Publication Data
A CIP catalogue record for this book is available from the British Library

ISBN 0–241–14052–8

This edition printed for

The Book People Ltd, Hall Wood Avenue, Haydock, St Helens, WA11 9UL

THE
BIG
PIG BOOK

Some other books by Dick King-Smith

THE CUCKOO CHILD
DODOS ARE FOREVER
DRAGON BOY
FIND THE WHITE HORSE
THE FOX BUSTERS
HARRY'S MAD
HOW GREEN WAS MY MOUSE
LADY DAISY
MAGNUS POWERMOUSE
MARTIN'S MICE
THE MERMAN
THE MERRYTHOUGHT
THE MOUSE BUTCHER
NOAH'S BROTHER
PADDY'S POT OF GOLD
PRETTY POLLY
THE QUEEN'S NOSE
SADDLEBOTTOM
THE SCHOOLMOUSE
THE STRAY
THE TERRIBLE TRINS
THE TOBY MAN
TREASURE TROVE
TUMBLEWEED
THE WATER HORSE

Picture book

THE SPOTTY PIG

For younger readers

ANIMAL STORIES
BLESSU
CLEVER DUCK
DUMPLING
GEORGE SPEAKS
THE GHOST AT CODLIN
CASTLE AND OTHER STORIES
THE HODGEHEG
A HODGEHEG STORY:
KING MAX THE LAST
THE INVISIBLE DOG
MR POTTER'S PET
A NARROW SQUEAK AND
OTHER ANIMAL STORIES
PHILIBERT THE FIRST AND
OTHER STORIES
SMASHER
THE SWOOSE

Read It Yourself books

HOGSEL AND GRUNTEL
HUGE RED RIDING HOOD
THE JENIUS
ROBIN HOOD AND
HIS MISERABLE MEN
THINDERELLA
TRIFFIC: A RARE PIG'S TALE

THE
SHEEP-PIG

Illustrated by Mary Rayner

CHAPTER I

"Guess my weight"

"What's that noise?" said Mrs Hogget, sticking her comfortable round red face out of the kitchen window. "Listen, there 'tis again, did you hear it, what a racket, what a row, anybody'd think someone was being murdered, oh dearie me, whatever is it, just listen to it, will you?"

Farmer Hogget listened. From the usually quiet valley below the farm came a medley of sounds: the oompah oompah of a brass band, the shouts of children, the rattle and thump of a skittle alley, and every now and then a very high, very loud, very angry-sounding squealing lasting perhaps ten seconds.

Farmer Hogget pulled out an old pocket-watch as big round as a saucer and looked at it. "Fair starts at two," he said. "It's started."

"I knows that," said Mrs Hogget, "because I'm late now with all theseyer cakes and jams and pickles and preserves as is meant to be on the Produce Stall this very minute, and who's going to take them there, I'd like to know, why you are, but afore you does, what's that noise?"

4

The squealing sounded again.

"That noise?"

Mrs Hogget nodded a great many times. Everything that she did was done at great length, whether it was speaking or simply nodding her head. Farmer Hogget, on the other hand, never wasted his energies or his words.

"Pig," he said.

Mrs Hogget nodded a lot more.

"I thought 'twas a pig, I said to meself that's a pig that is, only nobody round here do keep pigs, 'tis all sheep for miles about, what's a pig doing, I said to meself, anybody'd think they was killing the poor thing, have a look when you take all this stuff down, which you better do now, come and give us a hand, it can go in the back of the Land Rover, 'tisn't raining, 'twon't hurt, wipe your boots afore you comes in."

"Yes," said Farmer Hogget.

When he had driven down to the village and made his delivery to the Produce Stall, Farmer Hogget walked across the green, past the Hoopla Stall and the Coconut Shy and the Aunt Sally and the skittles and the band, to the source of the squealing noise, which came every now and again from a small pen of hurdles in a far corner, against the churchyard wall.

By the pen sat the Vicar, notebook in hand, a cardboard box on the table in front of him. On the hurdles hung a notice—'Guess my weight. Ten pence a go.' Inside was a little pig.

As Farmer Hogget watched, a man leaned over and picked it out of the pen. He hefted it in both hands, frowning and pursing his lips in a considering way, while all the time the piglet struggled madly and yelled blue murder. The moment it was put down, it quietened. Its eyes, bright intelligent eyes, met the farmer's. They regarded one another.

One saw a tall thin brown-faced man with very long legs, and the other saw a small fat pinky-white animal with very short ones.

"Ah, come along, Mr Hogget!" said the Vicar. "You never know, he could be yours for ten pence. Guess his weight correctly, and at the end of the day you could be taking him home!"

"Don't keep pigs," said Farmer Hogget. He stretched out a long arm and scratched its back. Gently, he picked it up and held it before his face. It stayed quite still and made no sound.

"That's funny," said the Vicar. "Every time so far that someone has picked him up he's screamed his head off. He seems to like you. You'll have to have a guess."

6

Carefully, Farmer Hogget put the piglet back in the pen. Carefully, he took a ten pence piece from his pocket and dropped it in the cardboard box. Carefully, he ran one finger down the list of guesses already in the Vicar's notebook.

"Quite a variation," said the Vicar. "Anything from twenty pounds to forty, so far." He wrote down 'Mr Hogget' and waited, pencil poised.

Once again, slowly, thoughtfully, the farmer picked the piglet up.

Once again, it remained still and silent.

"Thirty-one pounds," said Farmer Hogget. He put the little pig down again. "And a quarter," he said.

"Thirty-one and a quarter pounds. Thank you, Mr Hogget. We shall be weighing the little chap at about half past four."

"Be gone by then."

"Ah well, we can always telephone you. If you should be lucky enough to win him."

"Never win nothing."

As he walked back across the green, the sound of the pig's yelling rang out as someone else had a go.

"You do never win nothing," said Mrs Hogget at tea-time, when her husband, in a very few words, had explained matters, "though I've often thought I'd like a pig, we could feed 'un on scraps, he'd come just right for Christmas time, just think, two nice hams, two sides of bacon, pork chops, kidneys, liver, chitterling, trotters, save his blood for black pudding, there's the phone."

Farmer Hogget picked it up.

"Oh," he said.

CHAPTER 2

"There. Is that nice?"

In the farmyard, Fly the black and white collie was beginning the training of her four puppies. For some time now they had shown an instinctive interest in anything that moved, driving it away or bringing it back, turning it to left or right, in fact herding it. They had begun with such things as passing beetles, but were now ready, Fly considered, for larger creatures.

She set them to work on Mrs Hogget's ducks.

Already the puppies were beginning to move as sheep-dogs do, seeming to creep rather than walk, heads held low, ears pricked, eyes fixed on the angrily quacking birds as they manoeuvred them about the yard.

"Good boys," said Fly. "Leave them now. Here comes the boss."

The ducks went grumbling off to the pond, and the

five dogs watched as Farmer Hogget got out of the
Land Rover. He lifted something out of a crate in the
back, and carried it into the stables.

"What was that, Mum?" said one of the puppies.

"That was a pig."

"What will the boss do with it?"

"Eat it," said Fly, "when it's big enough."

"Will he eat us," said another rather nervously,
"when we're big enough?"

"Bless you," said his mother. "People only eat
stupid animals. Like sheep and cows and ducks and
chickens. They don't eat clever ones like dogs."

"So pigs are stupid?" said the puppies.

Fly hesitated. On the one hand, having been born and brought up in sheep country, she had in fact never been personally acquainted with a pig. On the other, like most mothers, she did not wish to appear ignorant before her children.

"Yes," she said. "They're stupid."

At this point there came from the kitchen window a long burst of words like the rattle of a machine-gun, answered by a single shot from the stables, and Farmer Hogget emerged and crossed the yard towards the farmhouse with his loping stride.

"Come on," said the collie bitch. "I'll show you."

The floor of the stables had not rung to a horse's hoof for many years, but it was a useful place for storing things. The hens foraged about there, and sometimes laid their eggs in the old wooden mangers; the swallows built their nests against its roof-beams with mud from the duckpond; and rats and mice lived happy lives in its shelter until the farm cats cut them short. At one end of the stables were two loose-boxes with boarded sides topped by iron rails. One served as a kennel for Fly and her puppies. The other sometimes housed sick sheep. Here Farmer Hogget had shut the piglet.

A convenient stack of straw bales allowed the dogs to look down into the box through the bars.

"It certainly looks stupid," said one of the puppies, yawning. At the sound of the words the piglet glanced up quickly. He put his head on one side and regarded the dogs with sharp eyes. Something about the sight of this very small animal standing all by itself in the middle of the roomy loose-box touched Fly's soft heart. Already she was sorry that she had said that pigs were stupid, for this one certainly did not appear to be so. Also there was something dignified about the way it stood its ground, in a strange place, confronted with strange animals. How

different from the silly sheep, who at the mere sight of a dog would run aimlessly about, crying "Wolf! Wolf!" in their empty-headed way.

"Hullo," she said. "Who are you?"

"I'm a Large White," said the piglet.

"Blimey!" said one of the puppies. "If that's a large white, what's a small one like?" And they all four sniggered.

"Be quiet!" snapped Fly. "Just remember that five minutes ago you didn't even know what a pig was." And to the piglet she said kindly, "I expect that's your breed, dear. I meant, what's your name?"

"I don't know," said the piglet.

"Well, what did your mother call you, to tell you apart from your brothers and sisters?" said Fly and then wished she hadn't, for at the mention of his family the piglet began to look distinctly unhappy. His little forehead wrinkled and he gulped and his voice trembled as he answered.

"She called us all the same."

"And what was that, dear?"

"Babe," said the piglet, and the puppies began to giggle until their mother silenced them with a growl.

"But that's a lovely name," she said. "Would you like us to call you that? It'll make you feel more at home."

14

At this last word the little pig's face fell even further.

"I want my mum," he said very quietly.

At that instant the collie bitch made up her mind that she would foster this unhappy child.

"Go out into the yard and play," she said to the puppies, and she climbed to the top of the straw stack and jumped over the rail and down into the loose-box beside the piglet.

"Listen, Babe," she said. "You've got to be a brave boy. Everyone has to leave their mother, it's all part of growing up. I did so, when I was your age, and my puppies will have to leave me quite soon. But I'll look after you. If you like." Then she licked his little snout with a warm rough tongue, her plumed tail wagging.

"There. Is that nice?" she said.

A little while later, Farmer Hogget came into the stables with his wife, to show her his prize. They looked over the loose-box door and saw, to their astonishment, Fly curled round the piglet. Exhausted by the drama of the day, he lay fast asleep against his new-found foster-parent.

"Well, will you look at that!" said Mrs Hogget. "That old Fly, she'll mother anything, kittens, duck-lings, baby chicks, she's looked after all of they, now

'tis a pig, in't he lovely, what a picture, good job he
don't know where he'll finish up, but he'll be big then
and we'll be glad to see the back of him, or the hams
of him, I should say, shan't us, wonder how I shall
get it all in the freezer?"

"Pity. Really," said Farmer Hogget absently.

Mrs Hogget went back to her kitchen, shaking her
head all the way across the yard at the thought of her
husband's soft-heartedness.

The farmer opened the loose-box door, and to save the effort of a word, clicked his fingers to call the bitch out.

As soon as Fly moved the piglet woke and followed her, sticking so close to her that his snout touched her tail-tip. Surprise forced Farmer Hogget into speech.

"Fly!" he said in amazement. Obediently, as always, the collie bitch turned and trotted back to him. The pig trotted behind her.

"Sit!" said Farmer Hogget. Fly sat. Babe sat. Farmer Hogget scratched his head. He could not think of anything to say.

CHAPTER 3

"Why can't I learn?"

By dark it was plain to Farmer Hogget that, whether he liked it or no, Fly had not four, but five children.

All the long summer evening Babe had followed Fly about the yard and buildings, aimlessly, it seemed to the watching farmer, though of course this was not the case. It was in fact a conducted tour. Fly knew that if this foster-child was to be allowed his freedom and the constant reassurance of her company for which he obviously craved, he must quickly learn (and patently he was a quick learner) his way about the place; and that he must be taught, as her puppies had been taught, how to behave like a good dog.

"A pig you may be, Babe," she had begun by saying, "but if you do as I tell you, I shouldn't be a bit surprised if the boss doesn't let you run about with us, instead of shutting you up. He's a kind man, the boss is."

18

"I knew that," said Babe, "when he first picked me up. I could feel it. I knew he wouldn't hurt me."

"You wait . . ." began one of the puppies, and then stopped suddenly at his mother's warning growl. Though she said nothing, all four of her children knew immediately by instinct what she meant.

"Wait for what?" said Babe.

"Er . . . you wait half a tick, and we'll take you round and show you everything," said the first puppy hastily. "Won't we, Mum?"

So Babe was shown all round the yard and the farm buildings, and introduced to the creatures who lived thereabouts, the ducks and chickens and other poultry, and the farm cats. He saw no sheep, for they were all in the fields.

Even in the first hour he learned a number of useful lessons, as the puppies had learned before him: that cats scratch and hens peck, that turning your back on the turkey-cock means getting your bottom bitten, that chicks are not for chasing and eggs are not for eating.

"You do as I do," said Fly, "and you'll be all right."

She thought for a moment. "There is one thing though, Babe," she said, and she looked across at the back door of the farmhouse, "if I go in there, you stay outside and wait for me, understand?"

"Aren't pigs allowed in there?" asked Babe.

"Not live ones," said one of the puppies, but he said it under his breath.

"No, dear," said Fly. Well, not yet anyway, she thought, but the way you're going on, I shouldn't be surprised at anything. Funny, she thought, I feel really proud of him, he learns so quick. Quick as any sheep-dog.

That night the loose-box in which Babe had first been put was empty. In the next door one, all five animals slept in the straw together. Though he did not tell his wife, Farmer Hogget had not had the heart to shut the piglet away, so happy was it in the company of the dogs.

At first the puppies had not been equally happy at the idea.

"Mum!" they said. "He'll wet the bed!"

"Nonsense," said Fly. "If you want to do anything, dear, you go outside, there's a good boy."

I nearly said "there's a good pup" she thought. Whatever next!

In fact, in the days that followed, Babe became so doglike, what with coming when Fly came and sitting when Fly sat and much preferring dog's food to anything else he was offered, that Farmer Hogget caught himself half expecting, when he patted the piglet, that it would wag its tail. He would not have been surprised if it had tried to accompany Fly when he called her to go with him on his morning rounds, but it had stayed in the stables, playing with the puppies.

"You stop with the boys, Babe," Fly had said, "while I see to the sheep. I shan't be long."

"What's sheep?" the piglet said when she had gone.

The puppies rolled about in the straw.

"Don't you know that, you silly Babe?" said one.

"Sheep are animals with thick woolly coats."

"And thick woolly heads."

"And men can't look after them without the help of the likes of us," said the fourth.

"Why do they need you?" said Babe.

"Because we're sheep-dogs!" they all cried together, and ran off up the yard.

Babe thought about this matter of sheep and sheep-dogs a good deal during the first couple of weeks of his life on the Hoggets' farm. In that time Fly's puppies, now old enough to leave home, had been advertised for sale, and Fly was anxious to teach them all she could before they went out into the world. Daily she made them practise on the ducks, while Babe sat beside her and watched with interest. And daily their skills improved and the ducks lost weight and patience.

Then there came, one after another, four farmers, four tall long-legged men who smelt of sheep. And each picked his puppy and paid his money, while Fly sat and watched her children leave to start their working life.

As always, she felt a pang to see each go, but this time, after the last had left, she was not alone.

"It's nice, dear," she said to Babe. "I've still got you."

But not for all that long, she thought. Poor little chap, in six months or so he'll be fit to kill. At least he doesn't know it. She looked fondly at him, this foster-child that now called her 'Mum'. He had picked it up, naturally enough, from the puppies, but it pleased her to hear it, now more than ever.

"Mum," said Babe.

"Yes, dear?"

"They've gone off to work sheep, haven't they?"

"Yes, dear."

"Because they're sheep-dogs. Like you. You're useful to the boss, aren't you, because you're a sheep-dog?"

"Yes, dear."

"Well, Mum?"

"Yes, dear?"

"Why can't I learn to be a sheep-pig?"

CHAPTER 4

"You'm a polite young chap"

After the last of the puppies had left, the ducks heaved a general sigh of relief. They looked forward to a peaceful day and paid no attention when, the following morning, Fly and Babe came down to the pond and sat and watched them as they squattered and splattered in its soupy green depths. They knew that the old dog would not bother them, and they took no notice of the strange creature at her side.

"They'll come out and walk up the yard in a minute," said Fly. "Then you can have a go at fetching them back, if you like."

"Oh yes please!" said Babe excitedly.

The collie bitch looked fondly at her foster-child. Sheep-pig indeed, she thought, the idea of it! The mere sight of him would probably send the flock into the next county. Anyway he'd never get near them on those little short legs. Let him play with the ducks for

24

a day or two and he'd forget all about it.

When the ducks did come up out of the water and marched noisily past the piglet, she half expected him to chase after them, as the puppies usually did at first; but he sat very still, his ears cocked, watching her.

"All right," said Fly. "Let's see how you get on. Now then, first thing is, you've got to get behind them, just like I have to with the sheep. If the boss wants me to go round the right side of them (that's the side by the stables there), he says 'Away to me'. If he wants me to go round the left (that's the side by the Dutch barn), he says 'Come by'. O.K.?"

"Yes, Mum."

"Right then. Away to me, Babe!" said Fly sharply.

At first, not surprisingly, Babe's efforts met with little success. There were no problems with getting round the ducks—even with his curious little see-sawing canter he was much faster than they—but the business of bringing the whole flock back to Fly was not, he found, at all easy. Either he pressed them too hard and they broke up and fluttered all over the place, or he was too gentle and held back, and they waddled away in twos and threes.

"Come and have a rest, dear," called Fly after a while. "Leave the silly things alone, they're not worth upsetting yourself about."

"I'm not upset, Mum," said Babe. "Just puzzled. I mean, I told them what I wanted them to do but they didn't take any notice of me. Why not?"

Because you weren't born to it, thought Fly. You haven't got the instinct to dominate them, to make them do what you want.

"It's early days yet, Babe dear," she said.

"Do you suppose," said Babe, "that if I asked them politely . . ."

"Asked them politely! What an idea! Just imagine me doing that with the sheep—'please will you go through that gateway', 'would you kindly walk into that pen?' Oh no, dear, you'd never get anywhere that way. You've got to tell 'em what to do, doesn't matter whether it's ducks or sheep. They're stupid and dogs are intelligent, that's what you have to remember."

"But I'm a pig."

"Pigs are intelligent too," said Fly firmly. Ask them politely, she thought, whatever next!

What happened next, later that morning in fact, was that Babe met his first sheep.

Farmer Hogget and Fly had been out round the flock, and when they returned Fly was driving before her an old lame ewe, which they penned in the loose-box where the piglet had originally been shut. Then they went away up the hill again.

Babe made his way into the stables, curious to meet this, the first of the animals that he planned one day to work with, but he could not see into the box. He snuffled under the bottom of the door, and from inside there came a cough and the sharp stamp of a foot, and then the sound of a hoarse complaining voice. "Wolves! Wolves!" it said. "They do never

leave a body alone. Nag, nag, nag all day long, go
here, go there, do this, do that. What d'you want
now? Can't you give us a bit of peace, wolf?"

"I'm not a wolf," said Babe under the door.

"Oh, I knows all that," said the sheep sourly.
"Calls yourself a sheep-dog, I knows that, but you
don't fool none of us. You're a wolf like the rest of
'em, given half a chance. You looks at us, and you
sees lamb-chops. Go away, wolf."

"But I'm not a sheep-dog either," said Babe, and he
scrambled up the stack of straw bales and looked over
the bars.

"You see?" he said.

"Well I'll be dipped," said the old sheep, peering up
at him, "no more you ain't. What are you?"

"Pig," said Babe. "Large White. What are you?"

"Ewe," said the sheep.

"No, not me, you—what are you?"

"I'm a ewe."

Mum was right, thought Babe, they certainly are
stupid. But if I'm going to learn how to be a
sheep-pig I must try to understand them, and this
might be a good chance. Perhaps I could make a
friend of this one.

"My name's Babe," he said in a jolly voice.
"What's yours?"

"Maaaaa," said the sheep.

"That's a nice name," said Babe. "What's the matter with you, Ma?"

"Foot-rot," said the sheep, holding up a foreleg. "And I've got a nasty cough." She coughed. "And I'm not as young as I was."

"You don't look very old to me," said Babe politely.

A look of pleasure came over the sheep's mournful face, and she lay down in the straw.

"Very civil of you to say so," she said. "First kind word I've had since I were a little lamb," and she belched loudly and began to chew a mouthful of cud.

Though he did not quite know why, Babe said nothing to Fly of his conversation with Ma. Farmer Hogget had treated the sheep's foot and tipped a drench down its protesting throat, and now, as darkness fell, dog and pig lay side by side, their rest only occasionally disturbed by a rustling from the next-door box. Having at last set eyes on a sheep, Babe's dreams were immediately filled with the creatures, all lame, all coughing, all, like the ducks, scattering wildly before his attempts to round them up.

"Go here, go there, do this, do that!" he squeaked furiously at them, but they took not a bit of notice, until at last the dream turned to nightmare, and they all came hopping and hacking and maa-ing after him with hatred gleaming in their mad yellow eyes.

"Mum! Mum!" shouted Babe in terror.

"Maaaaa!" said a voice next door.

"It's all right, dear," said Fly, "it's all right. Was it a nasty dream?"

"Yes, yes."

"What were you dreaming about?"

"Sheep, Mum."

"I expect it was because of that stupid old thing in there," said Fly. "Shut up!" she barked. "Noisy old fool!" And to Babe she said, "Now cuddle up, dear, and go to sleep. There's nothing to be frightened of."

She licked his snout until it began to give out a series of regular snores. Sheep-pig indeed, she thought, why the silly boy's frightened of the things, and she put her nose on her paws and went to sleep.

Babe slept soundly the rest of the night, and woke more determined than ever to learn all that he could from their new neighbour. As soon as Fly had gone out on her rounds, he climbed the straw stack.

"Good morning, Ma," he said. "I do hope you're feeling better today?"

The old ewe looked up. Her eyes, Babe was glad to see, looked neither mad nor hateful.

"I must say," she said, "you'm a polite young chap. Not like that wolf, shouting at me in the middle of the night. Never get no respect from they, treat you like dirt they do, bite you soon as look at you."

"Do they really?"

"Oh ar. Nip your hocks if you'm a bit slow. And worse, some of them."

"Worse?"

"Oh ar. Ain't you never heard of worrying?"

"I don't worry much."

"No no, young un. I'm talking about sheep-worrying. You get some wolves as'll chase sheep and kill 'em."

"Oh!" said Babe, horrified. "I'm sure Fly would never do that."

"Who's Fly?"

"She's my m . . . she's our dog here, the one that brought you in yesterday."

"Is that what she's called? No, she bain't a worrier, just rude. All wolves is rude to us sheep, see, always have been. Bark and run and nip and call us stupid. We bain't all that stupid, we do just get confused. If only they'd just show a bit of common politeness, just treat us a bit decent. Now if you was to come out into the field, a nice well-mannered young chap like you, and ask me to go somewhere or do something, politely, like you would, why, I'd be only too delighted."

CHAPTER 5

"Keep yelling, young un"

Mrs Hogget shook her head at least a dozen times.

"For the life of me I can't see why you do let that pig run all over the place like you do, round and round the yard he do go, chasing my ducks about, shoving his nose into everything, shouldn't wonder but what he'll be out with you and Fly moving the sheep about afore long, why dussen't shut him up, he's running all his flesh off, he won't never be fit for Christmas, Easter more like, what d'you call him?"

"Just Pig," said Farmer Hogget.

A month had gone by since the Village Fair, a month in which a lot of interesting things had happened to Babe. The fact that perhaps most concerned his future, though he did not know it, was that Farmer Hogget had become fond of him. He liked to see the piglet pottering happily about the yard with

33

Fly, keeping out of mischief, as far as he could tell, if you didn't count moving the ducks around. He did this now with a good deal of skill, the farmer noticed, even to the extent of being able, once, to separate the white ducks from the brown, though that must just have been a fluke. The more he thought of it, the less Farmer Hogget liked the idea of butchering Pig.

The other developments were in Babe's education. Despite herself, Fly found that she took pleasure and pride in teaching him the ways of the sheep-dog, though she knew that of course he would never be fast enough to work sheep. Anyway the boss would never let him try.

As for Ma, she was back with the flock, her foot healed, her cough better. But all the time that she had been shut in the box, Babe had spent every moment that Fly was out of the stables chatting to the old ewe. Already he understood, in a way that Fly never could, the sheep's point of view. He longed to meet the flock, to be introduced. He thought it would be extremely interesting.

"D'you think I could, Ma?" he had said.

"Could what, young un?"

"Well, come and visit you, when you go back to your friends?"

"Oh ar. You could do, easy enough. You only got

to go through the bottom gate and up the hill to the big field by the lane. Don't know what the farmer'd say though. Or that wolf."

Once Fly had slipped quietly in and found him perched on the straw stack.

"Babe!" she had said sharply. "You're not talking to that stupid thing, are you?"

"Well, yes, Mum, I was."

"Save your breath, dear. It won't understand a word you say."

"Bah!" said Ma.

For a moment Babe was tempted to tell his foster-mother what he had in mind, but something told him to keep quiet. Instead he made a plan. He would wait for two things to happen. First, for Ma to rejoin the flock. And after that for market day, when both the boss and his mum would be out of the way. Then he would go up the hill.

Towards the end of the very next week the two things had happened. Ma had been turned out, and a couple of days after that Babe watched as Fly jumped into the back of the Land Rover, and it drove out of the yard and away.

Babe's were not the only eyes that watched its departure. At the top of the hill a cattle-lorry stood

half-hidden under a clump of trees at the side of the lane. As soon as the Land-Rover had disappeared from sight along the road to the market town, a man jumped hurriedly out and opened the gate into the field. Another backed the lorry into the gateway.

Babe meanwhile was trotting excitedly up the hill to pay his visit to the flock. He came to the gate at the bottom of the field and squeezed under it. The field was steep and curved, and at first he could not see a single sheep. But then he heard a distant drumming of hooves and suddenly the whole flock came galloping over the brow of the hill and down towards him. Around them ran two strange collies, lean silent dogs that seemed to flow effortlessly over the grass. From high above came the sound of a thin whistle, and in easy partnership the dogs swept round the sheep, and began to drive them back up the slope.

Despite himself, Babe was caught up in the press of jostling bleating animals and carried along with them. Around him rose a chorus of panting protesting voices, some shrill, some hoarse, some deep and guttural, but all saying the same thing.

"Wolf! Wolf!" cried the flock in dazed confusion.

Small by comparison and short in the leg, Babe soon fell behind the main body, and as they reached the top of the hill he found himself right at the back in company with an old sheep who cried "Wolf!" more loudly than any.

"Ma!" he cried breathlessly. "It's you!"

Behind them one dog lay down at a whistle, and in front the flock checked as the other dog steadied them. In the corner of the field the tailboard and wings of the cattle-lorry filled the gateway, and the two men waited, sticks and arms outspread.

"Oh hullo, young un," puffed the old sheep. "Fine day you chose to come, I'll say."

"What is it? What's happening? Who are these men?" asked Babe.

"Rustlers," said Ma. "They'm sheep-rustlers."

"What d'you mean?"

"Thieves, young un, that's what I do mean. Sheep-stealers. We'll all be in thik lorry afore you can blink your eye."

"What can we do?"

"Do? Ain't nothing we can do, unless we can slip past theseyer wolf."

She made as if to escape, but the dog behind darted in, and she turned back.

Again, one of the men whistled, and the dog pressed. Gradually, held against the headland of the field by the second dog and the men, the flock began to move forward. Already the leaders were nearing the tailboard of the lorry.

"We'm beat," said Ma mournfully. "You run for it, young un." I will, thought Babe, but not the way you mean. Little as he was, he felt suddenly not fear but anger, furious anger that the boss's sheep were being stolen. My mum's not here to protect them so I must, he said to himself bravely, and he ran quickly round the hedge side of the flock, and jumping on to the bottom of the tailboard, turned to face them.

"Please!" he cried. "I beg you! Please don't come any further. If you would be so kind, dear sensible sheep!"

His unexpected appearance had a number of immediate effects. The shock of being so politely addressed stopped the flock in its tracks, and the cries of "Wolf!" changed to murmurs of "In't he lovely!" and "Proper little gennulman!" Ma had told them something of her new friend, and now to see him in the flesh and to hear his well-chosen words released them from the dominance of the dogs. They began to fidget and look about for an escape route. This was opened for them when the men (cursing quietly, for above all things they were anxious to avoid too much noise) sent the flanking dog to drive the pig away, and some of the sheep began to slip past them.

Next moment all was chaos. Angrily the dog ran at Babe, who scuttled away squealing at the top of his voice in a mixture of fright and fury. The men closed on him, sticks raised. Desperately he shot between the legs of one, who fell with a crash, while the other, striking out madly, hit the rearguard dog as it came to help, and sent it yowling. In half a minute the carefully planned raid was ruined, as the sheep scattered everywhere.

"Keep yelling, young un!" bawled Ma, as she ran beside Babe. "They won't never stop here with that row going on!"

And suddenly all sorts of things began to happen as those deafening squeals rang out over the quiet countryside. Birds flew startled from the trees, cows in nearby fields began to gallop about, dogs in distant farms to bark, passing motorists to stop and stare. In the farmhouse below Mrs Hogget heard the noise as she had on the day of the Fair, but now it was infinitely louder, the most piercing, nerve-tingling, ear-shattering burglar alarm. She dialled 999 but then talked for so long that by the time a patrol car drove up the lane, the rustlers had long gone. Snarling at each other and their dogs, they had driven hurriedly away with not one single sheep to show for their pains.

"You won't never believe it!" cried Mrs Hogget when her husband returned from market. "But we've had rustlers, just after you'd gone it were, come with a girt cattle-lorry they did, the police said, they seen the tyremarks in the gateway, and a chap in a car seen the lorry go by in a hurry, and there's been a lot of it about, and he give the alarm, he did, kept screaming and shrieking enough to bust your eardrums, we

41

should have lost every sheep on the place if 'tweren't for him, 'tis him we've got to thank."

"Who?" said Farmer Hogget.

"Him!" said his wife, pointing at Babe who was telling Fly all about it. "Don't ask me how he got there or why he done it, all I knows is he saved our bacon and now I'm going to save his, he's stopping with us just like another dog, don't care if he gets so big as a house, because if you think I'm going to stand by and see him butchered after what he done for us today, you've got another think coming, what d'you say to that?"

A slow smile spread over Farmer Hogget's long face.

CHAPTER 6

"Good Pig"

The very next morning Farmer Hogget decided that he would see if the pig would like to come, when he went round the sheep with Fly. I'm daft, he thought, grinning to himself. He did not tell his wife.

Seeing him walk down the yard, crook in hand, and hearing him call Fly, Babe was about to settle down for an after-breakfast nap when to his surprise he heard the farmer's voice again.

"Come, Pig," said Farmer Hogget and to his surprise the pig came.

"I expect it's because of what you did yesterday," said Fly proudly, as they walked to heel together up the hill. "The boss must be very pleased with you, dear. You can watch me working."

When they reached the lower gate, Farmer Hogget opened it and left it open.

"He's going to bring them down into the home paddock, away from the lane," said Fly quickly. "You be quiet and keep out of the way," and she went to sit waiting by the farmer's right side.

"Come by!" he said, and Fly ran left up the slope as the sheep began to bunch above her. Once behind them, she addressed them in her usual way, that is to say sharply.

"Move, fools!" she snapped. "Down the hill. If you know which way 'down' is," but to her surprise they did not obey. Instead they turned to face her, and some even stamped, and shook their heads at her, while a great chorus of bleating began.

To Fly sheep-talk was just so much rubbish, to which she had never paid any attention, but Babe, listening below, could hear clearly what was being said, and although the principal cry was the usual one, there were other voices saying other things. The contrast between the politeness with which they had been treated by yesterday's rescuer and the everlasting rudeness to which they were subjected by this or any wolf brought mutinous thoughts into woolly heads, and words of defiance rang out.

"You got no manners! . . . Why can't you ask nicely? . . . Treat us like muck, you do!" they cried, and one hoarse voice which the pig recognised called loudly, "We don't want you, wolf! We want Babe!" whereupon they all took it up.

"We want Babe!" they bleated. "Babe! Babe! Ba-a-a-a-a-be!"

Those behind pushed at those in front, so that they actually edged a pace or two nearer the dog.

For a moment it seemed to Babe that Fly was not going to be able to move them, that she would lose this particular battle of wills; but he had not reckoned with her years of experience. Suddenly, quick as a flash, she drove in on them with a growl and with a twisting leap sprang for the nose of the foremost animal; Babe heard the clack of her teeth as the ewe fell over backwards in fright, a fright which immediately ran through all. Defiant no longer, the flock poured down the hill, Fly snapping furiously at their heels, and surged wildly through the gateway.

"No manners! No manners! No ma-a-a-a-a-nners!" they cried, but an air of panic ran through them as they realised how rebellious they had been. How the wolf would punish them! They ran helter-skelter into the middle of the paddock, and wheeled as one to look back, ears pricked, eyes wide with fear. They puffed and blew, and Ma's hacking cough rang out. But to their surprise they saw that the wolf had dropped by the gateway, and that after a moment the pig came trotting out to one side of them.

Though Farmer Hogget could not know what had caused the near-revolt of the flock, he saw clearly that for some reason they had given Fly a hard time, and that she was angry. It was not like her to gallop sheep in that pell-mell fashion.

"Steady!" he said curtly as she harried the rear-guard, and then "Down!" and "Stay!" and shut the gate. Shepherding suited Farmer Hogget—there was no waste of words in it.

In the corner of the home paddock nearest to the farm buildings was a smallish fenced yard divided

into a number of pens and runways. Here the sheep would be brought at shearing-time or to pick out fat lambs for market or to be treated for various troubles. Farmer Hogget had heard the old ewe cough; he thought he would catch her up and give her another drench. He turned to give an order to Fly lying flat and still behind him, and there, lying flat and still beside her, was the pig.

"Stay, Fly!"said Hogget. And, just for fun, "Come, Pig!"

Immediately Babe ran forward and sat at the farmer's right, his front trotters placed neatly together, his big ears cocked for the next command.

Strange thoughts began to stir in Farmer Hogget's mind, and unconsciously he crossed his fingers.

He took a deep breath, and, holding it . . . "Away to me, Pig!" he said softly.

Without a moment's hesitation Babe began the long outrun to the right.

Quite what Farmer Hogget had expected to happen, he could never afterwards clearly remember. What he had not expected was that the pig would run round to the rear of the flock, and turn to face it and him, and lie down instantly without a word of further command spoken, just as a well-trained dog would have done. Admittedly, with his jerky little rocking-horse canter he took twice as long to get there as Fly would have, but still, there he was, in the right place, ready and waiting. Admittedly, the sheep had turned to face the pig and were making a great deal of noise, but then Farmer Hogget did not know, and Fly would not listen to, what they were saying. He called the dog to heel, and began to walk with his long loping stride to the collecting-pen in the corner. Out in the middle of the paddock there was a positive babble of talk.

"Good morning!" said Babe. "I do hope I find you all well, and not too distressed by yesterday's experience?" and immediately it seemed that every sheep had something to say to him.

"Bless his heart!" they cried, and, "Dear little soul!" and, "Hullo, Babe!" and, "Nice to see you again!" and then there was a rasping cough and the sound of Ma's hoarse tones.

"What's up then, young un?" she croaked. "What be you doing here instead of that wolf?"

Although Babe wanted, literally, to keep on the right side of the sheep, his loyalty to his foster-mother made him say in a rather hurt voice, "She's not a wolf. She's a sheep-dog."

"Oh all right then," said Ma, "sheep-dog, if you must have it. What dost want, then?"

Babe looked at the army of long sad faces.

"I want to be a sheep-pig," he said.

"Ha ha!" bleated a big lamb standing next to Ma. "Ha ha ha-a-a-a-a!"

"Bide quiet!" said Ma sharply, swinging her head to give the lamb a thumping butt in the side. "That ain't nothing to laugh at."

Raising her voice, she addressed the flock.

"Listen to me, all you ewes," she said, "and lambs too. This young chap was kind to me, like I told you,

50

when I were poorly. And I told him, if he was to ask me to go somewhere or do something, politely, like he would, why, I'd be only too delighted. We ain't stupid, I told him, all we do want is to be treated right, and we'm as bright as the next beast, we are."

"We are!" chorused the flock. "We are! We are! We a-a-a-a-a-are!"

"Right then," said Ma. "What shall us do, Babe?"

Babe looked across towards Farmer Hogget, who had opened the gate of the collecting-pen and now stood leaning on his crook, Fly at his feet. The pen was in the left bottom corner of the paddock, and so Babe expected, and at that moment got, the command "Come by, Pig!" to send him left and so behind the sheep and thus turn them down towards the corner.

He cleared his throat. "If I might ask a great favour of you," he said hurriedly, "could you all please be kind enough to walk down to that gate where the farmer is standing, and to go through it? Take your time, please, there's absolutely no rush."

A look of pure contentment passed over the faces of the flock, and with one accord they turned and walked across the paddock, Babe a few paces in their rear. Sedately they walked, and steadily, over to the corner, through the gate, into the pen, and then stood

51

quietly waiting. No one broke ranks or tried to slip away, no one pushed or shoved, there was no noise or fuss. From the oldest to the youngest, they went in like lambs.

Then at last a gentle murmur broke out as everyone in different ways quietly expressed their pleasure.

"Babe!" said Fly to the pig. "That was quite beautifully done, dear!"

"Thank you so much!" said Babe to the sheep. "You did that so nicely!"

"Ta!" said the sheep. "Ta! Ta! Ta-a-a-a-a-a!. 'Tis a pleasure to work for such a little gennulman!" And Ma added, "You'll make a wunnerful sheep-pig, young un, or my names's not Ma-a-a-a-a."

As for Farmer Hogget, he heard none of this, so wrapped up was he in his own thoughts. He's as good as a dog, he told himself excitedly, he's better than a dog, than any dog! I wonder . . . !

"Good Pig," he said.

Then he uncrossed his fingers and closed the gate.

CHAPTER 7

"What's trials?"

Every day after that, of course, Babe went the rounds with Farmer Hogget and Fly. At first the farmer worried about using the pig to herd the sheep, not because it was a strange and unusual thing to do which people might laugh at—he did not care about that—but because he was afraid it might upset Fly and put her nose out of joint. However it did not seem to do so.

He could have spared himself the worry if he had been able to listen to their conversation.

"That *was* fun!" said Babe to Fly that evening. "I wonder if the boss will let me do some more work?"

"I'm sure he will, dear. You did it so well. It was almost as though the sheep knew exactly what it was you wanted them to do."

"But that's just it! I asked them . . ."

"No use asking sheep anything, dear," interrupted Fly. "You have to *make* them do what you want, I've told you before."

"Yes, Mum. But . . . will you mind, if the boss uses me instead of you, sometimes?"

"Mind?" said Fly. "You bet your trotters I won't! All my life I've had to run round after those idiots, up hill, down dale, day in, day out. And as for 'sometimes', as far as I'm concerned you can work them every day. I'm not as young as I was. I'll be only too happy to lie comfortably in the grass and watch you, my Babe."

And before long that was exactly what she was doing. Once Farmer Hogget could see by her wagging tail and smiling eyes that she was perfectly happy about it, he began to use Babe to do some of her work. At first he only gave the pig simple tasks,

but as the days and weeks went by, Hogget began to make more and more use of his new helper. The speed with which Babe learned amazed him, and before long he was relying on him for all the work with the flock, while Fly lay and proudly watched. Now, there was nothing, it seemed, that the pig could not do, and do faultlessly, at that.

He obeyed all the usual commands immediately and correctly. He could fetch sheep or take them away, move them to left or right, persuade them round obstacles or through gaps, cut the flock in half, or take out one individual.

To drench Ma, for instance, there was no need for Hogget to bring all the sheep down to the collecting-pen, or to corner them all and catch her by a hindleg with his crook. He could simply point her out to the pig, and Babe would gently work her out of the bunch and bring her right to the farmer's feet, where she stood quietly waiting. It seemed like a miracle to Hogget, but of course it was simple.

"Ma!"

"Yes, young un?"

"The boss wants to give you some more medicine."

"Oh not again! 'Tis horrible stuff, that."

"But it'll make your cough better."

"Oh ar?"

"Come along, Ma. Please."

"Oh all right then, young un. Anything to oblige you."

And there were other far more miraculous things that Babe could easily have done if the farmer had only known. For example when it was time for the ewes to be separated from their lambs, now almost as big and strong as their mothers, Farmer Hogget behaved like any other shepherd, and brought the whole flock down to the pens, and took a lot of time and trouble to part them. If only he had been able to explain things to Babe, how easy it could have been.

"Dear ladies, will you please stay on the hill, if you'd be so kind?"

"Youngsters, down you go to the collecting-pen if you please, there's good boys and girls," and it could have been done in the shake of a lamb's tail.

However Babe's increasing skill at working sheep determined Farmer Hogget to take the next step in a plan which had begun to form in his mind on the day when the piglet had first penned the sheep. That step was nothing less than to take Pig with him to the local sheep-dog trials in a couple of weeks' time. Only just to watch of course, just so that he could have a look at well-trained dogs working a small number of sheep, and see what they and their handlers were required to do. I'm daft, he thought, grinning to himself. He did not tell his wife.

Before the day came, he put a collar and lead on the pig. He could not risk him running away, in a strange place. He kept him on the lead all one morning, letting Fly do the work as of old. He need not have bothered—Babe would have stayed tight at heel when told—but it was interesting to note the instant change in the atmosphere as the collie ran out.

"Wolf! Wolf!" cried the flock, every sheep immediately on edge.

"Move, fools!" snapped Fly, and she hustled them and bustled them with little regard for their feelings.

"Babe! We want Babe!" they bleated. "Ba-a-a-a-a-be!"

To be sure, the work was done more quickly, but at the end of it the sheep were in fear and trembling and the dog out of patience and breath.

"Steady! Steady!" called the farmer a number of times, something he never had to say to Babe.

When the day came for the local trials, Farmer Hogget set off early in the Land Rover, Fly and Babe in the back. He told his wife where he was going, though not that he was taking the pig. Nor did he say that he did not intend to be an ordinary spectator, but instead more of a spy, to see without being seen. He wanted Pig to observe everything that went on without being spotted. Now that he had settled on the final daring part of his plan, Hogget realised that secrecy was all-important. No one must know that he owned a . . . what would you call him, he thought . . . a sheep-pig, I suppose!

The trials took place ten miles or so away, in a curved basin-shaped valley in the hills. At the lower end of the basin was a road. Close to this was the starting point, where the dogs would begin their outrun, and also the enclosure where they would finally pen their sheep. Down there all the spectators would gather. Farmer Hogget, arriving some time before them, parked the Land Rover in a lane, and set off up the valley by a roundabout way, keeping in the shelter of the bordering woods, Fly padding behind him and Babe on the lead trotting to keep up with his long strides.

"Where are we going, Mum?" said Babe excitedly. "What are we going to do?"

"I don't think we're going to do anything, dear," said Fly. "I think the boss wants you to see something."

"What?"

They had reached the head of the valley now, and the farmer found a suitable place to stop, under cover, but with a good view of the course.

"Down, Fly, down, Pig, and stay," he said and exhausted by this long speech, stretched his long frame on the ground and settled down to wait.

"Wants me to see what?" said Babe.

"The trials."

"What's trials?"

"Well," said Fly, "it's a sort of competition, for

sheep-dogs and their bosses. Each dog has to fetch five sheep, and move them through a number of gaps and gateways—you can see which ones, they've got flags on either side—down to that circle that's marked out in the field right at the bottom, and there the dog has to shed some sheep."

"What's 'shed' mean?"

"Separate them out from the rest; the ones to be shed will have collars on."

"And then what?"

"Then the dog has to gather them all again, and pen them."

"Is that all?"

"It's not easy, dear. Not like moving that bunch of woolly fools of ours up and down a field. It all has to be done quickly, without any mistakes. You lose points if you make mistakes."

"Have you ever been in a trial, Mum?"

"Yes. Here. When I was younger."

"Did you make any mistakes?"

"Of course," said Fly. "Everyone does. It's very difficult, working a small number of strange sheep, in strange country. You'll see."

By the end of the day Babe had seen a great deal. The course was not an easy one, and the sheep were

very different from those at home. They were fast and wild, and, good though the dogs were, there were many mistakes made, at the gates, in the shedding-ring, at the final penning.

Babe watched every run intently, and Hogget watched Babe, and Fly watched them both.

What's the boss up to, she thought, as they drove home. He's surely never thinking that one day Babe might . . . no, he couldn't be that daft! Sheep-pig indeed! All right for the little chap to run round our place for a bit of fun, but to think of him competing in trials, even a little local one like to-day's, well, really! She remembered something he had said in his early duck-herding days.

"I suppose you'd say," she remarked, "that those dogs just weren't polite enough?"

"That's right," said Babe.

CHAPTER 8

"Oh Ma!"

Fly's suspicions about what the farmer was up to grew rapidly over the next weeks. It soon became obvious to her that he was constructing, on his own land, a practice course. From the top of the field where the rustlers had come, the circuit which he laid out ran all round the farm, studded with hazards to be negotiated. Some were existing gateways or gaps. Some he made, with hurdles, or lines of posts between which the sheep had to be driven. Some were extremely difficult. One, for example, a plank bridge over a stream, was so narrow that it could only be crossed in single file, and the most honeyed words were needed from Babe to persuade the animals to cross.

Then, in the home paddock, Hogget made a rough shedding-ring with a circle of large stones, and beyond it, a final pen, a small hurdle enclosure no bigger than a tiny room, with a gate to close its mouth when he pulled on a rope.

Every day the farmer would send Fly to cut out five sheep from the flock, and take them to the top of the hill, and hold them there. Then, starting Babe from the gate at the lower end of the farmyard, Hogget would send him away to run them through the course.

"Away to me, Pig!" he would say, or "Come by, Pig!" and off Babe would scamper as fast as his trotters could carry him, as the farmer pulled out his big old pocket watch and noted the time. There was only one problem. His trotters wouldn't carry him all that fast.

Here at home, Fly realised, his lack of speed didn't matter much. Whichever five sheep were selected were only too anxious to oblige Babe, and would hurry eagerly to do whatever he wanted. But with strange sheep it will be different, thought Fly. If the boss really does intend to run him in a trial. Which it looks as though he does! She watched his tubby pinky-white shape as he crested the hill.

That evening at suppertime she watched again as he tucked into his food. Up till now it had never worried her how much he ate. He's a growing boy, she had

thought fondly. Now she thought, he's a greedy boy too.

"Babe," she said, as with a grunt of content he licked the last morsels off the end of his snout. His little tin trough was as shiningly clean as though Mrs Hogget had washed it in her sink, and his tummy was as tight as a drum.

"Yes, Mum?"

"You like being a . . . sheep-pig, don't you?"

"Oh yes, Mum!"

"And you'd like to be really good at it, wouldn't you? The greatest? Better than any other sheep–pig?"

"D'you think there are any others?"

"Well, no. Better than any sheep-dog, then?"

"Oh yes, I'd love to be! But I don't really think that's possible. You see, although sheep do seem to go very well for me, and do what I ask . . . I mean, do what I tell them, I'm nothing like as fast as a dog and never could be."

"No. But you could be a jolly sight faster than you are."

"How?"

"Well, there are two things you'd have to do, dear," said Fly.

"First, you'd have to go into proper training. One little run around a day's not enough. You'd have to practise hard—jogging, cross-country running, sprinting, distance work. I'd help you of course."

It all sounded fun to Babe.

"Great!" he said. "But you said 'two things'. What's the second?"

"Eat less," said Fly. "You'd have to go on a diet."

Any ordinary pig would have rebelled at this point.

Pigs enjoy eating, and they also enjoy lying around most of the day thinking about eating again. But Babe was no ordinary pig, and he set out enthusiastically to do what Fly suggested.

Under her watchful eye he ate wisely but not too well, and every afternoon he trained, to a programme which she had worked out, trotting right round the boundaries of the farm perhaps, or running up to the top of the hill and back again, or racing up and down the home paddock. Hogget thought that Pig was just playing, but he couldn't help noticing how he had grown; not fatter, as a sty-kept pig would have done, but stronger and wirier. There was nothing of the piglet about him any more; he looked lean and racy and hard-muscled, and he was now almost as big as the sheep he herded. And the day came when that strength and hardness were to stand him in good stead.

One beautiful morning, when the sky was clear and cloudless, and the air so crisp and fresh that you could almost taste it, Babe woke feeling on top of the world. Like a trained athlete, he felt so charged with energy that he simply couldn't keep still. He bounced about the stable floor on all four feet, shaking his head about and uttering a series of short sharp squeaks.

"You're full of it this morning," said Fly with a yawn. "You'd better run to the top of the hill and back to work it off."

"OK Mum!" said Babe, and off he shot while Fly settled comfortably back in the straw.

Dashing across the home paddock, Babe bounded up the hill and looked about for the sheep. Though he knew he would see them later on, he felt so pleased with life that he thought he would like to share that feeling with Ma and all the others, before he ran home again; just to say "Hello! Good morning, everybody! Isn't it a lovely day!" They were, he knew, in the most distant of all the fields on the farm, right away up at the top of the lane.

He looked across, expecting that they would be grazing quietly or lying comfortably and cudding in the morning sun, only to see them galloping madly in every direction. On the breeze came cries of "Wolf!" but not in the usual bored, almost automatic, tones of complaint that they used when Fly worked them. These were yells of real terror, desperate calls for help. As he watched, two other animals came in sight, one large, one small, and he heard the sound of barking and yapping as they dashed about after the fleeing sheep. "You get some wolves as'll chase sheep and kill 'em"—Ma's exact words came back to Babe, and without a second thought he set off as fast as he could go in the direction of the noise.

What a sight greeted him when he arrived in the far field! The flock, usually so tightly bunched, was scattered everywhere, eyes bulging, mouths open, heads hanging in their evident distress, and it was clear that the dogs had been at their worrying for some time. A few sheep had tried in their terror to jump the wire fencing and had become caught up in it, some had fallen into the ditches and got stuck. Some were limping as they ran about, and on the grass were lumps of wool torn from others.

Most dreadful of all, in the middle of the field, the worriers had brought down a ewe, which lay on its side feebly kicking at them as they growled and tugged at it.

On the day when the rustlers had come, Babe had felt a mixture of fear and anger. Now he knew nothing but a blind rage, and he charged flat out at the two dogs, grunting and snorting with fury. Nearest to him was the smaller dog, a kind of mongrel terrier, which was snapping at one of the ewe's hindlegs, deaf to everything in the excitement of the worry.

Before it could move, Babe took it across the back and flung it to one side, and the force of his rush carried him on into the bigger dog and knocked it flying.

This one, a large black crossbred, part collie, part retriever, was made of sterner stuff than the terrier, which was already running dazedly away; and it picked itself up and came snarling back at the pig. Perhaps, in the confusion of the moment, it thought that this was just another sheep that had somehow found courage to attack it; but if so, it soon knew

better, for as it came on, Babe chopped at it with his terrible pig's bite, the bite that grips and tears, and now it was not sheep's blood that was spilled.

Howling in pain, the black dog turned and ran, his tail between his legs. He ran, in fact, for his life, an open-mouthed bristling pig hard on his heels.

The field was clear, and Babe suddenly came back to his senses. He turned and hurried to the fallen ewe, round whom, now that the dogs had gone, the horrified flock was beginning to gather in a rough circle. She lay still now, as Babe stood panting by her side, a draggled side where the worriers had pulled at it, and suddenly he realised. It was Ma!

"Ma!" he cried. "Ma! Are you all right?"

She did not seem too badly hurt. He could not see any gaping wounds, though blood was coming from one ear where the dogs had bitten it.

The old ewe opened an eye. Her voice, when she spoke, was as hoarse as ever, but now not much more than a whisper.

"Hullo, young un," she said.

Babe dropped his head and gently licked the ear to try to stop the bleeding, and some blood stuck to his snout.

"Can you get up?" he asked.

For some time Ma did not answer, and he looked

anxiously at her, but the eye that he could see was still open.

"I don't reckon," she said.

"It's all right, Ma," Babe said. "The wolves have gone, far away."

"Far, far, fa-a-a-a-a-ar!" chorused the flock.

"And Fly and the boss will soon be here to look after you."

Ma made no answer or movement. Only her ribs jumped to the thump of her tired old heart.

"You'll be all right, honestly you will," said Babe.

"Oh ar," said Ma, and then the eye closed and the ribs jumped no more.

"Oh Ma!" said Babe, and "Ma! Ma! Ma-a-a-a-a-a!" mourned the flock, as the Land Rover came up the lane.

Farmer Hogget had heard nothing of the worrying —the field was too far away, the wind in the wrong direction—but he had been anxious, and so by now had Fly, because Pig was nowhere to be found.

The moment they entered the field both man and dog could see that something was terribly wrong. Why else was the flock so obviously distressed, panting and gasping and dishevelled? Why had they formed that ragged circle, and what was in the middle of it? Farmer Hogget strode forward, Fly before him parting the ring to make way, only to see a sight that struck horror into the hearts of both.

There before them lay a dead ewe, and bending over it was the pig, his snout almost touching the outstretched neck, a snout, they saw, that was stained with blood.

CHAPTER 9

"Was it Babe?"

"Go home, Pig!" said Farmer Hogget in a voice that was so quiet and cold that Babe hardly recognised it. Bewildered, he trotted off obediently, while behind him the farmer picked up the dead ewe and carried it to the Land Rover. Then with Fly's help he began the task of rescuing those sheep that were caught or stuck, and of making sure that no others were badly hurt. This done, he left Fly to guard the flock, and drove home.

Back at the farm, Babe felt simply very very sad. The sky was still cloudless, the air still crisp, but this was a very different pig from the one that had cantered carefree up the hill not half an hour ago. In those thirty minutes he had seen naked fear and cruelty and death, and now to cap it all, the boss was angry with him, had sent him home in some sort of disgrace. What had he done wrong? He had only done his duty, as a good sheep-pig should. He sat in the doorway of the stables and watched as the Land Rover drove into the yard, poor Ma's head lolling loosely over the back. He saw the boss get out and go into the house, and then, a few minutes later, come out again, carrying something in the crook of one arm, a long thing, a kind of black shiny tube, and walk towards him.

"Come, Pig," said Farmer Hogget in that same cold voice, and strode past him into the stables, while at the same moment, inside the farmhouse, the telephone began to ring, and then stopped as Mrs Hogget picked it up.

Obediently Babe followed the farmer into the dark interior. It was not so dark however that he could not see clearly that the boss was pointing the black shiny tube at him, and he sat down again and waited, supposing that perhaps it was some machine for giving out food and that some quite unexpected surprise would come out of its two small round mouths, held now quite close to his face.

At that instant Mrs Hogget's voice sounded across the yard, calling her husband's name from the open kitchen window. He frowned, lowered the shiny tube, and poked his head around the stable door.

"Oh there you are!" called Mrs Hogget. "What dost think then, that was the police that was, they'm ringing every farmer in the district to warn 'em, there's sheep-worrying dogs about, they killed six sheep t'other side of the valley only last night, they bin seen they have, two of 'em 'tis, a big black un and a little brown un, they say to shoot 'em on sight if you do see 'em, you better get back up the hill and make sure ours is all right, d'you want me to fetch your gun?"

"No," said Farmer Hogget. "It's all right," he said.

He waited till his wife had shut the window and disappeared, and then he walked out into the sunlight with Babe following.

"Sit, Pig," he said, but now his voice was warm and kindly again.

He looked closely at the trusting face turned up to his, and saw, sticking to the side of Babe's mouth, some hairs, some black hairs, and a few brown ones too.

He shook his head in wonder, and that slow grin spread over his face.

"I reckon you gave them summat to worry about," he said, and he broke the gun and took out the cartridges.

Meanwhile Fly, standing guard up in the far field, was terribly agitated. She knew of course that some dogs will attack sheep, sometimes even the very dogs trained to look after them, but surely not her sheep-pig? Surely Babe could not have done such a thing? Yet there he had been at the centre of that scene of chaos, bloodstained and standing over a dead ewe! What would the boss do to him, what perhaps had he already done? Yet she could not leave these fools to find out.

At least though, she suddenly realised, they could tell her what had happened, if the shock hadn't driven what little sense they had out of their stupid heads. Never before in her long life had Fly sunk to engaging a sheep in conversation. They were there to be ordered about, like soldiers, and, like soldiers, never to answer back. She approached the nearest one, with distaste, and it promptly backed away from her.

"Stand still, fool!" she barked. "And tell me who chased you. Who killed that old one?"

"Wolf," said the sheep automatically.

Fly growled with annoyance. Was that the only word the halfwits knew? She put the question differently.

"Was it the pig that chased you? Was it Babe?" she said.

"Ba-a-a-a-abe!" bleated the sheep eagerly.

"What does that mean, bonehead?" barked Fly. "Was it or wasn't it?"

"Wolf," said the sheep.

Somehow Fly controlled her anger at the creature's stupidity. I *must* know what happened, she thought. Babe's always talking about being polite to these woolly idiots. I'll have to try it. I must know. She took a deep breath.

"Please . . ." she said. The sheep, which had begun to graze, raised its head sharply and stared at her with an expression of total amazement.

"Say that agai-ai-ai-ain," it said, and a number of others, overhearing, moved towards the collie.

"Please," said Fly, swallowing hard, "could you be kind enough to tell me . . ."

"Hark!" interrupted the first sheep. "Hark! Ha-a-a-a-ark!" whereupon the whole flock ran and gathered round. They stood in silence, every eye fixed wonderingly on her, every mouth hanging open. Nincompoops! thought Fly. Just when I wanted to ask one quietly the whole fat-headed lot come round. But I must know. I must know the truth about my Babe, however terrible it is.

"Please," she said once more in a voice choked with the effort of being humble, "could you be kind enough to tell me what happened this morning? Did Babe . . .?" but she got no further, for at the mention of the pig's name the whole flock burst out into a great cry of "Ba-a-a-abe!"

Listening, for the first time ever, to what the sheep were actually saying, Fly could hear individual voices competing to make themselves heard, in what was nothing less than a hymn of praise. "Babe ca-a-a-ame!" "He sa-a-a-aved us!" "He drove the wolves awa-a-a-a-ay!" "He made them pa-a-a-a-ay!" "Hip hip hooray! Hip hip hooray! Hip hip hoora-a-a-ay!"

What a sense of relief flooded over her as she heard and understood the words of the sheep! It had been sheep-worriers, after all! And her boy had come to the rescue! He was not the villain, he was the hero!

Hogget and Babe heard the racket as they climbed the hill, and the farmer sent the pig ahead, fearing that perhaps the worriers had returned.

Under cover of the noise Babe arrived on the scene unnoticed by Fly, just in time to hear her reply.

"Oh thank you!" she cried to the flock. "Thank you all so much for telling me! How kind of you!"

"Gosh, Mum," said a voice behind her. "What's come over you?"

CHAPTER 10

"Get it off by heart"

Because Babe had now saved the flock not only from rustlers but also from the worriers, the Hoggets could not do too much for him.

Because he was a pig (though Farmer Hogget increasingly found himself thinking of Pig as Dog and fed him accordingly), they gave him unlimited supplies of what they supposed he could not have too much of—namely, food.

Because he was strong-minded and revelled in his newfound speed, he ate sparingly of it.

Because there was always a lot left over, Fly became fat and the chickens chubby and the ducks dumpy, and the very rats and mice rolled happily about the stables with stomachs full to bursting.

Mrs Hogget even took to calling Babe to the back door, to feed him some titbit or other that she thought he might particularly fancy; and from here it was but a short step to inviting him into the house, which one day she did.

When the farmer came in for his tea, he found not only Fly but also Pig lying happily asleep beside the Aga cooker. And afterwards, when he sat down in his armchair in the sitting-room and switched on the television, Babe came to sit beside him, and they watched the six o'clock news together.

"He likes it," said Hogget to his wife when she came into the room. Mrs Hogget nodded her head a great many times, and as usual had a few words to say on the subject.

"Dear little chap, though you can't call him little no longer, he've growed so much, why, he's big enough to you-know-what, not that we ever shall now, over my dead body though I hopes it ain't if you see what I do mean, just look at him, we should have brought him in the house long ago, no reason why not, is there now?"

"He might mess the carpet," said Farmer Hogget.

"Never!" cried Mrs Hogget, shaking her head the entire time that she was speaking. "He's no more likely to mess than he is to fly, he'll ask to go out when he wants to do his do's, just like a good clean dog would, got more brains than a dog he has, why 'twouldn't surprise me to hear he was rounding up them old sheep of yourn, 'twouldn't honestly, though I suppose you think I'm daft?"

Farmer Hogget grinned to himself. He did not tell his wife what she had never yet noticed, that all the work of the farm was now done by the sheep-pig. And he had no intention of telling her of the final part of his plan, which was nothing less than to enter Pig in that sternest of all tests, the Grand Challenge Sheep Dog Trials, open to all comers! Never in his working life had he owned an animal good enough to compete in these Trials. Now at last he had one, and he was not going to be stopped from realising his ambition by the fact that it was a pig.

In a couple of weeks they would be competing against the best sheep-dogs in the country, would be appearing, in fact, on that very television screen they were now watching.

"No, you're not daft," he said.

But you won't half get a surprise when you sit here and watch it he thought. And so will a lot of other folks.

His plan was simple. He would appear at the Grand Challenge Trials with Fly, and at the last possible moment swap her for Pig. By then it would be too late for anyone to stop him. It didn't matter what

happened afterwards—they could disqualify him, fine him, send him to prison, anything—as long as he could run Pig, just one glorious run, just to show them all!

And they couldn't say they hadn't been warned —the name was there on the entry form. He had been worried, for he was a truthful man, that the heading might say 'Name of Dog', and then whatever he put would be a lie. But he'd been lucky. 'Name of Competitor' (the form said) . . . 'F. Hogget'. 'Name of Entry' . . . 'Pig'.

The simple truth.

Shepherds usually give their dogs short names, like Gyp or Moss—it's so much quicker and easier than shouting 'Bartholomew!' or 'Wilhelmina!'—and though someone might say "'Pig'? That's a funny name," no one in their wildest dreams would guess that simple truth.

The two weeks before the Grand Challenge Trials were two weeks of concentrated activity. Apart from Mrs Hogget who as usual was busy with household duties, everyone now knew what was going on. To begin with, Hogget altered the practice course, cutting out all the frills like the plank bridge over the stream, and building a new course as like as possible

to what he thought they might face on the day.

As soon as Fly saw this, she became convinced that the plan which she had suspected was actually going to be put into operation, and she told the sheep, with whom she was now on speaking terms.

Every night of course she and Babe talked endlessly about the coming challenge before they settled to sleep (in the stables still, though the Hoggets would have been perfectly happy for Babe to sleep in the house, so well-mannered was he).

Thoughtful as ever, Babe was anxious, not about his own abilities but about his foster-mother's feelings. He felt certain she would have given her dog-teeth to compete in the National Trials, the dream of every sheep-dog, yet she must sit and watch him.

"Are you *sure* you don't mind, Mum?" he asked.

Fly's reply was as practical as ever.

"Listen, Babe," she said. "First of all it wouldn't matter whether I minded or not. The boss is going to run you, no doubt of it. Second, I'm too old and too fat, and anyway I was only ever good enough for small local competitions. And lastly, I'll be the happiest collie in the world if you win. And you can win."

"D'you really think so?"

"I'm sure of it," said Fly firmly, but all the same she was anxious too—about one thing.

She knew that the sheep-pig, speedy as he now was, would still be much slower than the dogs, especially on the outrun; but equally she was confident that he could make this up by the promptness with which the sheep obeyed his requests. Here, at home, they shot through gaps or round obstacles as quick as a flash, never putting a foot wrong; the ones to be shed nipped out of the ring like lightning; and at the final penning, they popped in the instant that the boss opened the gate. But that was here, at home. What would strange sheep do? How would they react to Babe? Would he be able to communicate with them, in time, for there would be none to waste?

She determined to ask the flock, and one evening when Babe and the boss were watching television, she trotted off up the hill. Since that first time when she had been forced to speak civilly to them, they no longer cried "Wolf!" at her, and now they gathered around attentively at her first words, words that were carefully polite.

"Good evening," said Fly. "I wonder if you could be kind enough to help me? I've a little problem," and she explained it, speaking slowly and carefully (for sheep are stupid, she said to herself: nobody will ever persuade me otherwise.)

"You see what I mean?" she finished. "There they'll be, these strange sheep, and I'm sure they'll do what he tells them . . . asks them, I mean . . . eventually, but it'll all take time, explaining things. The last creature they'll be expecting to see is a pig, and they might just bolt at the sight of him, before he even gets a chance to speak to them."

"Password," said several voices.

"What do you mean?" Fly said.

"Password, password, Pa-a-a-a-assword!" said

many voices now, speaking slowly and carefully (for wolves are stupid, they said to themselves: nobody will ever persuade us otherwise.)

"What our Babe's got to do," said one, "is to larn what all of us larned when we was little lambs."

"'Tis a saying, see," said another, "as lambs do larn at their mothers' hocks."

"And then wherever we do go . . ."

". . . to ma–a–a–a–arket . . ."

". . . or to another fa–a–a–a–arm . . ."

". . . we won't never come to no ha–a–a–a–arm . . ."

". . . so long as we do say the pa–a–a–assword!"

"And if our Babe do say it to they . . ."

". . . why then, they won't never run away!"

Fly felt her patience slipping, but she controlled herself, knowing how important this information could be.

"Please," she said quietly, "please will you tell me the password?"

For a long moment the flock stood silent, the only movement a turning of heads as they looked at one another. Fly could sense that they were nerving themselves to tell this age-old secret, to give away —to a wolf, of all things—this treasured countersign.

Then "'Tis for Babe," someone said, "'tis for his sa–a–a–ake."

"Ah!" they all said softly. "A-a-a-a-a-a-ah!" and then with one voice they began to intone:

"I may be ewe, I may be ram,
I may be mutton, may be lamb,
But on the hoof or on the hook,
I bain't so stupid as I look."

Then by general consent they began to move away, grazing as they went.

"Is that it?" called Fly after them. "Is that the password?" and the murmur came back "A-a-a-a-a-a-a-a-a-ar!"

"But what does it all mean, Mum?" said Babe that night when she told him. "All that stuff about 'I may be you' and other words I don't understand. It doesn't make sense to me."

"That doesn't matter, dear," said Fly. "You just get it off by heart. It may make all the difference on the day."

CHAPTER II

"Today is the day"

The day, when it dawned, was just that little bit too bright.

On the opposite side of the valley the trees and houses and haystacks stood out clearly against the background in that three-dimensional way that means rain later.

Farmer Hogget came out and sniffed the air and looked around. Then he went inside again to fetch waterproof clothing.

Fly knew, the moment that she set eyes on the boss, that this was the day. Dogs have lived so long with humans that they know what's going to happen, sometimes even before their owners do. She woke Babe.

"Today," she said.

"Today what, Mum?" said Babe sleepily.

"Today is the day of the Grand Challenge Sheep-dog Trials," said Fly proudly. "Which you, dear," she added in a confident voice, "are going to win!" With a bit of luck, she thought, and tenderly she licked the end of his snout.

She looked critically at the rest of him, anxious as any mum that her child should be well turned out if it is to appear in public.

"Oh Babe!" she said "Your coat's in an awful mess. What have you been doing with yourself? You look just as though you've been wallowing in the duck-pond."

"Yes."

"You mean you have?"

"Yes, Mum."

Fly was on the point of saying that puppies don't do such things, when she remembered that he was, after all, a pig.

"Well, I don't know about Large White," she said. "You've certainly grown enormous but it's anyone's guess what colour you are under all that muck. Whatever's to be done?"

Immediately her question was answered.

"Come, Pig," said Hogget's voice from the yard, and when they came out of the stables, there stood the farmer with hosepipe and scrubbing brush and pails of soapy water.

Half an hour later, when a beautifully clean shining Babe stood happily dripping while Hogget brushed out the tassle of his tight-curled tail till it looked like candy-floss, Mrs Hogget stuck her head out of the kitchen window.

"Breakfast's ready," she called, "but what in the world bist doing with thik pig, taking him to a pig show or summat, I thought you was going to drive up and watch the Trials to-day, anybody'd think you was going to enter 'e in them the way you've got un done up, only he wouldn't be a sheep-dog, he'd be a sheep-pig wouldn't 'e, tee hee, whoever heard of such a thing, I must be daft though it's you that's daft really, carrying him about in the poor old Land Rover the size he is now, the bottom'll fall out, I shouldn't wonder, you ain't surely going to drive all that way with him in the back just so's he can watch?"

"No," said Farmer Hogget.

Mrs Hogget considered this answer for a moment with her mouth open, while raising and lowering her eyebrows, shaking her head, and drumming on the window-sill with her finger-tips. Then she closed her mouth and the window.

After breakfast she came out to see them off. Fly was sitting in the passenger seat, Babe was comfortable in

a thick bed of clean straw in the back, of which he now took up the whole space.

Mrs Hogget walked round the Land Rover, giving out farewell pats.

"Good boy," she said to Babe, and "Good girl," to Fly. And to Hogget, "Goodbye and have you got your sandwiches and your thermos of coffee and your raincoat, looks as if it might rain, thought I felt a spot just now though I suppose it might be different where you'm going seeing as it's a hundred miles away, that reminds me have you got enough petrol or if not enough money to get some if you haven't if you do see what I do mean, drive carefully, see you later."

"Two o'clock," said Hogget. And before his wife had time to say anything, added, "On the telly. Live," and put the Land Rover into gear and drove away.

When Mrs Hogget switched the television on at two o'clock, the first thing in the picture that she noticed was that it was raining hard. She dashed outside to fetch her washing in, saw that the sun was shining, remembered it wasn't washing-day anyway, and came back to find the cameras showing the lay-out of the course. First there was a shot of a huge pillar of stone, the height of a man, standing upright in the ground.

"Here," said the voice of the commentator, "is where each handler will stand, and from here each dog will start his outrun; he can go left or right, to get into position behind his sheep; today each dog will have ten sheep to work; they will be grouped near that distant post, called the Holding Post," (all the time the cameras followed his explanations), "and then he must fetch his sheep, through the Fetch Gates, all the way back to the Handler's Post, and round it; then the dog drives the sheep away—to the left as we look at it—through the Drive Away Gates, turns them right again and straight across the line of his fetch, through the Cross Drive Gates, and right again to the Shedding Ring, and when he's shed his sheep and collected them again, then finally he must pen them here."

"Mouthy old thing!" said Mrs Hogget, turning the sound off. "Some folk never know how to hold their tongues, keeping on and on about them silly gates, why don't 'e show us a picture of the spectators, might catch a glimpse of Hogget and Fly, you never knows, though not the pig, I hopes, he's surely not daft enough to walk about with the pig, can't see why he wanted to take un all that way just to lie in the back of the Land Rover, he'd have done better to leave un here and let un sit and watch it on the telly in comfort which is more than some of us have got time for, I

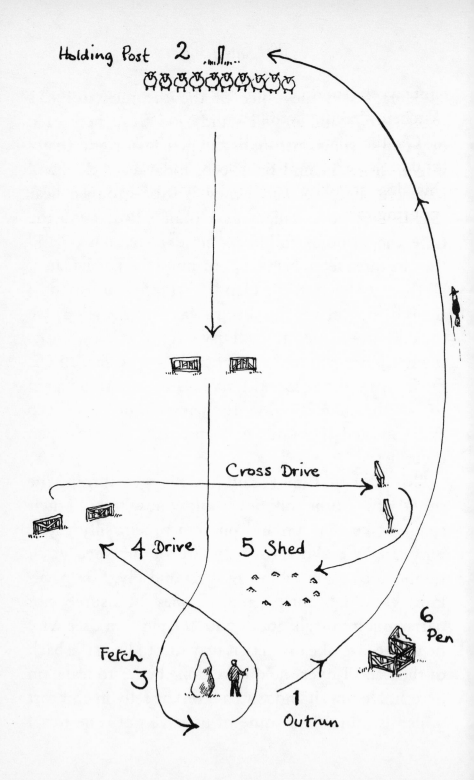

Holding Post 2

Cross Drive

4 Drive

5 Shed

6 Pen

Fetch
3

1

Outrun

got work to do," and she stumped off into the kitchen, shaking her head madly.

On the silent screen the first handler walked out and took up his position beside the great sarsen-stone, his dog standing by him, tense and eager in the pouring rain.

CHAPTER 12

"That'll do"

Hundreds of thousands of pairs of eyes watched that first dog, but none more keenly than those of Hogget, Fly and Babe.

The car-park was a big sloping field overlooking the course, and the farmer had driven the Land Rover to the topmost corner, well away from other cars. From inside it, the three so different faces watched intently.

Conditions, Hogget could see immediately, were very difficult. In addition to the driving rain, which made the going slippery and the sheep more obstinate than usual, there was quite a strong wind blowing almost directly from the Holding Post back towards the handler, and the dog was finding it hard to hear commands.

The more anxious the dog was, the more the sheep

tried to break from him, and thus the angrier he became. It was a vicious circle, and when at last the ten sheep were penned and the handler pulled the gate shut and cried "That'll do!" no one was surprised that they had scored no more than seventy points out of a possible hundred.

So it went on. Man after man came to stand beside the great sarsen-stone, men from the North and from the West, from Scotland, and Wales, and Ireland, with dogs and bitches, large and small, rough-coated and smooth, black-and-white or grey or brown or blue merle. Some fared better than others of course, were steadier on their sheep or had steadier sheep to deal with. But still, as Farmer Hogget's turn drew near (as luck would have it, he was last to go), there was no score higher than eighty-five.

At home Mrs Hogget chanced to turn the sound of the television back up in time to hear the commentator confirm this.

"One more to go," he said, "and the target to beat is eighty-five points, set by Mr Jones from Wales and his dog Bryn, a very creditable total considering the appalling weather conditions we have up here today. It's very difficult to see that score being beaten, but here comes the last competitor to try and do just that," and suddenly there appeared on the screen before Mrs Hogget's astonished eyes the tall long-striding figure of her husband, walking out towards the great stone with tubby old Fly at his heels.

"This is Mr Hogget with Pig," said the commentator. "A bit of a strange name that, but then I must say his dog's rather on the fat side . . . hullo, he's sending the dog back . . . what on earth? . . . oh, good heavens! . . . Will you look at that!"

And as Mrs Hogget and hundreds of thousands of other viewers looked, they saw Fly go trotting back towards the car-park.

And from it, cantering through the never-ending rain, came the long, lean, beautifully clean figure of a Large White pig.

Straight to Hogget's side ran Babe, and stood like a statue, his great ears fanned, his little eyes fixed upon the distant sheep.

At home, Mrs Hogget's mouth opened wide, but for once no sound came from it.

On the course, there was a moment of stunned silence and then a great burst of noise.

On the screen, the cameras showed every aspect of the amazing scene—the spectators pointing, gaping, grinning; the red-faced judges hastily conferring; Hogget and Babe waiting patiently; and finally the commentator.

"This is really quite ridiculous," he said with a shamefaced smile, "but in point of fact there seems to be nothing in the rule book that says that only sheep-dogs may compete. So it looks as though the judges are bound to allow Mr Hogget to run this, er, sheep-pig I suppose we'll have to call it, ha, ha! One look at it, and the sheep will disappear into the next

103

county without a doubt! Still, we might as well end the day with a good laugh!"

And indeed at that moment a great gale of laughter arose, as Hogget, receiving a most unwilling nod from the judges, said quietly, "Away to me, Pig," and Babe began his outrun to the right.

How they roared at the mere sight of him running (though many noticed how fast he went), and at the purely crazy thought of a pig herding sheep, and especially at the way he squealed and squealed at the top of his voice, in foolish excitement they supposed.

But though he was excited, tremendously excited at the thrill of actually competing in the Grand

Challenge Sheep-dog Trials, Babe was nobody's fool. He was yelling out the password: "I may be ewe, I may be ram, I may be mutton, may be lamb, but on the hoof or on the hook, I bain't so stupid as I look," he hollered as he ran.

This was the danger point—before he'd met his sheep—and again and again he repeated the magic words, shouting above the noise of wind and rain, his eyes fixed on the ten sheep by the Holding Post. Their eyes were just as fixed on him, eyes that bulged at the sight of this great strange animal approaching, but they held steady, and the now distant crowd fell suddenly silent as they saw the pig take up a perfect

position behind his sheep, and heard the astonished judges award ten points for a faultless outrun.

Just for luck, in case they hadn't believed their ears, Babe gave the password one last time. ". . . I bain't so stupid as I look," he panted, "and a very good afternoon to you all, and I do apologise for having to ask you to work in this miserable weather, I hope you'll forgive me?"

At once, as he had hoped, there was a positive babble of voices.

"Fancy him knowing the pa-a-a-a-a-assword!"

"What lovely ma-a-a-a-anners!"

"Not like they na-a-a-a-asty wolves!"

"What d'you want us to do, young ma-a-a-a-aster?"

Quickly, for he was conscious that time was ticking away, Babe, first asking politely for their attention, outlined the course to them.

"And I would be really most awfully grateful," he said, "if you would all bear these points in mind. Keep tightly together, go at a good steady pace, not too fast, not too slow, and walk exactly through the middle of each of the three gates, if you'd be good enough. The moment I enter the shedding-ring, would the four of you who are wearing collars (how nice they look, by the way) please walk out of it. And then if you'd all kindly go straight into the final pen, I should be so much obliged."

All this talk took quite a time, and the crowd and the judges and Mrs Hogget and her hundreds of thousands of fellow-viewers began to feel that nothing else was going to happen, that the sheep were never going to move, that the whole thing was a stupid farce, a silly joke that had fallen flat.

Only Hogget, standing silent in the rain beside the sarsen-stone, had complete confidence in the skills of the sheep-pig.

And suddenly the miracle began to happen.

Marching two by two, as steady as guardsmen on parade, the ten sheep set off for the Fetch Gates, Babe a few paces behind them, silent, powerful, confident. Straight as a die they went towards the distant Hogget, straight between the exact centre of the Fetch Gates, without a moment's hesitation, without deviating an inch from their unswerving course. Hogget said nothing, made no sign, gave no whistle, did not move as the sheep rounded him so closely as almost to brush his boots, and, the Fetch completed, set off for the Drive Away Gates. Once again, their pace never changing, looking neither to left nor to right, keeping so tight a formation that you could have dropped a big tablecloth over the lot, they

passed through the precise middle of the Drive Away
Gates, and turned as one animal to face the Cross
Drive Gates.

It was just the same here. The sheep passed through
perfectly and wheeled for the Shedding Ring, while
all the time the judges' scorecards showed maximum
points and the crowd watched in a kind of hypnotised
hush, whispering to one another for fear of breaking
the spell.

"He's not put a foot wrong!"

"Bang through the middle of every gate."

"Lovely steady pace."

"And the handler, he's not said a word, not even

moved, just stood there leaning on his stick."

"Ah, but he'll have to move now—you're never going to tell me that pig can shed four sheep out of the ten on his own!"

The Shedding Ring was a circle perhaps forty yards in diameter, marked out by little heaps of sawdust, and into it the sheep walked, still calm, still collected, and stood waiting.

Outside the circle Babe waited, his eyes on Hogget.

The crowd waited.

Mrs Hogget waited.

Hundreds of thousands of viewers waited.

Then, just as it seemed nothing more would happen, that the man had somehow lost control of the sheep-pig, that the sheep-pig had lost interest in his sheep, Farmer Hogget raised his stick and with it gave one sharp tap upon the great sarsen-stone, a tap that sounded like a pistol-shot in the tense atmosphere.

And at this signal Babe walked gently into the circle and up to his sheep.

"Beautifully done," he said to them quietly, "I can't tell you how grateful I am to you all. Now, if the four ladies with collars would kindly walk out of the ring when I give a grunt, I should be so much obliged. Then if you would all be good enough to wait until my boss has walked across to the final collecting pen over there and opened its gate, all that remains for you to do is to pop in. Would you do that? Please?"

"A-a-a-a-a-a-ar," they said softly, and as Babe gave one deep grunt the four collared sheep detached themselves from their companions and calmly, unhurriedly, walked out of the Shedding Ring.

Unmoving, held by the magic of the moment, the crowd watched with no sound but a great sigh of amazement. No one could quite believe his eyes. No one seemed to notice that the wind had dropped and the rain had stopped. No one was surprised when a single shaft of sunshine came suddenly through a hole in the grey clouds and shone full upon the great sarsen-stone. Slowly, with his long strides, Hogget left it and walked to the little enclosure of hurdles, the final test of his shepherding. He opened its gate and stood, silent still, while the shed animals walked back into the ring to rejoin the rest.

Then he nodded once at Babe, no more, and steadily, smartly, straightly, the ten sheep, with the sheep-pig at their heels, marched into the final pen, and Hogget closed the gate.

As he dropped the loop of rope over the hurdle stake, everyone could see the judges' marks.

A hundred out of a hundred, the perfect perform-ance, never before matched by man and dog in the whole history of sheep-dog trials, but now achieved by man and pig, and everyone went mad!

At home Mrs Hogget erupted, like a volcano, into a great lava-flow of words, pouring them out towards the two figures held by the camera, as though they were actually inside that box in the corner of her sitting-room, cheering them, praising them, congratulating first one and then the other, telling them how proud she was, to hurry home, not to be late for supper, it was shepherd's pie.

As for the crowd of spectators at the Grand Challenge Sheep-dog Trials they shouted and yelled and waved their arms and jumped about, while the astonished judges scratched their heads and the amazed competitors shook theirs in wondering disbelief.

"Marvellous! Ma-a-a-a-a-arvellous!" bleated the ten penned sheep. And from the back of an ancient Land Rover at the top of the car-park a tubby old black-and-white collie bitch, her plumed tail wagging wildly, barked and barked and barked for joy.

In all the hubbub of noise and excitement, two figures still stood silently side by side.

Then Hogget bent, and gently scratching Babe between his great ears, uttered those words that every handler always says to his working companion when the job is finally done.

111

Perhaps no one else heard the words, but there was no doubting the truth of them.

"That'll do," said Farmer Hogget to his sheep-pig. "That'll do."

ACE

Illustrated by Liz Graham-Yooll

CHAPTER I

A Pig with a Mark

"Well I never! Did you ever?" said Farmer Tubbs.

He was leaning on the wall of his pigsty, looking down at a sow and her litter of piglets. The sow was asleep, lying on her side, and six of her seven piglets slept also, their heads pillowed on their mother's huge belly.

But the seventh piglet was wide awake, and stood directly below the farmer, ears cocked, staring up at the man with bright eyes that had in them a look of great intelligence.

"I never seed one like you afore," said Farmer Tubbs. "Matter of fact, I don't suppose there's ever been one like you, eh?"

In reply the piglet gave a single grunt. Farmer Tubbs was not a fanciful man, but he did, just for a moment, fancy that the grunt sounded more like a 'No' than an 'Oink'. He half expected the piglet to shake its head.

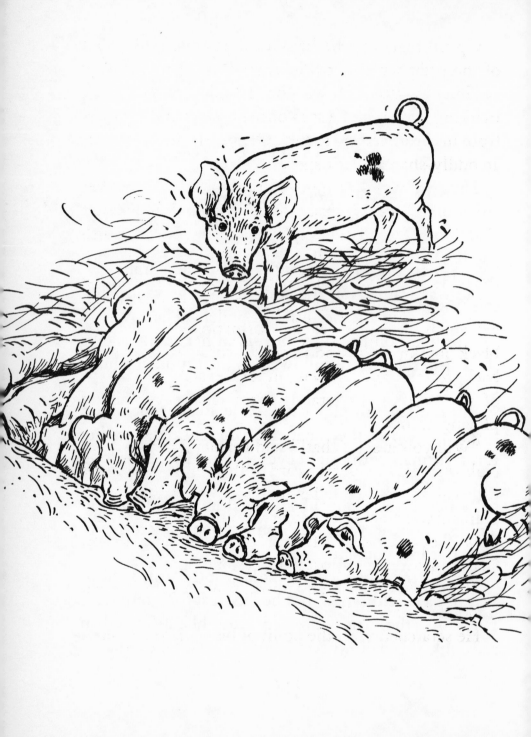

Up till that time he had not noticed anything out of the ordinary about this litter. But what was now catching his attention was the seventh piglet's strange marking, clearly to be seen once he was standing apart from his brothers and sisters. On his left side there was an oddly-shaped black spot.

The sow was a mongrel, numbering amongst her ancestors Large Whites, Saddlebacks and Gloucester Old Spots. Usually her piglets were white with bluish patches, but occasionally a baby would be born with the odd spot or two on it, so it was not remarkable that this piglet should have one. What was however extremely unusual was the formation of the single black marking. It stood out clearly against a white background, and it was almost exactly the shape of the symbol that stands for a club in a pack of playing-cards.

"Will you look at that!" said Farmer Tubbs. "It's a club, a single one! And a card with a single marking is called an ace, young feller-me-lad, d'you know that?"

In answer the piglet gave two quick grunts. Somehow they sounded different from the 'No' grunt, sharp, impatient, almost like 'Yes, Yes'.

"Fancy!" said Farmer Tubbs. "I wonder you never nodded at me."

He scratched with the point of his stick at the black

marking on the piglet's side.

"There be no doubt," he said, "what us shall have to call you. I don't never give names to piglets as a rule—they don't live long enough to make no odds—but us shall have to name you."

The piglet stood silent and motionless, apparently noting every word that was said.

"Your name," said Farmer Tubbs, "is written on you. The Ace of Clubs, that's who you be."

For some while longer the farmer stood leaning on the pigsty wall, chatting to the piglet. Farmer Tubbs enjoyed a nice chat, and since he lived alone and saw few other people, he spent a good deal of time talking either to himself or to his animals.

"If things had turned out different," he said now to the newly-named Ace of Clubs, "and I'd married when I were a young man, I'd likely have had six or seven children by now like your mum has. But I can't say as I'm sorry. Maybe it'd have been nice to have a wife to chat to, but you can have too much of a good thing. Only girl I ever fancied marrying, she were a good strong wench and she were a wonderful cook but, my, didn't she go on! Talk the hind leg off a donkey, she could, you couldn't never have a proper conversation with she, you wouldn't get a word in edgeways. We was engaged for a bit, but then she broke it off and went and wed a sheep farmer, long thin fellow name of Hogget. And I'll tell you a funny thing, young Ace of Clubs, are you listening?"

The piglet grunted twice.

"As well as sheep, Hogget had a pig, a huge old white boar, and that boar could round up sheep, just like a dog. You wouldn't never think that were possible, would you?"

The piglet grunted once.

"Well, 'tis true," said Farmer Tubbs, "and what's more, now I comes to think of it, that clever old boar was your great-grandfather! So you never knows, young Ace—you might be an extrahordinary pig when you'm full-grown."

Except you never will be full-grown, thought the farmer. I shall sell you and your brothers and sisters when you'm eight weeks old, and a few months after that you'll all be pork.

He was careful only to think all this and not to say it out loud. Why, he asked himself? Well, the piglet might understand what he was saying, this one might.

Farmer Tubbs's fat red face creased into a great smile and he shook his head and tapped his forehead with one finger.

"You'm daft, Ted Tubbs, you are!" he cried. "Who ever heard of a pig that could understand the Queen's

English! Can you imagine such a thing, Ace, eh, can you?"

The piglet grunted twice.

CHAPTER 2

A Pig with a Gift

"Mother?" said the Ace of Clubs one morning, six or seven weeks later.

"Yes, dear?"

"What's that noise outside the sty?"

"It's the farmer's pick-up truck, dear."

"What's he going to pick up, Mother?"

"You, dear. You and your brothers and sisters. To take you for a nice ride."

"Where to, Mother?"

Though the sow knew the correct answer to this question, she did not actually understand what it meant. Over the years, all her children had disappeared to this destination at a certain age, and, to be frank, she was always quite glad to see them go. Raising a litter of ever-hungry piglets was *so* demanding.

"You're going to Market," she said comfortably.

"Where's that?"

"It's a place," said the sow, "a very popular place for a holiday I should imagine, judging by the number of animals of all sorts that go to Market. You'll like it there. You'll make lots of new friends, I expect, and have a lovely time."

Ace's six brothers and sisters grew very excited at these words, and ran round the sty squealing. But Ace stood still and looked thoughtful.

"But Mother," he said. "Why do we have to go to Market? I like it here. I don't want to go. Why must I?"

"Why must you ask so many questions?" said the sow sharply, and she went into the inner part of the sty and flopped down in the straw with a sigh of relief at the thought of a bit of peace. She listened drowsily to the sounds of Farmer Tubbs catching up the squealing piglets and putting them into the net-covered back of the pick-up truck, and then the noise of it driving away. She closed her eyes and slept.

But when she woke later and went outside again, a shock awaited her. Ace had not gone to Market.

"Hullo, Mother," he said.

"Why have you not gone to Market?" asked the sow peevishly.

"I didn't want to. I told you."

"Didn't want to! It's not a question of what you want or don't want, it's what the farmer wants. Why didn't he take you?"

"I told him. He said to me, 'Do you want to go to Market?' and I said 'No'."

"You stupid boy!" said the sow. "How could he have possibly known whether you were saying 'Yes' or 'No'?"

Because I've been training him, thought Ace. Two grunts for a Yes, one grunt for a No. I think he's learned that now.

"And how could you possibly have understood what the man said?" went on his mother. "Pigs can't understand people's talk."

"Can't they?" said Ace.

That's odd, he thought. I can.

"No, they certainly cannot," said the sow. "No pig ever has and no pig ever will. I never heard such rubbish. But I still can't think why he took the rest and left you."

123

Just then they heard the sound of the truck returning. The engine was switched off, and footsteps
approached the sty.

"There!" said the sow with a sigh of relief. "He's
come back for you. He must have overlooked you
when he was catching them up. You didn't want to go
to Market indeed! You stupid boy!"

Farmer Tubbs's face appeared over the pigsty wall.

"Don't look so worried, old girl," he said to the
huffing, puffing, grumbly sow. "You'll get your rest
all right—I'm taking young Ace away now. Say goodbye to your mother, Ace."

"Goodbye, Mother," said Ace.

"Goodbye," said the sow, and then, feeling she had
been a trifle rough on him, added "dear", and "have
a nice time", and waddled inside to lie down again.

Farmer Tubbs waited a moment, elbows on the wall
top, and looked down at the piglet he had decided *not*
to take to market.

"Saved your bacon, I have, for the time being any
road," he said. "Not that you could know what I'm
talking about. Though I dare say you'll get to know
what you're called in a while, like a dog would. Eh?
Ace! Ace! That's your name, my lad. The Ace of
Clubs. Human beings like playing games, you see, and
you can play a lot of different games with a pack of

cards. Fifty-two of 'em there are in a pack, Spades, Hearts, Diamonds and Clubs. Though what good 'tis to tell you all that I ain't got no idea."

He opened the door of the sty and came inside, closing it behind him. The last thing he wanted was the piglet loose in the farmyard, dashing about all over the place. He expected that it might be a job to catch it even in the sty, and that when caught, it would squeal and kick and wriggle as its litter-mates all had.

"Steady now," he said as he approached it. "We don't want no fuss."

But Ace stood quite still, allowed himself to be picked up, and made no sound or struggle.

"You'm an extrahordinary pig, you are, young Ace," said Farmer Tubbs as he carried the piglet out.

Because it lay so quietly in his arms (and because it was already quite a weight to carry), the farmer decided to risk putting the piglet down on the ground outside, so that he could bolt the sty door the more easily.

"You sit there a minute, Ace, there's a good boy," he said without really thinking what he was saying, and when he turned round again, it was to find the piglet sitting waiting.

"Well I never! Did you ever?" said Farmer Tubbs. "Anybody would think . . . oh no, don't be so daft,

125

Ted Tubbs."

He stared at the Ace of Clubs for a long thoughtful
minute, and the Ace of Clubs stared back, sitting
silently on his hunkers.

Then Farmer Tubbs cleared his throat, nervously

126

it seemed, took a deep breath, and, turning away, said, "Walk to heel then, Ace," and set off across the yard. Looking down as in a dream, he saw on his left side the piglet marching steadily along, its pink snout level with his heels, the strangely-shaped black emblem upon its flank showing proudly for all to see.

And perhaps because Ace was marching so smartly, Farmer Tubbs was reminded of his own days as a soldier many years before, and he squared his shoulders and threw out his chest and pulled in his stomach. Left right, left right across the yard he went until they came to the door of a loose-box on the far side, and Farmer Tubbs automatically cried "Halt!"

Ace stopped dead.

Inside the loose-box, the farmer sat down hurriedly on a bale of straw. Strange thoughts rushed through his head, and his legs felt wobbly. He licked his lips, and once again taking a deep breath, said in a hoarse voice, "Ace. Lie down."

Ace lay down.

Farmer Tubbs swallowed. He took a large white-spotted red handkerchief from his pocket and mopped his brow.

"Ace," he said. "Listen to me, carefully now. I don't want to make no mistake about this. I don't know if I be imagining things or not. I might be going

127

around the bend. It might be just a cohincidence, or it might be . . . a miracle. But I got to know for certain sure. So you answer me honestly, young Ace of Clubs, you tell old Ted Tubbs the truth."

He paused, and then very slowly and clearly he said, "Can . . . you . . . understand . . . everything . . . that . . . I . . . say?"

The piglet grunted twice.

CHAPTER 3

A Pig and a Goat

I hope you can understand something that I'm going to say, thought Ace. Pigs are permanently hungry anyway, and he had not had a mouthful to eat since early that morning, long before the farmer had set out for Market. Now he was ravenous, and he let out a short but piercing squeal. Farmer Tubbs had not kept pigs all his working life without learning that a squeal like that meant either fury or fear or hunger. And since the piglet looked neither angry nor afraid, he got the message and hurried out to fetch food.

"He's not as stupid as he looks," said Ace out loud.

"He'd have a job to be," said a voice.

Ace spun round to see, standing in the gloom at the far side of the loose-box, a strange figure. It was covered in long greyish hair that hung down its sides like a curtain, and it wore a grey beard and a pair of sharp-looking curved horns.

The goat walked forward into the light and stood looking down at the piglet.

"What's your name?" she said.

"Ace. Ace of Clubs."

"Funny sort of name," said the goat. "How did you get that?"

Ace turned to show his left side.

"It's because of this mark on me," he said. "It's

something to do with some game that humans play, called cards.''

"How do you know that?'' said the goat.

"He told me. Ted Tubbs told me.''

"Ted Tubbs? Is that his name? How do you know it is?''

Ace felt like saying, "Why must you ask so many questions?'' as his mother had, but the goat, with that sixth sense that animals have, continued, "I hope you'll forgive me for asking so many questions, but I'm curious to know how you could possibly understand what the man says.''

The look in her golden eyes was kindly and mild.

"I just do,'' said Ace. "I don't know how. I thought all animals did but my mother said that no pig ever had.''

"Nor goat either,'' said the goat, "nor cow nor sheep nor horse nor hen, to the best of my knowledge. I've lived here all my life, all fifteen years of it, and the only word he says that I can recognise is my name.''

"What's that?''

"Nanny.''

Just then Farmer Tubbs opened the door and came in carrying a bucket of pigswill. He poured it into a trough in the corner of the loose-box and stood watching approvingly as Ace tucked into it.

"I'll tell you summat, Nanny," he said, patting the old goat's hairy back. "You'm looking at a most extrahordinary pig there. Not just his marking I don't mean—I'll swear blind that pig do understand what I do say to him."

He waited till Ace had licked the trough clean and turned to face him, and then he said, "Now then, young Ace, allow me to introduce you. This is Nanny, and I'm putting you in with her so's she can keep an eye on you and teach you a thing or two. She's brought up ever so many kids, Nanny has, and there ain't much she don't know. She'll be company for you, stop you feeling lonely."

"What was he on about?" said Nanny when the farmer had gone. "I heard my name a couple of times but the rest was just the usual gabble."

"He said you were very wise," said Ace.

"I wasn't born yesterday."

"And he said he was leaving me in here with you. I hope you don't mind?"

"Not a bit," said Nanny. "You'll be company for me, stop me feeling lonely." She pulled a wisp of hay out of the crib and munched it thoughtfully. "How come you never went to market this morning then?" she said. "I looked out and saw a bunch of pigs going off in the truck. Why did he leave you behind?"

133

"He asked me did I want to go," said Ace, "and I said 'No'."

"You mean to tell me that as well as you being able to understand the man . . . what did you call him?"

"Ted Tubbs."

"As well as you understanding Ted Tubbs, he can understand what *you* say?"

"Only three things," said Ace. "One grunt means 'No', two grunts mean 'Yes', and a sharpish squeal means 'Fetch food'. I think he's learned those all right."

"Going to teach him any more?"

"I don't know really. I suppose I could increase the grunts, three for this and four for that and so on, but I don't know if he could cope with it. What do you think, Nanny?"

"Might be beyond him," said Nanny. "He's not all that bright. Might be better to *show* him what you want."

"Like what?"

"Well, what d'you fancy doing?"

Ace thought.

"I wouldn't mind having a walk round the farm," he said. "You know, have a good look at everything, meet all the other animals. I've been stuck in a sty all my life so far and now I'm shut up in here."

"All right," said Nanny. "So you'd like to get out of this loose-box. I can't open the door, you can't open the door, he can. I can't tell him to open it, you can. By showing him what you want."

"How?"

"Listen," said Nanny, and she outlined a simple plan.

When Farmer Tubbs next opened the half-door of the loose-box and came in to fill Nanny's crib with hay for the night, the old goat bleated. To him it was just a bleat. To Ace she was saying, "Go on. Try it now."

Ace trotted up behind the farmer as he reached up to the crib, and butted him in the back of the leg with his snout.

"What's up with you, Ace?" said Farmer Tubbs, and for answer the piglet went to the door which the farmer had closed behind him, and butted it hard, several times, so that it shook on its hinges.

"You wants me to open it?"

Two grunts.

"Why?"

Ace marched round the box a couple of times, came back to the door and butted it again.

"You wants to go for a walk!" said Farmer Tubbs. "Well I never! Did you ever? What next? D'you want me to come with you?"

One grunt.

"Oh all right, then. But you come back when I calls you, understand?" and reassured by an affirmative answer, the farmer opened the door.

"And he will," he said to Nanny. "You don't understand what I'm saying because you're not all that bright. But that Ace—why, he can do everything bar talk. I suppose you could say he's too clever for words."

CHAPTER 4

A Pig and a Cat

Farmer Tubbs spent a worried time talking anxiously to himself as he went about his chores.

"You'm a fool, Ted Tubbs," he said. "Pigs is for pigsties, not to be let go wandering about wherever they fancies. Don't like to follow him around. Looks like I don't trust him. Whoever heard of trusting a pig, I needs my brains seeing to. But then he might hurt hisself, he might run away, he might get lost. Worth a bit of money a pig that size is, but 'tisn't the value if I'm honest. I've got real fond of that pig."

He kept looking at his watch, forcing himself to allow a full hour to pass, and when it had, he went and stood outside the loose-box, half-hoping that the pig would have made his own way back and be waiting there, safe and sound. But there was no sign of Ace.

Behind him there was a rattle as Nanny put her forefeet up on top of the half-door and peered out.

"Right then, Nanny," said Farmer Tubbs. "He's had long enough. It'll be dark afore long. We'll fetch him back, shall us?" and he called "Ace!" He waited a minute or two, but the piglet did not appear.

"Coop—coop—coop—coop—coop— come on then!" shouted Farmer Tubbs, the sounds he always made to call cows or sheep or chickens, but though there was some distant mooing and bleating in answer and a few old hens came scuttling hopefully across the yard, Ace still did not come.

"You'm a fool, Ted Tubbs," said the farmer. "What am I thinking of! There's only one proper way to get him back," and he cupped his hands to his mouth and took a deep breath and bellowed the summons that all pigmen have always used over the ages to bring their errant charges hurrying home, curling their tails behind them.

"PIG—pig—pig—pig—PIG!! Pig—pig—pig—pig—PIG!!" roared Farmer Tubbs, and in half a moment there was a distant rattle of little trotters and Ace came in sight, galloping as hard as he could go with that curious rocking-horse action that pigs have.

"What did I tell you!" said Farmer Tubbs triumphantly to Nanny, but inwardly he heaved a sigh of relief as he opened the door and let in the puffing, panting Ace of Clubs.

138

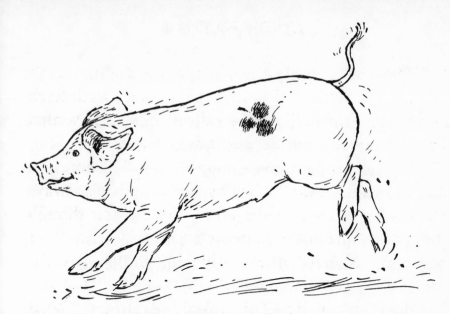

"Good boy!" he said, patting the piglet (just like he were a dog, he thought). "Good boy, Ace!"

But in reply there was only a rather breathless but none the less urgent squeal, so off he hastened to fetch food.

When the farmer (and the food) had finally disappeared, Nanny said, "How did you get on?"

"I had a lovely time," said Ace. "I made a speech to the sheep, had a conversation with the cows, a discussion with the ducks, a gossip with the geese, and a chat to the chickens. And by the way, you were right, Nanny. I asked all the different sorts of animals if they could understand what Ted Tubbs says to them, and they couldn't. They know some things, like to come when he calls them, but that's about all."

139

"The cows would know their names, I'm sure," said Nanny.

"Oh yes, they did. Called after flowers mostly, they are—Buttercup, Daisy, Primrose, that sort of thing. But I'll tell you a funny thing, Nanny—all the sheep had the same name."

"Really?"

"Yes. I said to one of them, 'What's your name?' and she said, 'Barbara'. But when I said to the next one, 'And what's your name?' the answer was 'Barbara'. I asked all of them in turn and they all said, 'Baaaabara'."

"How funny," said Nanny, straight-faced.

"Wasn't it?" said Ace.

He yawned hugely and snuggled down in the straw.

"Good-night then, Ace," said the old goat. "Sleep tight, mind the fleas don't bite," but the only reply was a snore.

Full-stomached, and tired out after all his exploring (for his legs were rather short), Ace slept soundly that night. When he woke, it was bright morning and the low early sun was streaming in over the half-door. Ace stood up and shook himself. Under the wooden crib Nanny lay, her jaws going round rhythmically.

"Morning, Nanny," said Ace.

"She can't answer," said a voice.

Looking up, Ace saw that there was a cat sitting on top of the crib. It was a large white cat, with one yellow eye and one green one.

"Why not?" he said.

"Because she's cudding," said the cat. "Chewing the cud. You're not supposed to talk with your mouth full, didn't your mother tell you?"

"No," said Ace. "Why not?" he asked.

"It's rude," said the cat.

At that moment Nanny swallowed noisily and got to her feet.

"Don't tease the lad, Clarence," she said. "He's only young," and to Ace she said, "This is an old friend of mine. His name is Clarence."

"How do you do?" said Ace.

"Pretty well, considering," said the cat.

"Considering what?"

The cat looked narrowly at him.

"MYOB," he said.

"What does that mean?"

"Mind your own business."

"Clarence!" said Nanny.

"Don't mind him," she went on to the piglet. "It's just his manner. He doesn't mean any harm."

"It's NSOMN," said Ace.

"What does that mean?" asked Clarence.

"No skin off my nose."

"But of a clever Dick, aren't you? What do they call you?"

"Ace of Clubs."

The white cat jumped easily down from the crib and walked slowly around the piglet. First he inspected

Ace's right (white) side with his left (yellow) eye, and then the left (marked) side with his right (green) eye.

"I've seen that odd black shape somewhere before," he said.

"It's something to do with a game the farmer plays," said Ace. "With some cards."

"Ah yes, that's it," said Clarence. "He sits down and lays all these bits of card out in rows, I've watched him. He lays them out on the table, some with black marks, some with red, some with pictures."

"Fifty-two of them, there are," said Ace. "Spades, hearts, diamonds and clubs. Funny though, isn't it? I thought you played games with other people—I used to with my brothers and sisters, chasing games, tag, that sort of thing. Strange for him to play on his own. He must have a lot of patience."

"Wait a minute, young know-all," said Clarence. "Are you telling me you've been inside the farm-house?"

"Oh no."

"Then how come you know all this stuff about fifty-two cards and hearts and clubs and all that?"

"He told me. Ted Tubbs told me."

"Ted Tubbs?"

"That's the man's name, Clarence," said Nanny. "You and I have never known what he's called but Ace found out. You see, he understands his language."

"Do you mean to tell me," said Clarence, "that you can understand every word that What's-his-name . . ."

". . . Ted . . ."

". . . Ted says to you?"

"Yes," said Ace. "I thought that all the animals could but it seems I'm a freak."

"You'll have to watch out, Clarence," said Nanny. "Next thing you know, you won't be the only one sitting in a comfy chair in the nice warm farmhouse watching Ted play cards. Ace will be in there too."

Clarence gave a loud miaow of amusement.

"Not for long," he said. "Young know-all wouldn't take much time to blot his copybook."

"What d'you mean?" said Ace.

"Only cats and dogs are allowed indoors, because only they can be house-trained."

"What does that mean?"

With a look of disdain on his face Clarence indicated a large lump of pig dung in the straw.

"You can't go doing that on the carpet," he said. "Or the other."

"Why not?"

"It's rude. Didn't your mother tell you? Humans don't mind if you do it outside but indoors it's simply not done. We cats bury that sort of thing anyway."

"Oh," said Ace. "Does Ted do it outside then?"

"No no no," said Clarence. "He has a special little room with a kind of white chair with a hole in it."

"He's almost as clean as a cat," said Nanny drily.

"That would be difficult," said Clarence smugly, and he leapt neatly on to the top of the half-door and was gone.

Ace thought about all this.

"Nanny," he asked, "are you house-trained?"

Nanny gave a loud bleat of laughter.

"Not likely," she said. "A goat's gotta do what a goat's gotta do!"

"Well d'you think I could be? I wouldn't mind seeing what it's like inside Ted's house. D'you think I could train myself?"

"Ace," said Nanny. "The more I see of you, the more I think you could do most things. Except fly."

CHAPTER 5

A Pig with a Plan

That day, and every day that followed, Farmer Tubbs let Ace out to run free. At first he bombarded the piglet with a whole list of Don'ts—don't go too far, don't go near the road, don't fall in the duckpond, don't chase the hens and so on. But gradually as time passed and Ace always behaved himself, the farmer just let him out without a word, confident now that he would not get into trouble and would return to the loose-box when called. It never occurred to him to say, "Don't go into the house."

In fact, Ace was not in a hurry to do that. He talked the matter over with Nanny, and she advised against haste.

"You don't want to rush him," she said. "Having a pig in the house is not something that humans are used to. He might take it amiss. And one thing's sure—you've got to keep on the right side of Ted Tubbs.''

"What's wrong with being on his left side?" said Ace.

"No, it's just an expression. To keep on the right side of someone means to keep in his good books."

"Good books? I don't understand."

"Sorry," said Nanny. "You're such a bright fellow that I forget how young and inexperienced you are. What I mean is that it's important for Ted to like you, to treat you as a pet."

"What's a pet?" said Ace.

"An animal that people keep for the pleasure of its company, like a dog or a cat."

"Are you a pet?"

"Sort of."

"What about the other animals on the farm—the cattle, the sheep and the poultry?"

"No, they're not pets. They all finish up as meat," said Nanny. "Sooner or later, young and old alike, they're all killed to provide meat for humans to eat."

Ace shuddered.

"My brothers and sisters," he said, "who went to Market . . . ?"

"Someone there will have bought them, to feed them up till they're fat enough to kill. And that could

147

still happen to you, Ace, if you rub Ted Tubbs up the wrong way."

"You mean," said Ace slowly, "if I . . . what was it Clarence said? . . . if I blot my copybook?"

"Exactly," said Nanny. "I'm not saying you won't be able to go into the farmhouse one day if that's what you want to do. But don't try to run before you can walk, don't rush your fences, look before you leap. The first thing to remember is that the farmer is not the only person who lives in that house."

"Why, who else is there?"

"Clarence, and Megan. Now Clarence won't be any problem—I'll have a word with him—but Megan's a different matter."

"Who's Megan?"

"Ted's dog. You may not have seen her. She's not too keen on taking exercise."

"I think I have," said Ace. "Brownish?"

"Yes."

"Short-legged?"

"Yes."

"With big sticking-up ears and a stumpy tail?"

"Yes."

"And very fat?"

"That's Megan. She loves her food, Megan does. She must be the fattest corgi that ever came out of Wales. Now you'll have to get her on your side. You see, cats don't really bother about people, they only care about themselves, but a dog reckons it's man's best friend. Megan could be very jealous. But if she takes a liking to you, I think you'll be home and dry."

"How can I make her like me?" said Ace.

"I'll tell you," said Nanny. "Megan, you see, is the most tremendous snob."

"What's a snob?"

"Someone who pretends to be much better-bred than other folk."

"And is she?"

"No, but she looks down her nose at all other dogs. They are common curs. She (she says), has Royal blood."

"And has she?"

"Ask her," said the old goat. "I'm not going to tell you any more about Megan, because the best thing you can do is to ask her yourself, very respectfully, mind, and remember to appear tremendously impressed by what she tells you. Oh, and don't call her 'Megan'. That would be much too familiar."

"What should I call her?" said Ace.

"Ma'am," said Nanny.

★

With all this in mind, Ace began to make changes in his routine. It had become his habit to make, each day, a grand tour of the farm, chatting to all the other animals (for he was a friendly fellow). Meeting the ducks and geese and chickens was easy for they all ranged freely. As for the cows, the barbed-wire fences that kept them in were no problem to Ace, who ran easily under the lowest strand. Sheep-fencing was a different matter, for by now Ace had really grown too big to be called a piglet and so too fat to squeeze through the wire-mesh. But this was no great loss, since none of them ever said anything to him but "Barbara".

At first he had always visited his mother to say good-morning, but lately he had given this up. For one thing, they could not see each other since the sty walls were too high, and for another she never really sounded pleased about his visits.

"I understood that you had gone to Market," she said when first she heard his voice again. She sounded disappointed. And before long the only answer he received to his cheery greeting was a grunt, so then he didn't bother. Now, he went straight towards the farmhouse as soon as he was let out in the morning, with the idea of meeting Megan in mind.

Behind the house was a piece of lawn bordered by

a shrubbery and in this he hid to watch what went on. It never varied, he found. Each day when Ted Tubbs had finished milking and gone indoors for his breakfast, the corgi would come out of the house on to the lawn and waddle about on the grass, making herself comfortable. If the weather was fine, she would then lie awhile in the sunshine, but any hint of rain or wind sent her hurrying in again as fast as her short legs would carry her stout body.

For a week or more Ace lay and watched and wondered how best to approach Megan. First impressions, he felt, might be very important. In the event, the matter was decided for him.

He was lying flat in the shrubbery one sunny morning, watching Megan through the leaves, when suddenly a voice said, "Peeping Tom, eh?"

Ace whipped round to see Clarence sitting a few feet away regarding him with a cold green-and-yellow stare.

"I don't know what you mean," he said in a flustered tone.

"Hiding in the bushes," said Clarence. "Spying on a lady. You can't do that."

"Why not?"

"It's rude. Didn't your mother tell you? Just exactly what are you up to, young know-all?"

Ace decided on honesty, not because he was aware that it was the best policy but because he was straight-forward by nature.

"Clarence," he said. "Will you do me a favour? Will you introduce me to Megan?"

"Why should I?"

"Well, you see I really am very keen to become a house-pig, you know, live in the farmhouse like you and Megan do. Nanny said that you wouldn't mind but that Megan might not like the idea."

Clarence combed his whiskers thoughtfully.

"You're an odd sort of a chap, you are," he said. "I don't care what you do. As far as I'm concerned it's . . . what was it you said?"

"NSOMN."

"Quite. And you haven't a hope of succeeding, in my view. Never mind what the man thinks of such an idea, I can tell you who won't stand for it, and that's HRH."

"HRH?"

"Her Royal Highness over there—Western Princess of Llanllowell."

"Is that Megan's real name?"

"Oh yes. Registered at the Kennel Club, ten champions in pedigree, all that tosh. It's enough to make a cat laugh," said Clarence, and he stood up and walked out on to the lawn towards the dog, Ace following.

"Megan," he said when he reached her, "this is Ace. Ace—Megan," and he sauntered off, waving his tail.

Ace stood smartly at attention in front of the corgi, his trotters neatly together. Close up, he could see that she was not merely brownish but a fine red-gold colour with a snowy-white chest.

Ears pricked, head raised, she favoured him with an

imperious stare. From her expression you would have thought there was a bad smell under her nose. Ace cleared his throat, and with downcast eyes he said, "Your servant, Ma'am."

CHAPTER 6

A Pig and a Dog

The corgi did not reply.

Glancing up, Ace fancied that the look in her eyes had softened a little. Was that a slight wag of her stumpy tail? Might as well go the whole hog, he thought.

"Please accept my apologies, Ma'am," he said, "for interrupting your walk. May it please Your Majesty."

Now the stump was really wagging.

"There's nice-mannered!" said Megan. "Sick and tired it is we are of being called plain 'Megan' by that cat. Who was it told you that we are of the blood-royal?"

"A friend, Ma'am. Nanny the goat."

"The goat!" said Megan scornfully. "A creature of no breeding whatsoever, look you. Common as muck. Surprised it is we are that she should even be aware of our rank. What did she tell you about us?"

Ace had never heard of the royal 'we', but he was becoming used to the way the dog spoke and to her unfamiliar lilting accent, so different from Ted Tubbs's broad tones.

"She said you had a very good pedigree, Ma'am," he said. "Though I don't quite know what that means, I'm afraid."

"We don't imagine for one moment that you would," said Megan.

She stared pointedly at the mark on Ace's left side.

"You're not pure bred, that's obvious, isn't it?" she said.

"I shouldn't think so," said Ace.

"Don't know anything about your ancestors, we presume?"

"No. Though I'm told my great-grandfather was a sheep-pig."

"Well there you are, see. Doesn't bear thinking about."

"But please," said Ace, "won't you tell me all about your family, Ma'am? If you would be so gracious, Your Majesty."

"There's ignorant you are," said Megan. "There's only one person in the whole country that is properly

addressed as 'Your Majesty', and that is the Queen.
She is the most important human being in the land,
see. Now the point about our family is not merely
to do with pedigree—plenty of dogs have pedigrees
a mile long even if not as distinguished. No, the reason
why we are head and shoulders above all the other
breeds is this. Corgis are the Queen's dogs. Buckingham Palace is bursting with them, and wherever she
goes—Windsor, Sandringham, Balmoral—she takes
them with her. Now the Queen's children are called
'Their Royal Highnesses'. In fact she made her eldest
son the Prince of Wales (because of her fondness for
corgis, no doubt). And so her own dogs are styled
princes and princesses every one, look you. Now it
so happens, see, that we personally are directly related
to the Royal corgis. Western Princess of Llanllowell,
that is our proper title."

"So should I call you 'Your Royal Highness'?" said
Ace.

"No no, that's for humans. Corgis were originally
bred as cattle-dogs, to nip at their heels. Now a tall dog
might get a good kick in the face doing that, but our
breed, see, has nice short legs to keep out of trouble. So
it's plain how you should address me, isn't it now?"

"How?"

"'Your Royal Lowness'," said Megan. "But you

need only do so at the start of a conversation. From then on, 'Ma'am' will suffice."

"Yes, Ma'am," said Ace.

"Now," said Megan, "the audience is at an end. You may attend on us tomorrow."

"Yes, Ma'am," said Ace.

He turned to go, but Megan said sharply, "Backwards, look you."

"Sorry?"

"It is customary to withdraw backwards when leaving the presence of royalty."

Ace could not wait to tell Nanny. He raced back to the loose-box and bashed on the door with his hard little snout so loudly that a puzzled Ted Tubbs came hurrying to let him in.

158

The farmer leaned on the half-door and looked over at the pig.

"What's the matter, my boy?" he said. "Did summat frighten you?" but receiving only a single grunt in reply, went off again about his business.

"What was he asking?" said Nanny.

"If something frightened me. No no, I was just in a hurry to come in because I've just met Megan and I'm bursting to tell you all about it," said Ace, and he did.

"'Your Royal Lowness' indeed!" said Nanny. "What a fraud! She really gets my goat with all her airs and graces. Are you going to be able to put up with all that stuff, Ace?"

"Oh yes, it's quite amusing really. I didn't realize a snob would be so funny."

"I suppose she said that you were common?"

"Oh yes, and you too."

Nanny gave a snort.

"D'you think," said Ace, "that Megan is really related to the Queen's corgis?"

"Shouldn't think so for a moment. What she has never realized is that it doesn't matter *who* you are. It's *what* you are that counts in this life, and you're worth ten of that silly fat thing. Snobbery apart, she's like all dogs, thinks she can understand what the man says. But like all dogs, she can't. Just a few commands that

159

she's learned to obey, that's about as far as it goes. Now you, you can understand his every word. Did you tell Megan that?"

"No."

There was a scratch of claws on the outside of the half-door and Clarence appeared over the top of it.

"She wouldn't believe you if you did," he said.

"Oh you heard that, did you?" said Nanny.

"Listening in to other people's conversation!" said Ace. "You shouldn't do that, Clarence."

"Why not?"

"It's rude. Didn't your mother tell you?"

Clarence did not answer this. Like all cats, he had the knack of making others feel uncomfortable by simply not reacting, by appearing, that is, to be taking no notice of what has been said. He jumped up on to the crib and began to wash his face, so that now it was Ace who felt that he had been rude by being cheeky. He

tried to make amends by making conversation.

"Why wouldn't Megan believe me, Clarence?" he said.

Clarence finished his washing before replying.

Then he said, "Because she only believes what she

wants to believe. Besides, if you succeed in your plan to get into the house, you could have the upper hand of her. You'll be able to understand the man. She won't. It could be amusing."

"Now Clarence," said Nanny. "I know what you're thinking. You'd like to take that dog down a peg or two, wouldn't you?"

Once again Clarence did not answer. He lay down and licked his black nose with his pink tongue. Then he wrapped his white tail around him, shut his yellow eye, shut his green eye, and went to sleep.

Next morning when Farmer Tubbs came out of the house after breakfast, he saw a strange sight. Sitting close together in the middle of the lawn were his dog, his cat and the Ace of Clubs. Anyone would think, he said to himself, that all three of them were household pets.

"You'll have to watch out, Megan, and you, Clarence," he said. "Next thing you know, you won't be the only ones sitting in comfy chairs in the nice warm farmhouse, watching me play cards. Ace will be in there too," and he walked away chuckling to himself at so ridiculous an idea.

CHAPTER 7

A Pig in the House

The farmer's words, Ace could see, were received quite differently by the other two animals. Clarence took absolutely no notice but stared absently into the distance. Megan looked up at the man, her ears flattened, and wagged her whole rump in pleasure at the sound of his voice.

Pity she can't understand what he said, thought Ace. She might ask me in. Ted's left the door wide open too. How am I going to wangle an invitation? He caught Clarence's eye (the yellow one, as it happened) and once again that telepathic sense that humans seldom, but animals so often, possess, came into play.

"He's left the door open," said Clarence. "Care to have a look round the house, Ace?"

"Oh could I?" said Ace. Clarence had never before called him by name, and he warmed to the white cat.

"You most certainly could not!" barked Megan

sharply. "A pig in the house! There's ridiculous! We never heard of such a thing!"

"I just thought you might like to show Ace your trophies, Megan," said Clarence smoothly.

The corgi's expression softened.

"Trophies?" said Ace. "What are they?"

"Awards that Megan won at dog shows," said Clarence. "Prize-cards, rosettes, that sort of thing."

"And a cup," said Megan. "You're forgetting that we won a cup in our younger days."

"So you did," said Clarence. "A little silver cup. Well, silvery-coloured anyway. Ace would be ever so interested, wouldn't you, Ace?"

"Oh yes, yes, I would! You must be very proud, Ma'am, to have won these things."

"We hardly expected to lose," said Megan, and she got up and waddled off into the farmhouse.

"Come on," said Clarence. "That's tickled her vanity. I knew it would. Follow me now, and don't speak till you're spoken to."

Inside, he led the way down a passage and into the living-room. On either side of the fireplace were two armchairs, and in the smaller one Western Princess of Llanllowell already lay in regal state.

On the wall beside this chair were fastened three cards, coloured red, with black writing on them, and pinned to each card was a blue rosette. On the mantel-shelf above the fireplace stood, amongst other knick-knacks, a very small cup, of a size suitable to contain a sparrow's egg.

Megan glanced up at these objects.

"The Royal Collection," she said offhandedly. "Beautiful, isn't it now?"

"Oh yes, Ma'am," said Ace in reverent tones. "It is an honour to see them." See them he could, but read what was written on them he could not. The inscription on the three prize-cards was in fact identical except for the dates, which spanned three successive years.

VILLAGE FETE
NOVELTY DOG SHOW
CLASS 10—FATTEST DOG
FIRST PRIZE

On the little cup was engraved:

DOG DERBY
ANY VARIETY 200 YARDS RACE
BOOBY PRIZE

"Impressive, aren't they?" said Clarence. He winked (the green eye) at Ace.

"Oh yes!" breathed Ace.

164

"Gracious of Her Lowness to compete, don't you think?" said Clarence, shutting his yellow eye.

"Royalty has its obligations, look you," said Megan modestly. "*Noblesse oblige.*"

She settled herself more comfortably in the armchair.

"The cat will take you on a conducted tour," she said. "We hope your feet are clean."

"Oh it was a scream. Nanny!" said Ace that evening, back in the loose-box. "Clarence just went out of the room of course, but I could see Megan watching me out of the corner of her eye so I walked out backwards. 'What does *noblesse oblige* mean, Clarence?' I said when I caught him up.

"'It's foreign talk,' he said.

"'What sort?' I said.

"'Double Dutch,' he said.

"So I wasn't any the wiser."

"Never mind," said Nanny. "What happened next?"

"Clarence showed me all over the house."

"Upstairs too?"

"Yes, though that was difficult. The stairs are steep. Megan can't get up them at all, Clarence says, she's too stout. I saw the bedrooms, and a room with a big white trough in it."

"That would be the bathroom," said Nanny.

"Yes, that's it, that's where Ted washes himself, and there was one of those white chairs with a hole in the middle of it too. There was another one in a very small room downstairs."

"You didn't . . . do anything, I hope?" said Nanny.

"Do anything?"

"Yes, you know . . ."

"Oh no," said Ace. "I went out on the lawn. 'I'll be in the kitchen when you've finished', Clarence said to me. He's nice when you get to know him, Clarence, isn't he?"

"Yes," said Nanny. "He lives in the kitchen, I know. He has a bed right by the Aga cooker, he's often told me how cosy it is in there on winter nights."

"That's right," said Ace. "I saw some other downstairs rooms but the kitchen's lovely, full of nice food smells. But still I think the living-room's the place for me, even though it means putting up with Her Lowness."

"Why?"

"Because in the living-room Ted Tubbs has got the most amazing thing, Nanny. You just can't imagine what an extrahordinary thing it is."

"What is?"

"The magic box!"

"Magic box?" said Nanny. "What are you talking about, Ace?"

"Well," said Ace, "when we'd finished the tour of the house we went back into the living-room and Megan asked Clarence if he'd showed me everything and Clarence said, 'Yes,' and Megan said, 'Upstairs too?' And then Clarence stared at her in that way he has and said, 'Oh yes, Your Lowness, the stairs weren't too high for Ace,' and Megan said, 'We are not amused,' and Clarence said, 'A cat may look at a princess,' and climbed into the other armchair.

"I waited a bit but neither of them said any more. In fact they both went to sleep, so I thought maybe I'd outstayed my welcome. But just as I was going out of the room I saw this thing in the corner. A big box it was, only one side was nearly all glass, like a window. So I walked up to it and had a look in this window but all I could see was myself looking back."

"That would be your reflection," said Nanny. "Like you get if you look in a puddle or in the duck-pond. Nothing magic about that."

"No, but wait," said Ace. "Below this glass window there were some knobs sticking out. So out of curiosity I pushed one of these knobs with my snout, and you wouldn't believe what I saw then, Nanny!"

"What did you see?"

"Inside that box," said Ace slowly and impressively, "there was a man, talking! He was talking about all kinds of different things, and as well as the man there were loads of different pictures, and the man talked about them too. Megan and Clarence didn't take a bit of notice, I suppose because they wouldn't have understood what the man was saying. But I could, of course, and it was ever so interesting, Nanny, honestly! I tell you, I simply couldn't take my eyes off that magic box!''

Thus it was that Farmer Tubbs, his morning's work finished, came in to his living-room to find the Ace of Clubs sitting on his hunkers in front of the television set, watching the BBC *One O'Clock News*.

CHAPTER 8

A Pig and the Television

After that, life was never really the same again for Farmer Ted Tubbs. All that afternoon he talked to himself in a bemused fashion.

"That pig," he said, "he were sat there watching the telly! Must have switched it on hisself. Never seed such a extrahordinary thing. I couldn't think of nothing to say. In the end I says to him, 'Anything interesting on the news then, Ace?' and he gives a couple of grunts, so I didn't like to turn it off. I goes and has my bit of lunch and when I comes back he's sat there watching *Neighbours*. What next, Ted Tubbs, what next?"

So stunned was the farmer by the pig's actions that the idea of forbidding him the house in future never crossed his mind, especially as, in the days that followed, Ace behaved faultlessly. All he did was to watch a great deal of television. He damaged nothing and made no messes anywhere (for Farmer Tubbs had

170

the sense always to leave the garden door open: he himself often did not bother to take off his wellies when he came in, so a few muddy trotter-marks did not signify). And at tea-time, before the farmer came in after finishing the afternoon milking, the pig would switch the television off with a prod of his snout, leave the house, and make his way back to the door of the loose-box. Here, if Farmer Tubbs did not hurry, a loud squeal would tell him that Ace wanted to be let in, fed, and left to spend the night with his friend Nanny the goat.

"Just as well, I suppose," the farmer said to himself (and to Megan and Clarence, though his reasoning meant nothing to them), "because if he stopped in the house we'd have the telly on all night long. 'Tisn't that I don't enjoy some programmes, but when there's rubbish on I likes to switch off and have a nice game of patience. Now if that pig was in nights, he'd be watching the *Midnight Movie* and then he'd have ITV on till 'twas time for milking again."

In point of fact, Ace was becoming very selective in his viewing. He had not been a house-pig many days before he found out, first by chance and then by trial and error, that pressing each of the five knobs below the window of the magic box produced a different result. One turned the thing off, and the other four controlled BBC 1, BBC 2, ITV and Channel Four. Ace of course had no idea that there were such things as different channels, but he soon found that the magic box offered a choice of pictures. His sense of time was good too, and before many weeks had passed, his viewing had taken on a definite pattern.

By experimenting with the control knobs, Ace found what programmes suited him and at what time of day. These, generally, were split into two parts, morning viewing and afternoon viewing. In between, he took a nice long nap, lying on the hearth-rug. He had the sense not to attempt to get into either of the armchairs.

For his morning watching, that is between the hours of roughly nine o'clock and eleven o'clock, he usually chose BBC 2. At this time there was a programme for schools called *Daytime on Two*, where there were items on such things as Science, Mathematics and a section called *Look and Read*. All of these Ace found fascinating, though on occasion he would switch to Channel Four's *Our World*, where there was often interesting information about Food.

In the afternoon, say between four o'clock and half-past five, he enjoyed Children's TV on either BBC or ITV. There were always plenty of animals, either live or in cartoons, and their antics amused him.

But though the afternoon's viewing was for fun, the morning's, because of his unique gift for understanding the human tongue, was, for Ace, highly educational, especially with regard to number and to language. Quick to learn, he began to recognise simple words. There were, for instance, items about Road Safety, using diagrams with large lettering, and soon Ace, had he been called upon, could have distinguished a sign that said STOP from one that said GO.

Soon too, he acquired a basic grasp of figures, becoming aware, for example, that he had one snout. one tail, two eyes, two ears and four legs, and that the sum of himself and the other two animals was three.

At first he feared that they might object to his generous use of the television set. By good fortune, however, he found that, though in general they were not interested, certain items appeared which were popular with them.

Clarence enjoyed the cat food advertisements in the commercial breaks on ITV, particularly one which showed a large white cat very like himself that fished meat from a tin with one paw, in the most elegant manner.

As to Megan, luck had it that quite early on, BBC 1 showed a repeat of a programme about the day-to-day life of the Royal Family. There were pictures of the Queen and her husband and her children and her grandchildren, at Buckingham Palace, at Windsor, at Sandringham and at Balmoral, and everywhere she was surrounded by corgis.

The moment Ace heard the programme announced, he woke Megan.

"Quickly, Your Lowness, quickly!" he cried. "The Queen is in the magic box!" and there, sure enough, she was, in the opening shot, walking in her garden with no less than six corgis.

Megan's growl at being disturbed changed to an eager whine.

"Oh there's lovely, see!" she said excitedly. "Our Aunt Olwen, that is, by the Queen's feet, we're nearly sure! And the one behind her looks ever so like our Cousin Myfanwy!"

She watched spellbound as the TV programme continued, silent except for an occasional yap at recognising an uncle or a grandparent, and when it was all over she actually, for the first time, addressed the pig by his name.

"Our thanks to you, Ace," she said graciously. "We shall be obliged if in the future you will draw our attention to any more pictures."

"Of the Royal Family, you mean, Ma'am?" said Ace.

"Of our royal family, yes. If the Queen appears without them, don't bother to wake us."

None of Ace's viewing bothered Ted Tubbs, for he was always busy about the farm. Like all farmers, he could not treat Sunday as a day of rest. The cows still needed milking morning and evening, babies were born regardless of the day of the week, and all the animals needed bedding, food and water. But Farmer Tubbs did treat Sunday differently in one way. He always tried to finish his morning's work by about eleven o'clock, and then he set about preparing and cooking himself a large traditional Sunday lunch.

It never varied. Roast beef and Yorkshire pudding, roast potatoes and green vegetables and lashings of thick gravy, followed by a jam roly-poly. And while this was cooking, the farmer would pour himself a quart mug of cider, and, sitting in the larger of the two armchairs with his feet up, would drink it slowly with much lip-smacking and a belch or two for good measure.

But on the very first Sunday after he had discovered Ace watching telly, the scene in his living-room was different.

Anyone looking in through the window would not have been surprised to observe the farmer in one chair and his dog in the other, but might well have been amazed to see, sitting at the farmer's side, a sizeable young pig, a white pig that bore on its left side a curious mark shaped like the Ace of Clubs.

Farmer Tubbs took a pull at his cider and addressed his house-pig.

"Now then, Ace," he said, "I bin telling myself, these last few days, that maybe old Ted Tubbs is going around the twist. You was sat in front of the telly when I come in t'other day, there's no doubt of that. And the telly was switched on, there's no doubt of that. But I must have left it running. I can't believe as 'twas you as switched it on."

He took another drink, nerving himself for what he had to do.

177

"I got to find out for sure," he said. "I don't never have the thing on this time of a Sunday, so I don't know what rubbish they be showing, but lunch won't be ready for another half-hour, so we might as well turn it on. Or rather you might as well turn it on, Ace. I hopes you can, for my peace of mind."

He raised his mug, took a long swallow, and then, pointing at the television set, said in as firm a voice as he could manage, "Switch it on, Ace. Any channel will do."

Later on, when Ace's morning lessons had taught him to read, beneath the control knobs, the numbers 1, 2, 3, 4 and finally the word OFF, he might have selected a channel. As it was, with luck once again on his side, he simply walked over to the set and pushed the middle one, 3.

"The time," said the announcer in the ITV studios as he swam into sight, "is exactly twelve-thirty. Time for our regular Sunday programme especially for those of you who earn their living from the land. Sit back and put your feet up and, for the next half-hour, enjoy *West Country Farming*, followed by the *Farmers' Weather Forecast*."

Ted Tubbs's mouth fell open. He stared in wonderment at Ace.

"Well I never!" he said. "Did you ever?"

CHAPTER 9

A Pig in a Pick-up

On a Sunday evening some months later, Ace lay in the straw of the loose-box, telling Nanny, as he always did, about the day's viewing.

No longer did he refer to 'the magic box'. He had learned that what he was watching was a television set, which could show pictures of things that were happening all over the world and indeed from space. How the television did this remained to him, as it does to most humans, a mystery, but he did not worry his head about that. It was full enough already of ideas and impressions and new-found knowledge.

Much of what he told the old goat meant little or nothing to her. Her experience of life was, after all, very limited, for she had never moved a step outside Ted Tubbs's farm; but she listened with interest to his stories of strange lands and peoples and customs and a host of other things shown on the schools programmes.

This particular day being a Sunday, Ace and Ted had, of course, watched *West Country Farming* while the lunch was cooking, and now the pig could not wait to tell Nanny all about the programme. It had upset him deeply. Indeed he left half his supper untouched, and his voice trembled as he told of what he had seen.

"Oh it was horrible, Nanny!" he said. "The first part wasn't too bad, it was about a market. I used to think that my brothers and sisters had gone to a town called Market, but these were pictures of pigs, sheep and cattle in pens, and people offering money for them. 'Bidding', it's called—the one who offers the most money gets the animals. I must say I'm glad I didn't go to market, but at least all the beasts there were still alive and well. But the second half of the programme—ugh!"

It wouldn't be true to say that a shudder ran through Ace's body. His flesh was much too solid for that, but if he could have shuddered, he would have.

"Why?" said Nanny. "What was it about?"

"An abattoir!" said Ace in a funereal voice. "A slaughterhouse, where animals are taken to be killed. They didn't show that bit, thank goodness, but they showed all the bodies. Rows and rows of them there were, all hanging head down, strung up by their back legs, cattle, sheep and pigs."

"Goats?" said Nanny.

"Don't think so. The cattle and the sheep weren't too dreadful because by then they were just sides of beef or carcasses of lamb, but the pigs still looked like pigs; dozens of them there were hanging there, all scrubbed and cold and still. I shan't sleep a wink tonight."

"Humans have always killed animals," said Nanny.

"Not only animals," said Ace gloomily. "You should just watch the television. Humans spend a lot of time killing other humans."

"Not for food, surely?" said Nanny.

"No, I don't think so, but the news is nearly always about people getting killed. Sometimes they do it on purpose, with guns and bombs, and sometimes they get killed by mistake on trains or aeroplanes or on the roads. And as well as that there are natural disasters, like earthquakes and floods, when thousands of people die."

"Sounds very depressing, watching television," said Nanny.

"Oh it isn't all like that," said Ace. "Sometimes it's quite funny. There's a cartoon programme that Clarence specially likes, called *Tom and Jerry*."

"Who are they?"

"Tom's a cat and Jerry's a mouse."

181

"Another programme about sudden death?"

"No, because you see Tom is stupid and Jerry's very smart, so Jerry always gets the best of things. Clarence likes the bits where Tom gets his tail caught in a door or gets beaten up by a bulldog, that sort of thing."

"Don't you ever feel," said Nanny, "that you'd like to stay in and watch the evening programmes? Or stay the night perhaps? I mean, don't think I'm trying to get rid of you—I love having you here—but there must be a lot of television you've never seen yet."

"No thank you," said Ace. "I did stay a bit later than usual one evening—it was after *Tom and Jerry* and Clarence was telling me at length how he would deal with Jerry and what a dumb cat Tom was—and I found that it's about then that Megan wakes up. She sleeps most of the day, but when it's getting near her supper-time she comes to life, and oh Nanny, she's such a *bore*! On and on about all the Champions in her pedigree and how her nephew won at Cruft's and

her niece was presented at Court and what the Queen Mother is supposed to have said to her Uncle Gareth. No wonder Clarence goes out every evening. No, daytime viewing is enough for me, and anyway I like talking it over with you afterwards. But I hope I don't have nightmares tonight. Ugh! That abattoir!"

"Look, Ace," said Nanny. "I am a great deal older than you. Which doesn't make me wiser, because you've already learned a whole host of things about the world that I had no idea of. But I do know one thing, which is this. Worrying does no one any good. Hundreds of thousands of pigs may get slaughtered, but you won't. With a bit of luck you and I are both going to die quietly and peacefully in our beds of old age. I shall die before you, just because I am a great deal older, but I don't worry about it. So finish your supper."

"I think I will," said Ace, and he did.

"Now then," said Nanny, "come and lie down."

She settled herself near him, but not too close, for he had grown so heavy.

"I shan't sleep," said Ace.

"Try counting sheep," said Nanny. "Live ones. That'll send you off."

"I don't think it will," said Ace, but it did.

Though Ace did not exactly have any nightmares, he did have a strange dream. He dreamed that he was riding in Farmer Tubbs's pick-up truck. The farmer was driving, and he, Ace, sat next to him on the passenger's side, held there by some kind of arrangement of straps. Where they were going he did not know, but in the dream he was able to get his tongue round some of the words of the English language that he had come to recognize on the *Look and Read* programme.

"Where are we going, Ted?" he said, and the farmer replied, "To market."

Two days later, a Tuesday, it was market day, and Ace stood in the yard, watching idly as Farmer Tubbs came out of a shed carrying a calf, which he put under the net in the back of the pick-up. Then he looked at Ace. Then he said, "I be going to market, Ace. Want to come?"

Remembering his dream, Ace replied with a single explosive grunt, a very definite "No!"

184

But by now, after many months of communication with the pig, Farmer Tubbs was completely confident that Ace understood every single word he said, in a way that no dog, let alone Megan, ever could, not even the most intelligent dog in the world. Now he came up to Ace and fondled the roots of his big ears, something that he knew the pig greatly enjoyed.

"Now you listen here, my boy," he said. "There ain't no need for you to come if you don't want to. I just said to myself, 'Ted Tubbs', I said, 'maybe Ace would enjoy the ride. And 'twould be company'. Now I reckon I know what's worrying you. You think I might be going to sell you, isn't that it?"

Two grunts.

"Never, Ace, never," said Farmer Tubbs earnestly. "You got my solemn oath on it. I won't never part with you and that's a promise. You believe that, don't you?"

Two grunts.

"That's all right then. Now then, time I was off," said the farmer, and he opened the passenger door.

"You coming?" he said, and to his delight Ace, with a final couple of grunts, jumped into the truck and sat upright while Farmer Tubbs carefully fastened the seat-belt around his fat stomach.

CHAPTER 10

A Pig in a Pub

The first pair of eyes to see Ace as he rode along in state in the pick-up truck were very short-sighted ones. They belonged to an elderly lady who was the village gossip. She lived with her sister in a cottage beside the road that led from the farm to the market town. All day she sat, and peered out between her lace curtains, minding everyone else's business.

"Quick!" she called as the pick-up approached. "Look at this!" but by the time her sister arrived, the truck had passed.

"Oh you're too late!"

"What was it?"

"Ted Tubbs on his way to market, I recognized his truck. And what d'you think, he had a woman with him! He's kept that quiet, hasn't he? These old bachelors! You can't trust them!"

"What did she look like?"

186

"Well I couldn't see her face too well, my sight's not what it was, but I can tell you she was a big stout piece, and no beauty neither."

A small boy playing in his front garden on the left-hand side of the road was the next to see Ace. The pig's bulk hid the man from the child's sight, and, greatly excited, he ran indoors, crying, "Mummy, Mummy, I've just seen a pig driving a lorry!"

"Don't be silly," said his mother.

"I did! I did!" yelled the boy angrily.

"Don't tell lies," said the mother, "and don't you shout at me like that," and she thumped him.

A minor accident was the only further thing that happened on the journey to market. A motorist approaching traffic lights suddenly caught sight of Farmer Tubbs's passenger. Goggle-eyed, he turned his head to watch them pass, and ran neatly into the back of the car ahead.

When Farmer Tubbs arrived in town and reached the market, he drove the pick-up into the car-park. This was close to the tavern, a pub called The Bull, used by all the farmers, dealers and drovers to quench their thirsts on market days.

"Now," said Farmer Tubbs to Ace, "I has to take this here calf in, and then I shall have a look around and see what the trade's like. So will you be all right stopping here for a bit?" And when he received the usual affirmative answer, he undid Ace's safety straps for greater comfort, and then, shutting the door, made off with the calf.

Ace looked all about him with curiosity, but though he could hear a good deal of mooing, bleating and grunting, he could not see much of interest through the windscreen except lots of cars, trucks and Land Rovers.

Presently, for something to do, he moved along the bench-seat and arranged himself on the driver's side. Often, on a Saturday, he had watched Formula One motor-racing on BBC's *Grandstand*, and though the pick-up was hardly a Grand Prix car there were certain likenesses. It had a steering-wheel, and a gear-lever, and an instrument panel. Raising his front legs, Ace rested his trotters on the steering-wheel, and gave himself up to a daydream of being the world's first Formula One pig racing-driver.

At that moment a red-faced man came rather unsteadily out of The Bull and began to weave his way across the car-park.

"Why, if 'tisn't old Ted Tubbs!" he cried as he neared the pick-up, but then the colour drained from his cheeks, leaving them as grey as cold porridge, and he staggered away, murmuring to himself, "Never again! Not another drop!"

After an hour or so, Farmer Tubbs returned. Though he had left the windows of the truck a little open, he found Ace panting, for the metal cab was not the coolest of places on a warm day.

"You'm hot, Ace!" said the farmer. "You'm thirsty too, I dare say?" and Ace assured him, in the normal way, that this was indeed the case.

"Tell you what," said Farmer Tubbs. "I always has a drink in The Bull afore I goes home on market day. You come in along of me, and we'll ask the landlord for some water for you. I gotta bucket in the back."

189

Thus it was that the patrons of the public bar at The Bull were treated to the sight of Farmer Tubbs entering with a large pig at heel.

"Now now, Ted," said the landlord. "You can't bring him in here. You seen the notice on the door."

"I did, Bob," said Ted Tubbs. "'No Dogs allowed', it says. This here's a pig."

"That's true," said the landlord thoughtfully. "The usual for you then? Half of scrumpy?"

"If you please," said the farmer.

Farmer Tubbs was a very moderate drinker. Cider was his tipple, but only on Sundays before lunch did he allow himself that quart mug. A half-pint was his usual ration, especially on market days when he was driving.

"What about your friend?" said the landlord.

The farmer held out his bucket.

"Put some water in here, will you, Bob?" he said.

"Go on, Ted!" someone shouted. "Buy 'im a beer. You can't bring the poor beast into a pub and not give him a proper drink."

"He shall have one on the house," said the landlord, and he drew a pint of beer and poured it into the bucket.

Ace, who had been listening carefully to these exchanges, noted with pleasure that the name on the

pump handle was that of a brand highly recommended
in the television advertisements.

He bent his head to the bucket.

The beer looked good.

He put his snout in the bucket.

The beer smelt good.

He drained the bucket.

The beer tasted good.

He gave a short happy squeal, and it was obvious to everyone what he meant.

There came a chorus of voices.

"He liked that!"

"That were a drop of good stuff, old chap, weren't it?"

"Same again, that's what he's saying!"

"He could do with the other half!"

"And one for the road!"

And the drinkers in the public bar rose, to a man, and poured their tankards of beer into Ace's bucket.

Almost before Farmer Tubbs had tasted his half-pint of scrumpy, the pig's bucket was empty again, and when they left, it was with some difficulty that the Ace of Clubs managed to get back into the pick-up truck.

"Good job you're not driving," said the farmer as he strapped the pig in.

Ace hiccuped.

At first the drive home was uneventful, but then Fate decreed that a police car should come up behind them just as Farmer Tubbs swerved wildly across the road. He swerved because Ace had fallen asleep and, despite the seat-belt, had lurched against him.

Next moment there came the sound of a siren, and then the police car, lights flashing, pulled in front of the pick-up and forced it to a stop.

One of the two policemen in the car got out and walked to the driver's side of the truck. Farmer Tubbs wound down his window. The smell of beer in the cab was overwhelming.

"Good-afternoon, Sir," said the policeman in the coldly polite way that policemen have on these occasions. "Having trouble with the steering, are we?"

"'Twasn't my fault," said Farmer Tubbs. "'Twas the pig."

"I see," said the policeman. He produced his breathalyser kit.

"Now, Sir," he said, "I'm going to ask you to blow into this tube. If you look at this machine, you'll see that there are three little lights on it—just like traffic lights, green, amber and red. Now then, Sir, if the green light comes on when you blow, that means you have had no alcoholic drink at all."

"Well I have had," said Farmer Tubbs. "A half of scrumpy, in The Bull."

The policeman raised his eyebrows at this. He wrinkled his nose at the reek of beer drifting out of the window.

193

"In that case," he said, "the amber light will come on. This is to show that you have drunk alcohol in some shape or form. But if, after forty seconds, that amber light should go off and the *red* light come on, then, Sir, you will be over the limit and I shall have to ask you to accompany me to the station for a blood test."

Farmer Tubbs shook his head in pity.

"You'm barking up the wrong tree, young man," he said. "I shan't never be over the limit."

"Just blow, Sir," said the policeman. "We'll see."

So he did, and they did.

The amber light came on. The policeman watched, waiting for it to give way to red, confident that here was yet one more drunken driver. A half of scrumpy indeed! But after forty seconds the amber light went out and no red light appeared.

"Told you," said the farmer.

"I don't understand it," said the policeman. He went and fetched the second constable from the police car.

"The stink of beer in here's enough to knock you down," he said to his mate.

"'Tis the pig," said Farmer Tubbs.

At this point Ace awoke, roused by the sound of voices. He looked happily at the six men he could see, four policemen and two Farmer Tubbs. He gave an enormous belch, and both policemen reeled backwards.

"Well I never! Did you ever?" said Farmer Tubbs. "Ace, you've been and gone and made a proper pig of yourself!"

A Pig in an Armchair

"Tell you one thing," said Farmer Tubbs as they drove on home. "With all that beer inside you, I reckons you better go straight in the loose-box. We don't want no accidents in the house, do we, Ace?"

Ace let out two sleepy grunts. He had meant to give a single one but he seemed not to be quite in control of things.

"Oh no we don't!" said Farmer Tubbs, and when they reached the farm he drew up outside the loose-box door.

"It don't matter," he said, "if you wets your bed in here."

Nanny was peering out.

"He's had a skinful, Nanny," said the farmer. "One over the eight."

Once the safety-belt was undone, getting out of the truck was more a matter of falling out for Ace, and he walked into the loose-box in a rather wobbly way. Nanny bleated anxiously.

"Don't you worry," said Farmer Tubbs. "He'll be all right when he's had a good sleep."

Ace did indeed fall fast asleep.

While he slept, Clarence came visiting.

"Oh Clarence, I'm worried!" said Nanny. "There's something the matter with Ace. He isn't acting at all naturally. What can it be?"

Clarence was a cat of the world. More than once he had courted the Blue Persian at the local pub, and the smell of drink was familiar to him.

"He's had a skinful, Nanny," he said. "One over the eight," and when the simple old goat still looked mystified, Clarence explained.

"Today," he said, "this little piggy went to market, and by the look of things, he's drunk a good deal of beer. He'll be all right when he's had a good sleep."

Neither farmer nor cat was quite correct. Ace did have a good sleep, but when he woke he was not quite all right. He had a hangover.

"Oh Nanny!" he groaned. "I've got an awful headache!" and after a while he explained all that had happened.

"I must have drunk a whole bucketful," he said.

"Why did you drink so much?" asked Nanny.

"I was so thirsty. And it did taste nice. But now I wish I hadn't."

"Well, you've learned a lesson," said Nanny. "A little of what you fancy does you good. But you can have too much of a good thing."

Clarence was in the kitchen when Ace went into the farmhouse the following morning. He got out of his bed by the Aga and walked round the pig, looking critically at him with first the green and then the yellow eye.

"Better?" he said.

"Oh yes thanks, Clarence," said Ace. "I'm afraid I made rather an ass of myself."

"Difficult for a pig," said the white cat. He sat down in front of Ace and gave him a quizzical green-and-yellow stare.

"Seen Megan yet this morning?" he said.

"No. Why?"

"She was wondering where you'd got to yesterday."

"Did you tell her?"

"Stupidly, I did."

"Why 'stupidly'?"

"Because I suspect Her Lowness is just longing to take you to task about your behaviour," said Clarence.

He gave a fair imitation of Megan.

" 'Going into a public house, look you, and drinking too much, see! There's *common*!' I should stay out here and give her a miss if I was you."

199

"Oh but it's Wednesday," said Ace.

"So?"

"There's *Paddington Bear* on BBC 1. I always watch that."

"I wish you luck," said Clarence.

Ace tiptoed into the living-room, hoping to find Megan asleep. She was, so he switched on BBC 1 very softly; he had long ago learned to turn the volume control with his teeth. But before Paddington could appear the telephone rang, something that always woke the dog, for she considered it her duty to boost its tones with a volley of barks.

This double summons brought Farmer Tubbs in from the yard, and when he had gone out again after answering the call and leaving mucky wellie-marks all across the carpet, Megan lost no time in speaking.

"We want a word with you, boyo," she said sharply.

The old Ace would have replied to this in the meek respectful way in which he had long been used to speaking to the corgi. "Yes, Your Lowness?" he would have said, and perhaps added, "What is it, Ma'am?"

But now a sudden flame of rebellion burned in Ace's broad breast. You stupid pompous little beast, he thought, with all your airs and graces, speaking to me as if I were no better than a . . . than a dog. Western Princess of Llanllowell my trotter! Why, you're just a mouthy little Welsh cow-hound. What am I doing kowtowing to you? And he did not answer.

"Did you hear what we said?" snapped Megan.

"Not now, Megan," said Ace firmly. "I'm busy."

There was a short stunned silence before the Western Princess found her voice.

Then, "Upon our word!" she spluttered. "'Not now' indeed! 'Busy' indeed! 'Megan' indeed! You will kindly address us in the proper fashion."

At that moment Paddington appeared on the screen in his funny blue hat.

"Oh shut up!" said Ace, and turned the volume up full.

"Oh Nanny, you should have seen it!" said Clarence that night. Often he came in the small hours for a chat with Nanny, who, like many old folk, did not sleep too well. Now he had jumped up to his usual perch on the crib, whence on occasion he launched himself upon an unwary loose-box mouse. Ace was fast asleep in the straw.

"Megan was jumping about in her chair," Clarence went on, "yapping her head off, practically frothing at the mouth, and Ace just turned his back on her and

sat watching till his programme was over. Then he switched it off and turned round.

"'What was it', he said very quietly, 'that you wanted to say to me?'

"Well by now her ladyship was so hopping mad at being treated so disrespectfully I thought she was going to have a fit.

"'How dare you tell us to shut up!' she yelled. 'How dare you!'"

"And what did Ace say to that?" said Nanny.

"Oh it was great!" said Clarence. "He got up and he walked slowly over to where she was sitting, in the smaller of the two armchairs, and he said, still very quietly, 'I'll tell you how I dare. It is because I have suddenly realised that I am no longer a little piglet, bowing and scraping to you, and having to listen to you waffling on about your piffling pedigree and your rotten relations and what the Princess of Wales said to your Great Aunt Fanny. I am now a large pig, about ten times as large as you, and I am fed up to the back teeth, of which I have a great many,' (and he opened his mouth wide) 'with all your silly snobbish nonsense.'"

"And what did Megan say?" asked Nanny.

"He didn't give her a chance to say anything," said Clarence. "He did all the talking. 'Now', he said,

'I want to watch *Time for a Story* on Channel Four, and I do not wish to be interrupted. On second thoughts, get out of this room. Just push off, quick!' and he gnashed his teeth together with a very nasty noise that sounded like 'Chop-chop! Chop-chop!' I shouldn't think Megan's moved so fast for years. She couldn't exactly put her tail between her legs, there isn't enough of it, but she was out of that room like a . . . like a . . .''

". . . scalded cat?" said Nanny.

"Exactly. And," said Clarence, "—and this is the best bit—Ace switched on Channel Four, and then he climbed up into Ted's big armchair and sat there watching. Then after the programme was over and all was quiet again, Megan came slinking back. Oh Nanny, how are the mighty fallen! She stuck her head round the door and gave a little whine, as if to say 'Please, can I come in?'"

"What did Ace say?" asked the old goat.

The white cat looked down with a certain fondness at the sleeping pig, the strange black mark on his side rising and falling to the rhythm of his breathing. Clarence was not one to give his affection easily, but he had grown to like the Ace of Clubs.

"I thought he handled it beautifully," he said. "He could have gone on being tough with her—'I'm bigger than you, watch your step', that sort of stuff. Or he could have got a bit of his own back on her for the way she's always patronized him—teased her or sneered at her for her high-and-mighty ways. But no, he just said, quite firmly but in a kindly voice, 'Come in, Megan. I've something to say to you.'

"'Yes, Ace', said Megan, rather uneasily. You could see she was expecting him to tell her off again, but instead he said, 'There's a documentary about Cruft's Dog Show on the telly this afternoon, they've just shown a clip of it and there were quite a lot of corgis there. I wondered if you'd like me to switch it on for you when the time comes?'"

"What did she say?" asked Nanny.

"She looked at him," said Clarence, "just like she looks at her master. She put her ears flat and she wagged her rump and she said in a humble voice, 'Oh we should like that, Ace! There's kind of you.'

"Oh I wish you could have seen him, Nanny, sitting in that big armchair, looking for all the world like Ted Tubbs's twin brother. He sat there staring down at Megan, and what d'you think he said, to round it all off?"

"What?"

"'There's a good dog, Megan. There's a good dog.'"

CHAPTER 12

A Pig in the Papers

On market day the following week, the public bar at The Bull was, as usual, full of farmers and dealers and drovers. In addition there was a very young man who had just started in his first job as a cub reporter for the local newspaper, the *Dummerset Chronicle*.

One of his duties was to cover the market and take note of the fatstock prices, not the most interesting of work. So that he pricked up his ears, as he sat in a corner nursing a glass of shandy, at a conversation between the landlord and some of the customers.

"Ted Tubbs been in with that pig, Bob?" asked one.

"Ain't seen him today," said the landlord.

"I never seen nothing like that afore," said another.

"A pig, drinking beer like that!" said a third.

"I reckon he put down more than eight pints," said the landlord.

"He had a skinful," said the first man. "One over the eight."

A pig drinking beer, said the reporter to himself. Though he had not been long in the job, he knew that an interesting item of news which you got before anyone else was called a 'scoop', and he hastily swallowed his drink and hurried off to the newspaper offices.

"It might make a story," said his editor in the tired bored way that editors have. "Go and see this Farmer Tubbs and find out what you can."

When the cub reporter arrived at the farm and rang the front doorbell, no one answered. This was partly because Farmer Tubbs was busy with the afternoon milking, and partly because the bell hadn't worked for years. So the reporter walked round the side of the farmhouse, where he found the garden door open. Someone had the television on, he could hear, so he walked in, calling, "Hallo? Excuse me! Can I come in?"

From the nearest room a dog barked, but then came the sound of a single loud grunt and the dog immediately fell silent.

Nervously, for he felt that perhaps he had already gone too far, the young man opened the door of the room.

Though in later years, as a much-travelled newspaper man, he saw many strange sights in many strange countries, he never forgot the scene that now met his eyes.

On the television was the cartoon *Tom and Jerry*.

Directly in front of the set sat a white cat, its tail swishing angrily (for Jerry had just caught the tip of Tom's tail in a mousetrap).

In a small armchair lay a very fat corgi.

In a big armchair sat a large pig.

All three were watching the cartoon.

All three took not the slightest notice of him.

"Oh I like *Tom and Jerry*!" said the cub reporter. "Can I watch, please?" and almost as though it was some sort of reply, the pig grunted twice.

"Who was that?" said Ace, when the young man had left to try to find the farmer.

"Haven't a clue," said Clarence, and, "We don't know, we're sure," said Megan.

"He likes *Tom and Jerry* anyway," said Ace.

"How do you know?" said Megan.

"He said so."

"Of course!" said Megan. "We were forgetting," for she now knew of Ace's great gift. The old Megan would never have believed in the possibility of such a thing. The new, Ace-worshipping Megan had no

209

doubt at all of his powers.

Across the yard, the hum of the milking-machine suddenly stopped.

"I'm going for my supper," said Ace. "Shall I switch the telly off?"

"Sure," said Clarence, and, "There's kind of you!" said Megan, so he did.

Hardly had the reporter found the farmer and introduced himself than there came the sound of a loud urgent squeal.

"Just a minute, my lad," said Farmer Tubbs. "Time and tide and Ace wait for no man," and he hurried off to fetch the pig's supper.

The old man and the young leaned on the half-door of the loose-box, watching.

"He's enjoying that," said the cub reporter. "Is there any beer in it?"

"Bless you, no!" said Farmer Tubbs. "Why ever . . . ? Oh I see. You've heard tell, have you? When he had a few, in The Bull?"

"Yes. And I'd like to do a story on it, for *The Chronicle*, if you don't mind, Mr Tubbs. A pig that drinks beer, that'll make a nice little item, half a column maybe, and it'd be quite a scoop for me. I've not been long in the job, you see."

"Who told you?" asked the farmer. "The police?"

"The police? No, I heard it in The Bull. What's the pig's name, by the way?"

"The Ace of Clubs."

The reporter looked at the mark on the pig's side.

"Oh yes, I can see why," he said. "If I write about it, it would be good publicity for you, Mr Tubbs. You should get a really good price for him then."

"I shall never sell him," said Farmer Tubbs. "He's a pet. A house-pig, that's what he is."

"That reminds me," said the reporter. "You must have left your TV set running. I couldn't get an answer so I went in through a side door and the pig was watching TV, along with your dog and your cat."

"He enjoys a bit of telly," said the farmer.

"That'll make the story even better. You'll be telling me next that he selects the channels and switches it on himself, ha, ha!"

"Ha, ha!" said Farmer Tubbs.

"By the way," said the reporter, "the pig was sitting in an armchair, your armchair, I dare say."

"Ah, now that explains something," said the farmer. "Lately I said to myself, 'Ted Tubbs, you must be putting on weight something cruel—the springs in this chair have gone flat. You'll have to go on a diet,' I said. Ah well, that's a relief."

By now Ace had finished his supper. He stood and

looked up at the two men with bright eyes that had in them a look of great intelligence, and when Farmer Tubbs said, "Did you enjoy that, old chap?" he grunted twice.

"Anyone would think he could understand what you were saying!" said the reporter.

If only you knew, thought the farmer, but you ain't going to. You can write a piece about him having a drink or watching the telly, but nobody except me is ever going to know that my Ace do know every word that I do say to him. Folk would never believe it, any road. They'd take me away from here and put me in the funny farm.

"You write your piece, young man," he said, "and mind and let us have a copy."

And sure enough the very next day a copy of the *Dummerset Chronicle* was delivered to the farm.

At lunchtime that day Ted Tubbs read this out to Ace (who later translated it for Clarence and Megan, and that evening, for Nanny).

"I shall have to have that framed," said the farmer, "and put on the wall alongside Megan's prize-cards. Pity they never done a photograph. I'd like to have a good one of you."

The very next day Farmer Tubbs's wish was granted, for a phone call came from one of the national

A pig in a million

Of all the pigs in England's green and pleasant land, surely none can compare with the Ace of Clubs, belonging to local farmer Ted Tubbs.

Not only does Ace have the freedom of Mr Tubbs's picturesque old farmhouse, he also enjoys watching television, sitting at his ease in the farmer's armchair.

The Ace of Clubs has been to market, but only as a passenger in Farmer Tubbs's truck. Not only does his unusual pet enjoy the outing, he also savours a refreshing drink of ale at the market's popular hostelry, the Bull Inn. But not for Ace the pint pot. He drinks his beer by the bucket.

"I'll never part with him," Farmer Tubbs told our reporter. "He's a pig in a million."

daily newspapers, wanting to send an interviewer and a photographer; and in due course a large section of the British public opened their copies of the *Daily Reflector* at breakfast time to see a fine picture of Ace, carefully positioned in profile to show his distinguishing mark to best advantage. The picture was accompanied by a generous, if somewhat inaccurate, piece which stated that Ace drank a gallon of beer with every meal, that he not only sat in an armchair but slept in the spare bed, and that his favourite programmes were *University Challenge* and *Mastermind*.

But this was not all.

A week later the BBC rang.

"Mr Ted Tubbs?" said a voice.

"Speaking," said the farmer.

"This is the producer of *That's The Way It Goes*."

"Oh yes."

"You have heard of the programme, of course."

"Can't say I have."

"You haven't heard of *That's The Way It Goes*, presented by Hester Jantzen on Sunday evenings at half-past nine?"

"Oh bless you, young man, I don't watch telly that time of night. I be abed by nine. I has to get up early to milk the cows. Early to bed, early to rise, makes a man healthy and wise if it don't make him wealthy."

"Well this won't exactly make you wealthy, Mr Tubbs," said the producer, "but we can offer you a fee and certainly pay all your expenses for first-class travel and four-star accommodation if you and your pig would be willing to come to London."

"Whatever for?"

"Why, to appear on *That's The Way It Goes*. Hester Jantzen is greatly looking forward to interviewing you both."

"Well I never!" said Farmer Tubbs. "Did you ever?"

CHAPTER 13

A Pig on the Stage

A little later there came a letter from the BBC, giving date and times and various arrangements. Farmer Tubbs told Ace all about it, and afterwards Ace told his friends.

"What d'you think!" he said excitedly to Clarence and Megan. "Ted and I are going to London!"

"To see the Queen, is it?" cried Megan.

"No, no, we're going to be on the telly. Just think, you'll be able to sit here and see us on the box."

"Except that we can't switch the thing on," said Clarence.

"I'll show you how to do it, Clarence," said Ace. "Look, just put your paw on this knob—where it says 'One'—and push. See?"

"How in the world are you going to get to London, Ace?" asked Megan. "It's a long way, look you."

"Oh the BBC is fixing everything," said Ace.

"They're sending one of the big estate cars that their film crews use—Volvos they are, you've seen them on the telly ads, there'll be loads of room for me in the back—and that will take us straight to the studios. Then when we've done the programme, they've booked a room for Ted for the night, in ever such a posh place."

"Buckingham Palace?" said Megan.

"No, no, a big hotel, near Regent's Park."

"Where will you sleep?" asked Clarence.

"Well," said Ace, "they seemed to think I might not be happy in the hotel, so I shall be sleeping in the London Zoo. Remember, you've seen pictures of it on the telly? And in the Zoo they have what they call Pets' Corner. That's where I'm going. And then next morning we'll be picked up and driven back home again."

"That's all very well," said Megan with a return of some of her old spirit, "but who'll be looking after us?" (And by 'us', she meant, of course, herself.)

"One of Ted's friends is coming in," said Ace, "to do the milking on Sunday afternoon and Monday morning, and feed all the animals. It'll be a lovely break for Ted."

Because for many months now the dog and the cat had had so much explained to them of what appeared on television, they were able to imagine what Ace would be doing. But trying to explain things to Nanny was not so easy.

"They're going to put me on the television," he said to her that evening after supper.

Nanny of course had never in her long life set hoof inside the farmhouse, so that the only idea of the television she had was what Ace had originally told her—it was a big box with one side nearly all glass, like a window.

"Put you on the television?" she said. "But surely you'll smash the thing? It'll never bear your weight."

Ace tried his best to explain to the old goat all that was going to happen, but so many words that he used—'Volvo', 'London', 'studio', 'cameras', 'hotel', 'Zoo'—meant nothing to her.

"Oh well, just as long as you enjoy yourself, Ace dear," she said, "that's all that matters."

And enjoy himself the Ace of Clubs most certainly did when the day came.

What a day it was!

First, there was the journey. His trips in Ted Tubbs's rattlebang old pick-up truck had not prepared Ace for the luxury of travel in a huge, modern, warm, silent, comfortable car speeding eastwards along the motorway; and because of his modest ability in reading and number and his interest in Road Safety programmes on the box, there were many signs and notices that caught his eye; though one, at roadworks, puzzled him. DEAD S OW, it said, and the missing L led him to fear the worst.

Oh but when they reached London—the streets, the houses, all the thousands of buildings! Their numbers filled him with amazement. In all his six months of life he had only been in two houses, a private one—the farmhouse, and a public one—The Bull, and he stared in wonder at the acres of concrete and tarmac.

But London, he could see, was not completely built over. There were a number of large grassy spaces with fine trees, and as they passed through one of these Parks, Farmer Tubbs asked the driver to stop for a moment. It occurred to him that this Hester Jantzen

219

person might not be best pleased if Ace should have an accident during the interview, and so he let him out for a little walk.

Then at last they arrived at the BBC Studios!

How the onlookers gaped as the pair of them stepped from the staff car to make their entry.

Ted Tubbs was dressed up to the nines. Bathed, and shaved so closely that his chins bore several little cuts, he had attired himself in his best. Not only was his shirt clean but it had attached to it something he never normally wore—a collar. More, he had put on his one and only tie (a black one, so useful for funerals), and in place of wellies he was shod in a pair of old but well-polished black leather boots.

But the crowning glory was his suit. It was his only suit, of a colour best described as sky-blue, that he had bought as a young man. There was no hope of button-ing the jacket, though by letting the back-straps of the waistcoat right out, he had been able to do that up. As to the trousers, most of the fly-buttons were safely in position, and, where the top ones refused to meet he wore, concealed beneath the waistcoat, a carefully attached short length of binder-twine.

And if the man was at his smartest, what of the pig?

Ace positively shone. Not only had Farmer Tubbs hosed him down and soaped and scrubbed him all

over, but then, when the soap was rinsed away and
Ace had dried in the sunshine, the farmer had produced
a big bottle of vegetable oil and oiled the pig all over.

Gleamingly clean, the single mark on his left side
showing up more blackly than ever under its sheen,
Ace marched proudly into Reception at his master's
heels, and they were conducted to the Hospitality
Room.

Farmer Tubbs was asked what he would like
to drink.

"You won't be on camera for a while yet," they
said. "So can we offer you some refreshment?"

It being Sunday, Ted had had his quart of cider
before lunch as usual, but he felt thirsty after the
journey, and anyway it struck him that a drink might
lend him Dutch courage, for he was nervous.

"Well thank you," he said. "I'll have a half
of scrumpy."

"Sorry?" they said.

"Cider," he said. "Dummerset cider. We come
up from Dummerset where the cider apples grow.
And the pig'll have a pint of best bitter."

The cider, when they brought it, was horrid, weak,
sweet stuff, but Ace had no complaints about the beer.
They poured it into a bowl for him and he thoroughly
enjoyed it. But he remembered Nanny's words—

"A little of what you fancy does you good. But you can have too much of a good thing"—and when they offered him another pint, he just gave one grunt.

"He don't want no more," said Farmer Tubbs. "And neither do I."

For a while longer they waited in the Hospitality Room (whence all but they had fled). Farmer Tubbs grew steadily more nervous. The sweet cider had done him no good. Ace on the other hand was on top of the world. The pint of beer had made him feel happy and carefree, and he could not wait to go in front of the cameras. The thought that many millions of people would be watching did not worry him, because he didn't realize they would be. He was simply thinking of Clarence and Megan at home, hoping that Clarence would remember to switch on, and only sorry that dear old Nanny wouldn't see him.

So that when they came to the Hospitality Room to tell Ted Tubbs it was time to go on stage, Ace hurried out ahead of his master. Brushing past the guide who was to take them to the set of *That's The Way It Goes*, he heard a woman's voice saying, "And now, ladies and gentlemen, allow me to introduce . . . [that's me, he thought, and pushing through some curtains, arrived on stage just as a lady with her back to him completed her introduction] . . . Farmer Ted Tubbs!"

There was a huge roar of laughter from the studio audience as a large pig appeared.

Hester Jantzen (for it was she) clapped her hand to her mouth in astonished embarrassment, and a second roar of laughter came as Farmer Tubbs, helped on his reluctant way by a push, arrived on the stage looking, apart from his clothes, like the pig's twin brother.

Hester Jantzen took her hand from her mouth and smiled, revealing, Ace could see, a fine set of teeth. She was dressed in a silk frock of a shade of emerald green that clashed horribly with the farmer's sky-blue suit, and for a moment it seemed as though a clash of a different kind might occur; for Farmer Tubbs did not know why everyone was laughing at him, and whatever the reason, he did not like it. Already nervous, and uncomfortable in his too-tight clothes, he now felt the heat of the studio lights, and his red face turned redder still.

Miss Jantzen, professional to her painted finger-tips, took command of the situation. Gliding forward, she shook the farmer's large sweaty hand, and said with another flashing smile, "Welcome to *That's The Way It Goes*, Mr Tubbs. How good of you to come, and to bring your famous pig, the Ace of Clubs."

She turned to camera.

"Many of you watching," she said, "will have read

in the newspapers about Farmer Tubbs's pet, Ace to
his friends. We've had some unusual animals on *That's
The Way It Goes* before, but never one as big, I think."

She made a half move as though to give Ace a pat
as he stood patiently in the middle of the stage, but
the sheen of oil on his bristly back deterred her, not
to mention his size. His teeth, she noticed, were even
larger than her own.

"He's a whopper, Mr Tubbs," she said with a light
laugh. "How heavy is he?"

"Ten score," grunted the farmer.

"Ten score? What does that mean?"

Farmer Tubbs took out a large spotted handkerchief
and mopped his streaming brow. These London folk,
he thought angrily, they don't know nothing.

"Don't you know what a score is, young woman?"
he said.

"Why yes, twenty."

"Well now we're getting somewhere," said Farmer
Tubbs. "A score be twenty pound, so ten score be two
hundred. Not difficult, is it, really?"

The audience roared.

Now they were laughing at her, not him, and
he sensed this. He began to think he might enjoy
himself, and Miss Jantzen sensed that.

"Silly me!" she said. "Tell us some more about him.

I'm told he likes a drink of beer. Would he like one now?"

"He's had one, out the back," said Farmer Tubbs. "That's enough to be going on with."

Hester Jantzen put on her most roguish smile.

"Just as well," she said. "We don't want this little piggy to go wee-wee-wee all the way home."

"Don't you fret, young woman," said Ted Tubbs. "He'm house-trained, like you and me."

When she could speak above the studio audience's laughter, Hester Jantzen said, "I'm told that the Ace of Clubs does a number of remarkable things, apart from beer-drinking, such as sitting in an armchair watching television?"

"He's a extrahordinary animal," said the farmer.

"I can see that. People don't realize how knowing pigs are. I believe it was Sir Winston Churchill who said, 'A dog looks up to man, a cat looks down to man, but a pig will look you in the eye and see his equal'."

"He knowed a thing or two, old Winnie did," said Farmer Tubbs. "You have a good look in Ace's eyes, young woman. You'll see what he meant."

Gamely, Miss Jantzen forced herself to approach the Ace of Clubs. They stared at one another, and it was she who looked away first.

"He has a look of great intelligence," she said a little shakily. "Tell us, Mr Tubbs, what else can Ace do?"

"Whatever I wants him to."

"You mean, like sitting down or lying down or coming when he's called?"

"Them's easy things," said the farmer. "Sit down, Ace," and Ace sat down.

"Take the weight off your feet, my lad," and Ace lay down, on his left side as it happened.

There was loud applause from the studio audience, and Hester Jantzen clapped her hands.

"Roll over, Ace," said Farmer Tubbs, "and show them how you got your name," and as Ace obeyed, one of the cameramen quickly zoomed in to show a close-up picture of that extremely unusual single black marking for all the millions of viewers to see.

"Good boy," said Farmer Tubbs. "Now in a minute or two, I want you to go over to Miss Wozzername there and say, 'Thank you for having me'."

"You're not going to tell me," giggled the presenter, "that Ace can speak!"

"No, nor fly neither," said the farmer, "but he'll shake hands with you. Go on, Ace, say 'thank you' to the lady."

And then, before the wondering gaze of the studio audience and of all the viewers across the length and breadth of the country who were watching *That's The Way It Goes*, the Ace of Clubs walked solemnly across the stage, and sitting down on his hunkers, raised one forefoot and politely offered his trotter to Hester Jantzen.

Bravely, the lady grasped it.

"Goodbye, Ace," she said. "I do hope you've enjoyed yourself. Have you?" and the pig grunted twice.

CHAPTER 14

A Very Important Pig

As soon as the BBC staff car dropped them back at the farm on the Monday morning, Ted Tubbs hurried to change into his greasy old overalls and his dungy old wellies, to go round and make sure that his animals had not suffered any harm while in the charge of a stranger.

Ace made his way to the living-room, where he found Megan alone.

"Hullo, Megan!" he cried. "We're back! Did you enjoy the programme?"

"Indeed to goodness, no!" said Megan.

"Why not?"

"Never saw it, see. Clarence must have pressed the wrong knob. Sat there for ages waiting for you to appear, we did, and all they showed was a lot of cowboys and Indians."

Later, when the cat appeared, he favoured the pig with a rather cold green-and-yellow stare, as though

daring him to mention the matter, so Ace didn't. But
Fortune decreed that nothing was lost. When Farmer
Tubbs came in for his lunch, he switched on the BBC
One O'clock News, and farmer, pig, dog and cat sat and
watched as, at the end of it, the newsreader said,
"Finally, for those who say the News is all doom and
gloom nowadays, here is a clip from last night's
edition of *That's The Way It Goes*," and there was Ace
having his trotter shaken by Hester Jantzen.

"A nationally-known celebrity," said the newsreader, "greets a brand-new one."

In the days and weeks that followed it became apparent
just what a celebrity Ace had become. Only once,
many years before, had a pig appeared on TV and
attracted anything like as much publicity, and that was
when Ace's great-grandfather had defeated all the best
dogs in the land to win the Grand Challenge Sheep-
dog Trials.

Farmer Tubbs was bombarded with letters and
phone calls. Fan letters made up much of the mail,
addressed to:

The Ace of Clubs
c/o Mr T. Tubbs

and as well as invitations to Ace to open fêtes or even
new supermarkets, or to appear at functions as a VIP

(Very Important Pig), there were many offers to buy him for large sums of money, from farmers everywhere and from more than one circus proprietor. There was also an offer of marriage (for Mr T. Tubbs) from a lady in Weston-super-Mare.

But Farmer Tubbs refused all these things.

The thought of parting with his pig never crossed his mind.

"You got your health and strength, Ted Tubbs," he told himself, as he finished the afternoon milking one day, "and you got your livestock to see to, and your pets—old Nanny and Megan and Clarence and above all that there Ace of Clubs. What good would any amount of money be to you if you had to part with him? Why, you wouldn't have no one to watch *West Country Farming* with. You wouldn't have no one to keep you company in the old pick-up. You wouldn't have no one to enjoy a drink with at The Bull."

He switched off the milking-machine, and almost at once he heard, from the direction of the loose-box, a short but piercing squeal, a squeal that he well knew was not of fury or of fear but of hunger, and he hurried away obediently to prepare a bucket of pigswill.

As for Ace, success did not spoil him. He had his friends, his favourite television programmes both educational and entertaining, his occasional pint, his comfortable bed. After supper that evening he lay thankfully down in it, ready for a good twelve hours of sleep. It was odd, but he always slept on his right side, as though to show to all whom it might concern that mark emblazoned on his left.

"'Night, Nanny," he said, yawning.

Dimly he heard the old goat reply, as she always did, "Sleep tight. Mind the fleas don't bite," and then, with a last couple of grunts, the Ace of Clubs drifted happily into dreamland.

DAGGIE
DOGFOOT

Illustrated by Mary Rayner

CHAPTER I

Taken Away

"Oh, no!" cried Mrs Barleylove miserably. "Oh no!"

"What is it, my dear?" came the voice of Mrs Gobblespud next door. "One dead?"

"No," said Mrs Barleylove. "Not yet anyway."

Mrs Barleylove was a pedigree Gloucester Old Spots, a flop-eared white pig spotted with a number of roundish black blobs of colour, as though a giant had flicked his paint-brush at her. During the night she had given birth to eight babies, seven of them all of a size, round and strong-looking and already plumped out with their first milk. But the eighth, she now saw, was a poor spindly little creature, half as big as the rest, with a head too large for its scrawny body and a look of hopelessness on its face.

It was a runt, a piglet born for some reason far smaller and weaker than its brothers and sisters. In different parts of England they are called by different names—cads, wasters, or nesslegraffs. In Gloucestershire they call them dags.

There was a rustling and a scrabbling in the next sty, and Mrs Gobblespud's head appeared over the wall.

"Oh dearie me," she said. "Oh dearie me, Mrs B. Oh, I am sorry. 'Tisn't just a smallish one, is it?"

"No," said Mrs Barleylove. "'Tis a proper dag."

Now most of the Old Spots sows in the range of nine sties had probably had a dag at some time in their careers as mothers. It wasn't thought of as a disgrace, something to be whispered about, because it didn't seem to be anyone's fault. But it was thought to be a pity, a great pity, for every sow's ambition was to rear a fine litter of healthy evenly-matched youngsters; and as the news spread that morning, there was much worried grunting and rolling of eyes and shaking of long droopy ears.

The servant wouldn't like it either, they said to each other. They thought of the pigman as a servant since he did nothing but minister to their wants; he fed them, he watered them, he cleaned them out and brought them fresh bedding. When the showing season came round, it was his duty to brush and comb and oil those taking part, to bring them to the peak of plump beauty. They spoke of him—and to him, though he could not understand this—simply as "Pigman", as a Roman noble might have said "Slave". Pigman wouldn't be pleased about Mrs Barleylove's dag, for dags, if they survived, grew very very slowly, and were more trouble than they were worth.

Mrs Barleylove's neighbour on the other side was

called Mrs Swiller and she was leaning over her wall, gossiping with the next lady down the line, Mrs Swedechopper.

" 'Tain't just that it's a dag, Mrs Swedechopper," she said sadly. "From what I can see of the poor little soul, it's deformed."

"Deformed, Mrs Swiller?" said Mrs Swedechopper in a tone of horror. "Why, whatever do you mean?"

"Well, its front feet ain't right."

"Not right?"

"No. They do turn inwards. And they don't look like pig's trotters. More like dog's feet."

Mrs Gobblespud too had noticed this further piece of misfortune for poor Mrs Barleylove, and had told her neighbour, Mrs Maizemunch; and everywhere heads were sticking up as the sows rested their forefeet comfortably upon their boundary walls and discussed the situation. Only at Number Five, in the centre of the row of sties, was no head raised, for Mrs Barleylove still stood sadly contemplating her misshapen child, while its seven brothers and sisters squeaked greedily around her legs, begging her to lie down and give them more milk. When she did so, the dag was knocked down in the general rush, and lay for a moment upside down in the straw, his curious clubfeet waving helplessly.

Even when he righted himself and tried to feed, he was continually pushed aside by the others and got very little. From Mrs Troughlicker at Number One to Mrs Grubguzzle at Number Nine everybody was convinced of one thing. Pigman would never let this one stay.

"Pigman'll 'ave 'e," they said.

"No doubt about it."

"Stands to reason—with feet like that."

"Poor little mite."

"Pigman'll take un away, for sure." And gloom hung over the pigsties like a black cloud.

The sows never quite knew what happened to a dag, or for that matter a piglet badly hurt by being stepped or lain on by its mother. They knew that the servant came and removed such an unfortunate, so they simply spoke of it as being 'taken away'; they were unaware of the hardwood club which the pigman kept in his meal-shed to deal out merciful death to the weak and the wounded.

Before long, the distant clank of buckets and good smells blowing on the wind told them that the servant was bringing breakfast and the low grunts of concern changed to loud impatient yells as the dag was forgotten in the excitement of feeding time.

"Hurry up, Pigman!" shouted the sows.

"Stir your stumps, you lazy article!"

"Fair starved, I am!"

" 'E'm too slow to catch a cold!"

And Mrs Troughlicker at Number One, who

would be the first fed, champed her jaws with a noise
like clapping hands, and great dribbles of spit ran out
of her mouth.

When the pigman had completed his duties and
Mrs Grubguzzle's head was deep in the trough at
Number Nine, he returned to Mrs Barleylove. Earlier
that morning he had seen that the birth was finished
and all seemed well, but he had not yet examined the

litter. Of course he immediately saw the dag and without hesitation picked it gently up and popped it into the deep pocket of his old coat, unnoticed by the sow busy at her breakfast. Had he wanted to examine or remove a healthy piglet, he would have clamped its mouth shut to prevent its squeals bringing the mother rushing to its defence; but this one, he thought, hadn't the strength for even a squeak.

In the meal-shed he looked more closely at it. In all his long experience he had never seen a piglet with such funny forefeet. The little 'clicks' or points of the tiny hooves were turned inward towards one another, so that the shape of the foot was not sharp but rounded as Mrs Swiller had said, like a puppy's.

Now Gloucester Old Spots are a rare breed of pig, and the pigman occasionally gave in to the temptation to spare the life of a dag if it was a female. A little sow-piglet, or 'gilt' as he called it, just might grow, even if very slowly, to make a breeding sow one day. But little boar-piglets, called hogs, he wanted nothing to do with if they were born weakly.

Not only was this one a hog. It also had those awful feet. Hanging upon a rusty nail was his hardwood club, and the pigman reached up for it.

CHAPTER 2

Not 'It', but 'He'

Strangely enough, people who keep pigs very often seem to look like them. The pigman was a huge fat person, with short legs and a big stomach. His face had several chins, a squashed nose, and little dark glinty eyes. He also had enormous hands, and in one of these he held the dag as one might hold a bunch of flowers, its bony sad-looking head and curious fore-feet sticking out above his curled fingers. He shifted his grasp to hold the creature by its hindlegs, its head now hanging down, and took a good grip on his club with the other hand. At that very moment, he heard a scuttling noise at the other end of the shed, and, turning, he saw a rat running across the top of one of his meal bins.

Now if there was one thing the pigman hated, it was a rat. Rats, as far as he was concerned, were worthless greedy cunning thieves, plotting from dawn to dusk to steal the food of his beloved pigs, and the sight of a rat was enough to make him forget everything else. He dropped the dag head first upon the floor and lumbered towards the meal bin, grunting with fury.

The first thing the dag saw, when it had picked itself up, was bright sunlight outside the door; and it tottered towards it and fell down the concrete steps into the yard. Once outside, it heard in the distance the contented noises of full-fed sows and the squeals of piglets fighting for a place at the milk-bar, and it turned that way. It was weak and confused and hungry and unhappy. But it was also determined, and wanted its mother and was going to find her even if, as seemed likely, it killed it.

It plodded on on its dogfeet and eventually reached the door of Number One, where it had just enough strength left for some feeble squeaking. Mrs Trough-licker's head appeared over the door.

"'Pon my soul!" she cried. "'Tis that little dag that Pigman took away! Mrs Barleylove! Mrs Barleylove! 'Tis thy dag! 'Tis little Daggie Dogfoot!"

There was uproar along the row as every sow lurched to her feet, those with piglets shaking them off and scattering them in screaming confusion. Soon upon every front door there rested a pair of trotters, and above each a large drop-eared face gazed down at the object outside Mrs Troughlicker's sty.

Above the hubbub came the deep urgent grunting of little Daggie Dogfoot's mother at Number Five. When Mrs Barleylove had finished breakfast, she had nosed her newborn litter and, though she could not count, had found them all fat and level and had known that Pigman had taken one away. Now, by some miracle, here he was again, not a dozen yards from home.

"Daggie!" she called, "Daggie! Come on, my son! Don't give up now."

Slowly the exhausted baby began to cover the last lap, wobbling along past Mrs Boltapple at Number Two, then Mrs Swedechopper, then Mrs Swiller, till at last it stood swaying with weariness at the door of Number Five.

"Mammie," said Daggie Dogfoot. "I'm tired. And I'm hungry. Let me in."

Mrs Barleylove would have broken down the door without a second thought had she been able to, but it was stout, and opened inwards. Rooting frantically at the bottom of it in a vain attempt to lift it off its hinges, she discovered that there was a narrow gap between its lower edge and the concrete, a gap not wide enough to get her snout through or to allow a fat piglet out, but just sufficient perhaps to let a very thin piglet in. She scraped away all the straw from it and snorted madly under it as though she were trying to sniff Daggie in like a vacuum cleaner.

"Come on, my baby," she said. "Only just get your head through, and the rest'll follow easy."

"Go on, littlun!" shouted Mrs Grubguzzle at Number Nine, and she was echoed by Mrs Grazegrass, Mrs Maizemunch, and Mrs Gobblespud, as well as by the ladies whose doors Daggie had already passed.

"Go on, love!" they shouted. "We'm all behind you!"

And before the combination of their support and his mother's urging and his own determination, with

a last desperate effort, Daggie Dogfoot somehow squeezed his head beneath the door and scrabbled with his funny forefeet and pushed with his skinny hindlegs and found himself at last back home. He lay exhausted while with tender grunts his mother carefully licked him all over. All down the line there rose up a chorus of snorts of relief, and Mrs Swiller and Mrs Gobblespud got off their doors and up on to their boundary walls for final words of congratulation.

"Love it!" cried Mrs Gobblespud. "What a brave little pig it is!"

Mrs Barleylove looked up from her licking.

"Begging yer pardon, Mrs Gobblespud," she said slowly and severely, "'tisn't an 'it'. He's a 'he'."

"She's right," said Mrs Swiller. "And not just a 'he'. I do reckon he's a hero." And with a few last good wishes both ladies returned to their duties.

Fortunately, by the time Daggie had made his way back to the pigsties, his mother had not only finished her own breakfast but had also given his brothers and sisters theirs. Now therefore she was able to push and prod and nose their well-fed little bodies into the inner covered part of Number Five, to barricade the opening with her great spotted back, and to offer the whole range of the milk-bar to one thin tired little body.

And how he drank! Moving along the line, scrabbling at his mother's side with his puppy's feet, he drank and drank and drank. And as he drank, so colour seemed to come into his skin, and his tummy blew out like a drum, and some sparkle crept into his dull eyes. Ten minutes later, when the pigman looked over the door, he found it hard to recognise his late intended victim.

The pigman's pursuit of the rat had led to much moving of bins and sacks, which in turn had exposed other rats. And from this followed much swearing and heavy breathing and wild swiping with the hardwood club, and cries of "Dratyer!" and "Dangyer!" and "Blastyer!" At the end of it all he was hot and sweaty, and the rats were laughing in their runways, and quite a lot of time had passed.

He looked about the doorway end of the meal-shed, expecting to find the dag hiding somewhere, then searched the yard, and finally, seeing no sign of it, walked down to the sties in case it could by any chance have found its way home. He leaned on the door of Number Five and shook his head till his three chins wobbled.

"Never credit it," he said to himself, mopping his face with a red spotted handkerchief, "little chap's got some guts. But all the same he'll never be no use to no one, nohow. He'll 'ave to go," and he slid back the bolt.

Now Mrs Barleylove busy at breakfast and un-aware of the fact—though resigned to the possibility

—that one of her children was to be taken away, was one thing. Mrs Barleylove interrupted while feeding that hero of a child was another; interrupted moreover by an impudent servant who had no right in her house except at feeding or cleaning-out times, and who was clearly intending to try to take her baby away once more.

Heaving herself to her feet with a violence that threw a surprised Daggie far to one side, she ran at the servant, swinging her head and champing her jaws together so that a froth of bubbles ran out over her tusks. The champing and her furious grunting combined to make a noise that sounded to the pigman like "Out! Out! Out!" which in fact was exactly what she was saying. At the same time, Mrs Swiller and Mrs Gobblespud reared up on to their walls and also shouted angrily at the servant.

"You leave 'im alone, Pigman!" they roared.

"Poor little feller."

"Tackle somebody your own size!"

"Dirty fat man!"

For just as we say 'dirty as a pig' or 'fat as a pig', so pigs repay the insult the other way round. And all along the row, from Mrs Troughlicker to Mrs Grubguzzle the cry went up "Dirty fat man! Let un alone! Get off out of it!" while nine pairs of jaws champed and nine pairs of eyes glistened.

The pigman was indeed out of Number Five

remarkably quickly for a man of his size. He knew all about the damage an angry sow can cause, and it was a different kind of sweat which he now wiped from his brow.

"Dratyer!" he cried, and "Dangyer!" and "Blast-yer!"

He waited until the fuming Mrs Barleylove had got down off the top of her door, and then bolted it, and lumbered off grumbling to himself. Let her keep the 'orrible little dag, he thought, it'll die soon enough and save me the trouble. Cussed old sows!

And as men often do when they feel that women-folk are too much for them, he walked across the yard to seek the company of another male, for the Gloucester Old Spots boar lived opposite. The boar came to his door, and gave his usual order.

"Hey you, Pigman. Scratch my back." And the servant of course obeyed. "He's not a bad chap really," thought the boar. "Does what he's told."

"Now he's a good old chap," thought the pigman. "Aren't you, old man?" he said. "Not like they cussed old sows."

And indeed, excepting that one was spotted and one was not, they looked very alike as they stood and chatted, each in his own tongue.

CHAPTER 3

Pigs Might Fly

Time passed, and Daggie Dogfoot not only survived but grew. He did not expand visibly like his litter-mates, but by cunning and agility he secured a fair share of his mother's milk. For example, he would persuade her to lie across a corner in which he was already waiting, or stand alongside the concrete feeding-trough so that he could scramble on to its rim for a high-level drink which the others couldn't reach; their slippery sharp-hooved forefeet did not allow them to balance there.

The pigman became resigned to Daggie's survival, and persuaded himself he had kept the creature out of kindness, as a mascot. Well aware of the look in Mrs Barleylove's eye and the sound of her threatening grunts, he left the dag severely alone.

Mrs Barleylove's neighbours spent a lot of their spare time leaning over their respective walls to watch. Unlike the pigman, who was merely pretend-ing as an excuse, they really did regard Daggie as a mascot, as indeed did all the other mothers; no piglet before had ever been 'taken away' and then come back, and there seemed something magical, mystical almost, about this, and also about his feet which appeared at the moment to be an advantage to him rather than the reverse.

"Love him!" said Mrs Gobblespud one morning, after watching Daggie do his king-of-the-castle trick on the trough. "He's growed ever so smart, an't 'e, Mrs B?"

Mrs Barleylove only grunted but inwardly she swelled with pride. She had never believed in having favourites among her many children, but she had to admit to herself that this one was very . . . special.

"No offence," said Mrs Swiller, "but his little feet have altered, an't they?" And indeed, though the hooves on Daggie's hindfeet remained normal, the grotesquely inward-curving horny parts on his front feet had fallen off, leaving even more puppy-like round pads. This seemed to make him more sure-footed, so that when the litter played a game of tag, racing round the smooth clean-washed concrete of the outer enclosure after Pigman had mucked out, it was always Daggie who kept his feet while his stronger brothers and sisters often slipped and skidded on to their sides.

Mrs Barleylove was half minded to take offence at such a personal remark, but she quickly realised that it was well-meant; and anyway she badly wanted her neighbours' opinions.

"Yes, he has growed. And they have altered," she said. "Tell you the truth, ladies, I'd be mortal glad to know what you do think. You might say I'm daft, but I've caught meself wondering if he ain't somehow . . ." she paused and looked round to make sure that Daggie was not listening but he had run off with the rest for a rough-and-tumble in the straw inside, so she went on ". . . somehow . . . special?"

"Special?" said Mrs Swiller.

"Well, born for some purpose."

"Purpose?" said Mrs Gobblespud.

"What I mean to say is," said Mrs Barleylove, "he was taken away, wasn't he?"

"Must-a been," they said.

"And yet he come back?"

"For certain sure," they said.

"So that's kind of . . . special?"

Long droopy ears slap-slapped against fat faces as the two ladies nodded vigorous agreement.

"And his front feet?" said Mrs Barleylove.

"Different," said Mrs Swiller.

"Curious," said Mrs Gobblespud.

"Special?" asked Mrs Barleylove. There was a pause.

"Do you mean," said her neighbours, "special feet . . . for some purpose?"

It was Mrs Barleylove's turn to nod. There was another pause, during which the neighbours glanced a little anxiously at each other over her head. It occurred to them simultaneously that this was going a bit too far. Mrs Barleylove's concern for her dag was leading her to flights of fancy. Special feet for some purpose? No, no, that was too much of a good thing.

"Well . . . no, dear, not really," said Mrs Gobble-spud in a kindly voice, "I mean, I know they're not like other piglets' front feet are, but . . ."

"What Mrs G means, dear," said Mrs Swiller soothingly, "is that you shouldn't worry yourself overly about the little chap's feet. I mean I don't personally think they're going to be a hindrance to him, quite the contrary, but as to having been made like that for some purpose, well, that's about as likely as that . . ."

". . . pigs might fly," finished Mrs Gobblespud.

As Mrs Swiller had hesitated, Daggie Dogfoot had been on the point of coming out from the inner part of the sty, impelled as children often are by the certain feeling that adults are talking about them. All he heard in fact were the last three words. What's more, his mother and her friends fell silent the moment they saw him, so he felt sure he had been right.

"Good morning, Auntie Swiller, good morning, Auntie Gobblespud," he said politely. And then, "Can I have a milk shake, please, Mammie—quick, before the others come back?"

The sows' conversation thus abruptly terminated,

the neighbours dropped back off their walls, and Mrs Barleylove lay hastily down, anxious to please her darling.

Even as he gollupped down milk, Daggie was thinking hard. Pigs might fly, he thought, and they were definitely talking about me; that must mean *I* might fly. The other piglets came dashing out at that moment, and scrambled and shoved and stamped all over him, but he hung on determinedly until he was finished, and then climbed up and lay down on the huge rubbery cushion of his mother's side.

He looked at his curious feet about which the others already teased him, though he did not mind for he was glad to be alive. He looked up at the blue sky. A sparrow flew over the sty with a whirr of wings; a little higher, a flock of starlings made their way across the yard; higher still, the swallows and martins cut lovely circles in the fly-filled air and above them all, so high that his baby eyes could barely see them, the swifts raced black and crescent-shaped, screaming their joy at the wonder of flight.

I . . . might fly, thought Daggie Dogfoot. He sat up on his mother and beat his forelegs together experimentally, but nothing happened. Perhaps it's taking off that's difficult, he thought. Perhaps once you get up there, it's easier. He looked up into the sky again and tried to imagine himself up there, legs beating away somehow or other, ears flapping, curly tail

stretched out straight behind him as he soared and glided and swooped.

Perhaps if I got up somewhere high, he thought, so that I could jump off and then start flying. I'm sure they were talking about me. I'm sure I could do it. I will do it, you see if I don't. Just give me half a chance.

CHAPTER 4

The Squire

The boar was of course the most important person around, partly because he was an incredibly well-bred and aristocratic Gloucester Old Spots, and partly because he was the father of all the children born. His real name was Champion Imperial Challenger III of Ploughbarrow, but the sows all knew him as the Squire. His sty, which was opposite the row of nine, had a sloping verandah-type roof to keep the rain off his noble back, and the pigman, being large, had to duck down under this whenever he went in; the sows appreciated the fact that the servant always bowed low before the master.

The Squire kept in touch with his wives by means of occasional conversations across the yard when he felt like it and the wind was not too strong. He would stand against his door and poke his head out under his verandah roof and shout at them in his bluff jolly way. Sometimes he would address them generally, and then everyone who was not actually engaged at that moment in feeding babies would come respectfully to their front doors and bob their heads up and down deferentially. Sometimes he would single out an individual, to enquire after the latest arrivals perhaps.

One morning some weeks after Daggie Dogfoot's birth, his deep coughing grunt was heard, and the rattle of his door as he heaved his bulk up on to it. "'Tis the Squire!" they all said to their neighbours, and waited in awestruck silence. The boar cleared his throat.

"Ah, hhhrm, Mrs Barleylove, dear lady. A word with you."

"Here I be, Squire," said Mrs Barleylove. "What was you wanting?"

"The latest children, my dear. I hear from sparrow-talk that you have a litter?" The sparrows carried all the gossip round the farm.

"Y-yes, Squire."

"All well, I trust? Bonny? Bouncing? Chips off the old block, what?" There was a moment's pause and a shudder of anticipation ran down the sties. But Mrs Barleylove was equal to the occasion.

"All well, I thank you, Squire," she replied, with hardly a tremor in her voice. "Thanking yer honour for your kindness in enquiring."

"Good show," said the Squire. "Fine effort, doncherknow. Keep up the good work, what?" and he got down off his door, while all the ladies ducked their heads again and disappeared with a whistling sound which was made up of eight small sighs of relief and one large one.

It was not that the Squire didn't know about dags. He knew only too well, because a litter-sister of his had been one. He had never forgotten waking up one morning when he was a baby, to find the poor spindly little thing stretched out cold and lifeless beside him; and because of this he was always terrified that one of his own children might be born a dag.

So he always asked the same question "Chips off the old block, what?", and the sows never let him down. He never knew that occasionally the chips were very small, and either died or were taken away; and as for the occasional gilt whose life the pigman saw fit to spare, the Squire would not set eyes on it until it was weaned and on its way to other quarters. If it survived that long, it would have caught up a bit in size and be nothing worse than the smallest of the litter. But what on earth would he say to Daggie Dogfoot?

Mrs Barleylove's neighbours tried to find a tactful way to approach the subject. They began with praise.

"Ain't he active?" said Mrs Gobblespud admiringly as she watched Daggie, his mind on flight, leap from his mother's back and land upside down in the remains of breakfast at the bottom of the trough. "You must be proud of him, Mrs B."

"Any mother would be proud of him," said Mrs

Swiller. And then, greatly daring, she added defiantly,
"And any father too."

There was a long awkward pause, and it seemed to
the neighbours that Mrs Barleylove's white parts
grew a little pink and her spots turned slightly
blacker.

"I don't rightly know what to do, ladies," she said at last. "Squire's bound to clap eyes on him sooner or later. He'll go raving mad."

" 'Tis more sooner than later though, ain't it?" said Mrs Gobblespud. "They'll be crossing the yard in a week or so, won't 'em?"

'Crossing the yard' meant weaning time, when the eight-week-old piglets left their mothers and went to the store pens on either side of the boar's sty; later the hogs would go to the fattening pens, and the gilts to other quarters till big enough to be sold for breeding.

Daggie, though he had not been listening to the conversation properly, had, like children everywhere, picked up the awkward bits.

"Who's Squire, Mammie?" he asked.

"The Squire is your father, dear, a very fine gentleman."

"Why will he go raving mad?"

"Oh, your father's a hot-tempered person," said Mrs Swiller quickly. "He gets very angry with the servant if his meals are late."

"Well, what's 'crossing the yard' mean, Auntie Swiller?"

"Oh, you'll like that, Daggie," put in Mrs Gobblespud soothingly. "That's when all you young 'uns go off on a lovely holiday and your mother gets a nice rest."

Mrs Barleylove's other seven piglets jumped about excitedly at this, and ran about the sty squealing "A lovely holiday! A lovely holiday!" But Daggie Dogfoot sat on his thin backside, and a tear ran down the side of his big head.

"I don't want to leave my Mammie," he said, and another tear ran down the other side.

At that moment Mrs Barleylove made up her mind, quite firmly, that she would not allow this humble undersized deformed child of hers to cross the yard. Always before, like all the other mothers, she had allowed the servant to drive the weaners away without protest, indeed with a sigh of relief after two months' hard work. This time it would be different, for this child was different, and her heart ached at the sight of those two great tears. The servant could take the other seven, but not her Daggie. Just let him try.

A fortnight later he tried. He opened the door of Number Five, and holding a sheet of corrugated iron in front of him like a shield, he hooshed Mrs Barleylove into the inner part of the sty while the litter ran out into the yard. A grunt and a rattle on the other side told everyone that the Squire was at his door to inspect his offspring as they crossed. But when the

pigman had shut up Number Five again, he could only count seven fat weaners frisking about outside. He looked back in and saw the dag peeping out from between his mother's legs. He started to open the door again but immediately Mrs Barleylove rushed forward, champing and snorting, fierce as one of her wild woodland ancestors.

"Dirty fat man!" she shouted. "Let un alone!"

"Dratyer!" cried the pigman, and "Dangyer!" and "Blastyer!"

But he backed away quickly, and then turned and lumbered off after the rest.

"Keep the mizzable thing then!" he shouted back over his shoulder. " 'Twill never be no use to no one, nohow!"

He rounded up the others, drove them into a V-shaped funnel of hurdles which he had put up, and so into one of the store pens, and shut them in. He mopped his face with his red spotted handkerchief and went to talk to Champion Imperial Challenger III of Ploughbarrow.

"Hey you, Pigman. Scratch my back," said the Squire. And, as usual, the servant obeyed. They held a conversation, and it was fortunate that they spoke different languages.

"Damn fine bunch of youngsters that, Pigman," said the Squire, "fat as you are by the time they're finished, I shouldn't wonder."

"You got an 'orrible little dag left over there, old feller," said the pigman. "That bad-tempered old sow's welcome to him."

And what a welcome Daggie Dogfoot was having, for his mother still had plenty of milk left for one, and now the whole milk-bar was his and his alone.

At last, full to the brim, he fell asleep by his mother's side, and dreamed that he and she and his father the Squire were all flying, trotter in trotter, through a warm and milky sky.

CHAPTER 5

Resthaven

The sows usually had two litters of babies each year, in the Spring and in the Autumn; and so twice a year, after weaning her piglets, every mother enjoyed what Mrs Gobblespud had called 'a good rest'. As soon as a newly-weaned litter had 'crossed the yard', the sow would expect the servant to open her door and then a gate at the upper end of the cluster of farm buildings. This gate was the entrance to a small field which the pigman unimaginatively called 'the Pig Ground', but to which the ladies always referred as 'Resthaven'.

"Not long now," a harassed mother would say to her neighbour at about the seventh week of nursing. "Soon be going to Resthaven."

"Oh, that'll be nice for you, dear."

"Lovely and quiet there."

"The air's good too. So bracing."

"Not but what I shan't miss the kiddies, mind."

"No, but you got to get away. Besides, it gives that lazy Pigman time to give the house a good clean-up."

Resthaven was a small triangular patch of roughish hillside, sloping down from a point at the top to a long base bounded by a brook. The other two sides were fenced with stout pig-wire, and right in the centre stood a great old oak. Most of the upper part of the little field was dotted with ant heaps.

The morning after Daggie's brothers and sisters had left, the pigman came to Number Five and opened the door. Normally on these occasions one or two heads might pop up along the row, and one or two shouts be heard of "Have a nice time!" or "Happy holidays!" But this time it was different, for no one remembered a piglet ever going to Resthaven, much less a dag. By the time Daggie had politely said goodbye to Auntie Swiller and Auntie Gobblespud, every other head was up to see this strange baby. And as Mrs Barleylove made her stately way off after the lumbering servant, with Daggie trotting behind her, many and heartfelt were the good wishes that followed them, though softly spoken so as not to wake the Squire.

For Daggie, everything was new and wonderful. No sooner had the servant closed the gate than the little piglet cried, "Oh, Mammie! Isn't it exciting? Can I go off and explore?"

"Go where you like, my love," said his mother. "But mind and be careful of the water at the bottom of the field. Pigs can't swim, you know."

Pigs might fly though, thought Daggie Dogfoot gleefully to himself as he ran away over the summer grasses. Specially if they could find somewhere high enough to jump off.

Mrs Barleylove, watching her darling with pride, was quite amazed to see how fast he made his way around Resthaven, scampering down to the brook to peer at the glistening tinkling water, rushing up through patches of reed and coarse grass to scratch himself against the rough trunk of the oak, and skipping on and off the ant heaps more like a lamb than a piglet. Doggy little forefeet and skinny long hindlegs he might have, but he was quicker and more active, she thought, than any of the dozens of fat rolypoly babies she had had in her long life of motherhood.

Finally, as she watched, Daggie arrived at the very top of the wedge-shaped field and climbed upon the highest of all the ant heaps. He turned to face down-hill and saw his mother looking up towards him. "Watch me, Mammie!" he yelled, and leaped off. He nosedived into the grass, turned a somersault, rolled over a couple of times on the steep slope, and fetched up against the next ant heap six feet away.

"Yes, dear. Very clever," called Mrs Barleylove tenderly, and went to the oak to look for acorns.

By the end of that first thrilling day Daggie was pretty sore. He had climbed on to and jumped off everything he could find, every bank and ridge in the rough field, every ant heap, and several stumps of

felled elms. He had even somehow climbed to the highest part of a big dead branch that lay on the ground beneath the oak, and taken off from a height of perhaps four feet. But every effort had resulted in a crash landing, and now, in the warmth of the August evening, he was not only bruised but a little despondent.

He and his mother had just left a shallow place at the brook's edge where they had drunk their fill, and now they stood together at a point further along the bank, a high point where the stream had cut away the side over the years as it made a swirling turn. Here they were about fifteen feet above the water, and behind them the slope of Resthaven was steep and short-grassed for some distance.

Suppose I started back up there and ran really fast,

thought Daggie. "Mammie," he said, "did you say pigs couldn't swim?"

Mrs Barleylove, like all her kind, had been brought up to believe the old sows' tale that a pig attempting to swim will cut its own throat by the awkward action of its sharp-hooved forefeet; and she explained this to her son. She was comfortably full of acorns and roots and grasses and berries, as well as the ration of pig-nuts which the servant had brought, and she gazed dreamily down at the winking water without really thinking what she was saying.

"But I haven't got . . ." began Daggie, and then some instinct checked him.

"What, dear?" said Mrs Barleylove absently.

"Er, I haven't heard that before," said Daggie quickly. "I mean, I didn't know that."

"There's lots of things you don't know, my son," said his mother in the way that mothers always do.

And there's something that you don't know too, thought the dag to himself. Which is that if I started back up there and ran really fast . . . Pigs *might* fly, he said to himself, Auntie Gobblespud said so. I just wish I had the chance to consult an expert before trying. Daggie had thought a good deal about getting expert advice, and had often asked the birds who hopped around Number Five. But the sparrows, when he questioned them, only answered "Cheap! Cheap!" in an impudent way, and the starlings simply piped rudely at him; once a big carrion crow had pitched on the sty wall but in reply to the piglet's enquiries only said "Garn!"

Suddenly, as he stood by his mother high above the brook, there was a whistle of wings and over their heads flew a black-and-white bird with a bright red bill and cheek-patches, and wide webbed feet with sharp claws at the ends of the toes. Beating its wings rapidly, it braked and dropped upon the surface in a shower of water-drops that gleamed golden in the sunlight. Wagging its tail feathers from side to side, it swam rapidly about, first drinking, and then showering itself with water by splashing with its wings.

Flying *and* swimming, thought Daggie. Too much!

"What's that bird, Mammie?" he asked. "I've never seen one like that before."

"There's lots of things you've never seen before, dear," said his mother in the way that mothers always do. "That's a duck."

"Where does it come from?" asked Daggie.

"Oh, Pigman keeps some, I believe," said Mrs Barleylove. "For their eggs, I think. After all," she went on reflectively, "even servants have to eat, I suppose. Let them eat eggs."

"Can I talk to it, Mammie?" said Daggie Dogfoot eagerly. "It won't hurt me, will it?"

"Won't hurt you," said his mother. "But I don't

suppose you'll get much out of it. They'm stupid things. Probably won't understand a word you say.'' But when Daggie ran down to the shallow place and called to the duck, it immediately turned and swam towards him with a pleasant expression on its neat face.

CHAPTER 6

Felicity

"Good-mor-ning-duck," said Daggie Dogfoot very slowly and loudly, the proper way to address foreigners, "can-I-ask-you-some-thing-please?" The duck, which had been walking towards him up the sandy shallows with a quick rolling gait, hopped up on to a low willow branch, gripped it comfortably with her clawed feet, settled her feathers, and considered the piglet with bright eyes.

"Absolutely anything you like," she answered in a quiet musical voice.

"Oh," said Daggie, surprised, "Mammie said you wouldn't . . ." He stopped, confused.

". . . wouldn't understand a word you said?" chuckled the duck. "Well, your mother obviously doesn't know much about Muscovy ducks."

Daggie gulped. "Please," he said, "what is a . . . Muscovy duck?"

"Well," said the duck, "we're a tree-perching variety—that's what these are for," and she raised one foot to show the curved claws. "Originally from South America."

Daggie's world had expanded enormously since leaving Number Five, but it was still very small. He imagined South America to be the next field beyond Resthaven.

"Anyway," said the duck, "what did you want to ask me?"

Daggie took a deep breath. He looked up at the steep bank above to see if his mother was there, but she had moved away.

"Do you think," he said slowly and carefully, "that pigs might fly?" The duck opened her bill wide, and then hastily closed it again. Then she opened and closed it rapidly perhaps a dozen times, making a soft quot-quot-quotting noise.

"Well, do you?" asked Daggie.

"I think," said the duck, "that almost anything *might* happen. Though I have never actually heard of a flying pig. Who put the idea in your head?"

"My Auntie," said Daggie. "Well, she was our next-door neighbour really but I called her Auntie. She said it, you see, and I'm pretty sure they were all talking about me."

"So it's you that's going to . . . fly?" said the Muscovy.

"Hope so."

"Have you tried yet?"

"Oh yes, quite a few times. But I can't seem to get airborne. That's why I'm so excited about this place."

And Daggie proceeded to explain to his new friend his idea of the steep downhill take-off and the leap from the top of the high bank into glorious soaring flight. "D'you think I could do it?" said Daggie Dogfoot.

The bright-eyed duck looked consideringly at this strange creature before her. She looked at his big head and his hard thin little body and his skinny backside. She looked down at the sand and saw the three sets of prints in it, her own webs, the deep slots of the heavy sow, and the third strange set of tracks of two tiny slots and two pawmarks. The idea of a modest lecture on the qualities necessary for flight occurred to her, but she dismissed it immediately in the face of the determination which shone from the piglet's features.

"I think you're going to try," she said. And looking at the deep pool which the current had gouged out below the steep bank, she added, "It's not a bad place to try either. I presume you can swim?"

Daggie looked puzzled.

"Pigs can't swim," he said. "I should have thought you would have known that. I'm not talking about swimming. I'm talking about flying."

The duck hopped off the willow branch and walked over to Daggie. Pretending to squatter in the damp sand with her bill, she shot a close look at the piglet's forefeet. I wonder, she thought. His high-flown ambitions are going to flop, that's for sure. But something else quite novel might come out of it.

"Tell you what," she said. "I'd love to see the . . . er, maiden flight. Would you mind?"

"Not a bit," replied Daggie excitedly. "That's exactly what I wanted—an expert to be around to give me tips. I mean it isn't just the take-off. I may need some help with landing."

Once again the duck made that soft quot-quot-quotting noise with her bill.

"Yes," she said. "Though coming down is really the easiest bit. By the way, what does your mother think about all this?"

"Oh she doesn't know," said Daggie. "I thought I'd try it very early in the morning while she's having her lie-in. How about tomorrow?"

"All right," said the duck. "I'll be in the pool here at sunrise tomorrow. By the way, I don't know your name?"

"Daggie Dogfoot," said the piglet.

"Right," said the duck. She slipped into the water and began to paddle off upstream.

"Wait a minute," called Daggie after her. "How will you get here that early? Won't you have to wait till Pigman lets you out?"

The duck stopped paddling and floated back towards him on the current.

"Pigman?" she said.

"Yes, the servant," said Daggie. "You know, that dirty fat man."

"Oh, Duckman you mean," said the Muscovy. "Oh no, I don't go in the shed at nights with the rest of them. I roost in a tree."

You might suppose Duckman just keeps us for the eggs we lay, she thought, but I've seen him before now go into the shed with an empty sack and come out with it full and kicking. I'm not taking any risks. And off she swam once more. She was almost round the next bend in the stream before Daggie realised he did not know her name. He ran through the shallow water on to the bank and galloped along till he came level with her.

"What are you called?" he shouted down.

"Felicity," said the duck.

"That's a funny name," shouted Daggie. "What's it mean?"

"Happiness," said the duck, and paddled away past the boundary of Resthaven and out of the piglet's sight.

Happiness, thought Daggie, as he made his way towards his mother who was lying under the oak tree, life seems to be full of it. Living in this lovely place, and making such a nice friend, and to-morrow . . . wheeeee! Mrs Barleylove woke up from her nap at his squealing arrival.

"Where you bin, my baby?" she asked. "Talking to that duck?" and she grunted with amusement.

"Yes, Mammie," said Daggie excitedly, "and she's ever so nice and she's called Felicity and . . ." he took a deep breath ". . . she's a Muscovy from South America."

"Fancy!" said Mrs Barleylove. "There's nice."

What an imagination, she thought fondly. Just sees an old duck in the brook, and he comes out with all that fairy story. Bless his little heart.

"You come and have a nice rest," she said. "You don't want to overtire yourself. Tomorrow's another day."

But as Daggie Dogfoot lay by his mother's side and dozed in the sheltered warmth of Resthaven while the afternoon shadows lengthened, he knew that to-morrow wasn't just another day. Tomorrow was the day he had been planning for ages and ages, a whole two weeks, a quarter of his life. Tomorrow was the day he would fly. And Felicity would be there to help him. His mouth screwed into a grin of pure joy, he fell soundly asleep.

CHAPTER 7

Gosh!

Felicity woke early next morning on her usual perch. This was the thin branch of an alder tree sticking out over the stream. She had chosen it not only because it was completely fox-proof, but because she liked the never-ending music of the running water, singing her to sleep with its bubbling lullaby and waking her each day with its gurgling song.

She stretched her wings, one after the other, pushing out each in its turn to its fullest extent so that the big flight feathers stood apart from each other, as a human might stretch his fingers wide. Then she flapped her wings very vigorously as she stood upon the branch and shook herself all over. She felt very happy.

She began to think about her new friend Daggie Dogfoot. He's in for a ducking, she thought with amusement, and then it suddenly struck her that a ducking might easily turn into a drowning. She jumped off her alder branch and flew rapidly downstream towards Resthaven. She was suddenly worried that the piglet might have been too impatient to wait for her.

However as soon as she reached the little sloping field she could see that everything was in order. Under the oak lay a mountain of spotted flesh, which was Mrs Barleylove having her lie-in. And at the top of the steep slope above the high bank, a small spotty figure positively danced with impatience, pawing at the ground with his round front feet as though he were a puppy on an invisible leash.

"Hallo, Felicity!" cried Daggie as the duck glided over his head. "Take-off in two minutes. OK?"

A minute and three-quarters later the first rays of the rising sun came over the eastern bank of Resthaven and shone upon the rough bark of the oak tree and upon the smooth, closed, white-lashed eyelids of Mrs Barleylove. She opened her eyes, stretched, heaved herself to her feet, and looked about for her beloved boy. Hardly had she focused upon him, high above her on the slope, than to her absolute horror she saw him begin to run downhill at great speed, faster, faster, faster, till at last he leaped out over the high bank of the stream, and disappeared from her sight.

Felicity had positioned herself close under the Resthaven bank of the brook, directly underneath the take-off point. She knew that the impetus of his downhill run would take Daggie well out into the middle of the pool, and, head cocked upwards, she waited ready to go instantly to his aid.

Suddenly the quiet of the morning was shattered by an anguished scream from the horrified watcher under the oak tree, and in the same instant, high above the waiting duck, a small spotted shape shot out from the top of the bank and seemed for a frozen fraction of time to hang suspended against the clear blue sky. Legs working frantically, ears streaming behind his head, ridiculous tail whipping round and round like an egg-whisk, Daggie Dogfoot enjoyed a

split second of level flight. Then his heavy head came down to point him at the pool, a squeal of fright burst from him as the dark water rushed up to greet him, and "Eeeeeeeek—kersplosh—glug!" he was gone from view.

When he rose to the surface, he was facing the opposite bank and could not see the reassuring figure of the Muscovy duck who had by now swum close to him. He could see nothing but what seemed an ocean of water of which he had already swallowed a lot, and on top of the newfound knowledge that pigs couldn't fly came the awful realisation that they couldn't swim either. He knew this. Mammie had said so. Mammie, whom he would never see again.

"Heeeelp!" he squealed. "Heee-gurgle-glug!" and down he went again. As soon as he surfaced for the second time he heard two voices. One was his mother's, shouting desperately from the shallows where she stood belly-deep after a thundering gallop from the oak tree.

"Save him! Save my boy!" yelled Mrs Barleylove in agony.

The other was a quiet voice which spoke in his ear.

"Keep still," said the quiet voice. "Don't struggle. Don't talk. Keep your mouth tight shut. Breathe through your snout. Run after me. Just run as though you were on dry land," and Felicity set off for the far bank which was by now the nearer of the two,

283

wagging her tail encouragingly and glancing back over her shoulder at the piglet.

Because of the confidence in the duck's voice, because he had spirit and courage still in the midst of his panic, and because there was nothing else to do, Daggie obeyed. He clenched his teeth together, tipped up his head so that his nostrils pointed skywards like the twin guns of a surfaced submarine, kicked with his hindlegs and paddled like mad with his doggy feet, trying hard to imagine that he was galloping through the grass.

To his amazement, he began to move forward through the water after the duck, at first slowly, then faster as he gained momentum and confidence, and finally so fast that before they reached the far bank he was level with her and they touched bottom together in a little reedy inlet.

They looked at one another and their eyes shone, Felicity's with amusement and pleasure, Daggie's with relief and triumph as realisation swept over him.

"Pigs can't fly," said Daggie. Felicity shook her head.

"But there's one pig," said Daggie quietly, "that can," said Daggie more loudly, "SWIM!" shouted Daggie Dogfoot at the top of his squeaky voice, and off he set, all by himself, towards his mother on the Resthaven bank.

Mrs Barleylove had continued throughout to yell

"Save my boy!" pausing only when it seemed he had reached safety. Now here he was back in deep water again, and she began to squeal as before, until two voices reached her ears.

"Calm yourself, missus," said one as the duck, who had flown quickly across over the head of the swimmer, landed beside her. "He's all right. Just listen to him." And as the sow quietened, she heard the other voice, the voice of her fast-approaching son.

"Mammie! Mammie!" came the cry over the gentle lapping of the pool. "Look at me! I can swim! It's easy! Watch!" and as she stared, open-mouthed, the small figure came paddling nearer and nearer, pushing up a little bow wave in front of it with the speed of its progress.

Still Mrs Barleylove did not really understand what had happened since the sun had woken her. As soon as Daggie was out of the brook and shaking himself like a water-spaniel, she turned and made off up the bank towards the summit, scolding as she went in the way that mothers do when their children have given them a bad fright.

"Silly boy!" she said. "Naughty boy! Come quickly and run about in the sunshine or you'll catch your death of cold. I told you not to go down by the water. You'm never to go there again, d'you understand? Never. I don't know what your father would say if he knew," and so on, until, receiving no reply, she turned and found that she had been talking to herself.

Below her, as she stood at the take-off point on the top of the high bank, two figures swam happily about the pool. One was white with black patches, and one was white with black spots, and as Mrs Barleylove watched giddily from the height they made a series of patterns in the pool, first one leading, then the other. Circles they made, and figures-of-eight, and zigzags, and criss-crosses, till the surface frothed and little wavelets lapped and slapped against the banks.

Slowly the incredible truth dawned upon Mrs Barleylove. Her poor undersized deformed child was swimming, really swimming, swimming beautifully. 'Special feet for some purpose', eh? If only the neighbours could see him now.

"Oh, Daggie my love!" she called down. "How clever you be!"

How happy I am, thought Daggie, to have such a lovely mother, to swim in this beautiful sparkling stuff, to be with my friend whose very name means happiness. And he paddled madly about, while every little fish in the pool formed its mouth into a perfect round o of wonder. The moorhens in the reeds tut-tutted their amazement. The heron on the top of a downstream willow squawked his disbelief. A brilliant kingfisher gave an admiring whistle, and a passing green woodpecker laughed hysterically. And up the line of the brook flew a solitary swan, the sound of his great wings expressing exactly the surprise of all. "Gosh!" was the noise they made. "Gosh! Gosh! Gosh! Gosh!"

CHAPTER 8

The Truth Comes Out

The news travelled fast, by air mail of course, for the woodpecker shouted it to his mate in her nesting hole, and starlings resting in upper branches heard it; later they discussed it in wheezy whistles as they bathed in the yard trough; sparrows searching the floor for small seeds listened to the starlings, and then of course told everybody. By midday there was only one creature who did not know the story of the swimming piglet, and that of course was the pigman, too stupid to understand animal language. The Squire knew, as the sows soon found out.

Mrs Swiller and Mrs Gobblespud were conversing across the empty outer run of Number Five, now brushed and scraped and washed clean by the servant, and smelling strongly of disinfectant. They were recalling a conversation of a couple of weeks ago.

"Do ee recall what she said, Mrs G?" grunted Mrs Swiller.

"That I do, Mrs S," replied Mrs Gobblespud, "that I do. Special, she said. Special feet, that's what she said. And do you remember what we said?"

"That I do, Mrs G," answered Mrs Swiller. "Sure as my name's Rosie Swiller, I do. 'Special feet for some purpose', that's what we asked if she meant. Rubbish, we thought."

"Just fancy!" said Mrs Gobblespud. She paused, consideringly.

"Wouldn't cut his throat, see," she went on.

"Not with feet like that," said Mrs Swiller.

"Always said he were a clever little chap."

"And brave with it."

"Never heard of any Ploughbarrow pig swimming, never."

"Never heard of any pig swimming."

"What'll Pigman say when he finds out?"

There was a short silence, and then with one horrified voice they said, "What'll Squire say when he finds out?"

The words were hardly out of their mouths when they heard the deep grunt and the rattle of the door on the other side of the yard. Mrs Swiller and Mrs Gobblespud slid back off their walls and stood very still in their sties, heads lowered, breath held. If they had had fingers, they would have crossed them. Neither wanted in the least to hear her name called if the boar started asking questions. As it turned out, no one was to escape.

"Ladies!" barked the Squire in his loudest voice. "A word with you all, if ye please. My apologies if any of you are in the midst of your duties, but I want you all on parade in one minute."

At these stern words there was a tremendous noise of hustling and bustling and shuffling mixed with the squeals of rudely disturbed piglets, and within thirty seconds eight pairs of trotters reared up on to eight front doors, and above them eight large anxious faces peered across at the lord and master.

Only at Number Five of course was there no face, and it seemed to the nervous sows that the Squire's angry gaze was directed at this space rather than at any one of them. After a moment however he shifted his look to Number One, and then slowly, deliberately, swung his heavy head to scrutinise in turn each face, all the way to Number Nine.

At last he spoke. "It has come to my notice," he said, "that something very strange has been going on, doncherknow. What?"

No one answered, so he went on, "Now I'm going to get to the bottom of this, dammit, so I shall ask you all in turn. And I don't want any shilly-shallying, what? Understood?"

"Yes, Squire," chorused eight worried voices.

The Squire looked directly at Number One again. "Mrs Troughlicker," he said. "The damned sparrows are talking about a swimming pig. What d'ye know about it, eh?"

"Not a great deal, Squire," said Mrs Troughlicker

uncomfortably, "there's rumours."

"Mrs Boltapple?"

"Don't hardly seem possible, Squire."

"Mrs Swedechopper?"

"Well, Squire, perhaps somebody was mistook."

"Mrs Swiller?"

Mrs Swiller hesitated, and glanced nervously across at Mrs Gobblespud.

"Well, Mrs Swiller?"

"Tidn't one of mine, Squire, they'm all here, dry as a bone, every one," and Mrs Swiller forced a kind of snorting laugh.

"No laughing matter," said the Squire severely. "Mrs Gobblespud?"

"Pigs can't swim, Squire, we all knows that," said Mrs Gobblespud in a strained voice. "Not if they'm normal," she added thoughtlessly.

"Normal? Normal?" said the Squire loudly. "What child of mine has ever been other than normal? What? Eh? What are you talking about? What's she talking about, Mrs Maizemunch?"

"Don't know, Squire."

"Mrs Grazegrass?"

"Can't say, Squire."

"Mrs Grubguzzle?"

"Don't ask me, Squire."

"But I do ask you," shouted the Squire angrily. "I do ask you, dammit. I'm asking all of you. Except of course Mrs Barleylove," and he shifted his gaze back to the door of Number Five.

Nobody said anything.

"Now lookee here," said the Squire. "If none of you ladies is willing or able to tell me about this business, I can only presume that it's connected with Mrs Barleylove, what?"

Still no one said anything.

"Well, she's at Resthaven, ain't she?" said the Squire. Eight heads nodded. The Squire began to lose patience again.

"You're not telling me," he shouted, "that Mrs Barleylove's been swimming in the brook, eh? What? What?"

Eight heads shook and eight faces struggled to keep straight at this question.

"Well then, dammit!" roared the Squire. "I saw her last litter cross the yard with me own eyes, not a couple of days ago, and a damn fine bunch they were. Any father would be proud of them. And," he added as an afterthought, "any mother too. So if she's not swimming, and she's got no youngsters with her, will you kindly tell me who in the name of St Anthony is this swimming pig?"

Now St Anthony is the patron saint of pigmen, and when the sows heard the Squire swear so dreadfully, they knew that the issue could no longer be avoided. It would have had to have come out sometime. It had

better come out now. Mrs Troughlicker, Mrs Boltapple, and Mrs Swedechopper looked inwards
towards Mrs Swiller, Mrs Grubguzzle, Mrs Graze-
grass, and Mrs Maizemunch looked inwards towards
Mrs Gobblespud.

"Well?" said the Squire.

"Well, Squire," said Mrs Swiller and Mrs Gobblespud together. "This last litter, Mrs Barleylove . . .

had a . . . dag," they finished in a kind of whisper.

There was an awful silence, broken only by the sound of the Squire grinding his tusks. The sows could not see his eyes, hidden by his drooping ears, and of this they were glad.

At last he spoke, very softly. "Go on," he said.

Mrs Swiller swallowed. "Usually, you see, Squire," she said, "when a . . . dag's born. . ."

"Usually?" interrupted the Squire in the same soft voice.

"Don't happen very often, of course," put in Mrs Gobblespud hastily, "but most of us, one time or another. . ."

"I see," said the Squire heavily.

"And then," said Mrs Swiller, "the servant takes it away."

"Takes it away?"

"Well, the mother never do see un no more."

"But this un came back!" said Mrs Gobblespud excitedly, and at this the rest could not contain themselves but joined in in a babble of voices.

"I seen it!"

"Brave little love!"

"Wouldn't be beat!"

"Squeezed under the door!"

"Then Pigman come again!"

"Dirty fat man!"

"We told un!"

"And later on he come again!"

"When t'others crossed the yard!"

"And she told un!"

At last the hubbub died down, and there was silence again, this time unbroken.

After a while the Squire spoke. It seemed to the sows that he sounded old and tired.

"This . . . dag, then," he said slowly, "is down at Resthaven with Mrs Barleylove, what?"

"Yes, Squire," they all replied.

"It must be the swimmer, then?"

"Yes, Squire."

"Extraordinary. Extraordinary. Boy or gel?"

"Boy, Squire."

"Boy, eh? What's he called?"

"Daggie Dogfoot."

"Daggie what?"

"Dogfoot."

"Because. . . ?"

"Yes, Squire."

"Which is presumably how he. . . ?"

Eight heads nodded, and nine brains imagined the scene in the brook. "Extraordinary," said the Squire. "Extraordinary, what?"

His natural courtesy reasserted itself, and he said in his normal bluff hearty voice, "I'm obliged to you, ladies. Pray return to your duties, doncherknow."

But after the sows had disappeared from sight, the

boar still leaned upon his gate. He felt shocked, as we all are when we learn home truths about ourselves. But he also felt in some way relieved, for it is better to admit some facts, even hard bitter facts, than to go on pretending that they don't exist. Most of all perhaps, as he stood there in the late afternoon sunshine, he began to feel proud.

Daggie Dogfoot, eh? he thought to himself. Taken away but fought his way back, what? Wouldn't be beaten, doncherknow. And swimming! Swimming like a damned fish, apparently! Extraordinary! By St Anthony, said the Squire to himself, I'd like to meet the little chap.

CHAPTER 9

The Race

Daggie spent nearly all that day in the water, only coming out for a drink of milk or to eat some of the pig-nuts which the servant threw down. The pigman noticed nothing. We only see what we expect to see, and he did not dream that he was the slave of a swimming pig.

Mrs Barleylove had already come to look upon Felicity as a kind of combination of nurse, aunt, instructress and lifeguard. She stood upon the bank watching teacher and pupil with a silly grin on her big fat face.

Felicity concentrated on Daggie's streamlining, to begin with. She wanted him lower in the water, but he was having trouble with his nose. Like all pigs, his nostrils faced directly forwards out of the flat end of his snout and the water simply rushed up them.

"Why doesn't the water go up *your* nose?" spluttered Daggie, after much trial and error.

"Oh, we've got a sort of valve thing we can shut to stop it," said the duck. "Just like you can shut your eyes if you don't want to see something." She paused, considering. "Perhaps you've got one too?" she said.

"Try and see, my love," called Mrs Barleylove. "After all, my dear," she addressed Felicity, "I can put my snout deep in a trough full of slops, and gobble away without having to take it out."

So Daggie tried, first on dry land, thinking very hard about pinching the insides of his nostrils together, while Felicity peered up his nose. After a bit she thought it was working so they went in the water, and it was!

Then Felicity re-designed Daggie's swimming action. His otter-like forefeet were just fine for the job; all he needed to be taught was to reach and pull instead of paddling. But his hindfeet, used as though running on dry land, hadn't the necessary drive.

The duck taught him a different method—to stick his hindlegs straight out behind him and beat them up and down in the water alternately, as fast as he could, keeping them stiff, barely breaking the surface.

They reached this stage by the end of the first day, and a long day it seemed to a very tired piglet curling up by his mother's warm side under the oak tree at dusk.

Oddly enough, as the Muscovy was settling to sleep on her alder branch, she heard, further up the valley, a thin hard cry in the coming darkness. "I-zaak!" it sounded like, "I-zaak!" Must warn Daggie about otters, she thought drowsily. Don't want him mistaken for a big fish.

For the next couple of days they worked hard at improving Daggie's style, and on the morning of the fourth day Felicity swam down early from her alder tree and found Daggie already practising in the pool. She hid behind some bulrushes and watched. Nor was she alone. From holes in the bank the blunt heads of water voles poked out. Moorhens peeped from among the reeds. The kingfisher sat on a brookside root, forgetting his fishing in his interest. And above, taking time off from mousing, a kestrel hung in fascination over the swimming pig.

He's good, thought Felicity, watching him slice through the water, low and straight, only his eyes and the dome of his head showing except when he tipped up his nostrils for a quick breath, hindlegs beating rhythmically, those curious forefeet pulling strongly. She left the bulrushes and swam into the pool.

"Hullo, Felicity!" shouted Daggie. "I've just been warming up. You said something about a final trial today."

"Well," said Felicity, "I thought we might have a race. I mean you've taken to the water like a duck, as the saying goes. Let's see if you can beat one."

"Hey, steady on!" Daggie said. "You're a proper swimmer. You've been doing it all your life. I'm only a beginner. You'll wallop me."

I'm not so sure of that, thought the Muscovy.

"It's only a bit of fun," she said. "Just to see how

299

you perform over a longer distance. I thought we could start from the tail of the pool and swim upstream as far as the Resthaven boundary fence. The current's not running all that strongly because we haven't had rain for a long time. And it's a pretty straight course. About two hundred yards overall, I should think. OK?"

"I'm game!" said Daggie. "Wait while I fetch
Mammie to watch."

"Well, don't bring her here," said Felicity. "Ask
her if she'd be kind enough to go to the finish. Ask
her to stand on the bank by the fence and act as
judge."

Five minutes later duck and pig floated side by side
at the lower end of the pool, and, in the distance, they
could see the big spotted shape of Mrs Barleylove
come down to the bank and stand waiting. A little
way up the kingfisher sat on his root.

"We'll use him as a starting signal," said Felicity.
"When he moves, swim."

They fixed their eyes on the blazing little bird, and
Daggie braced his hindfeet against the bank behind
him, ready to get a good push-off. He quivered all
over with excitement.

Suddenly, in a burning streak of colour, the kingfisher flashed away upstream, and they were off!

For a time they were level, and Felicity, thrusting as hard as she could with her broad webs, began to think that she had overestimated this prodigy; for though she could see from the corner of her eye that he was swimming beautifully, doing everything that he'd been taught in perfect style, she felt she had the measure of him. For a moment she even considered slacking off a bit, to let him win and give him confidence. Then she caught his eye, and it seemed to have a twinkle in it.

Suddenly, at about the halfway stage, Daggie Dogfoot changed gear, and Felicity realised that he'd only been playing with her. Twice as low as before went his body in the water, twice as hard as before pulled those otter's feet, twice as fast as before beat those outstretched hindlegs, and he shot away in front of her with the speed of a salmon. She could hear Mrs Barleylove behaving as an impartial judge certainly should not, urging Daggie on to further efforts with loud proud squeals, and saw her jump for joy, all four feet off the ground, as he crossed the finishing line, fifty yards ahead.

By the time the duck finished, the piglet had been able to climb out of the brook, shake himself all over, be licked by the judge, and call encouragement to his puffing panting teacher. He isn't even out of breath, thought Felicity as she clambered out and waddled up to mother and son.

"How about that then, missus?" she puffed. "Aren't you proud of him?"

"Any mother would be," said Mrs Barleylove. And any father too, she thought. At least I hope he will.

CHAPTER 10

Izaak

A mile upstream was a mill, the very mill that ground the barley meal for the pigs, and beside it was a great pond that gave the water-power to drive the mill-wheel. It was from this pond, some nights before, that the thin hard cry had reached Felicity's ears as she dropped off to sleep. The animal that had made the cry was a big dog-otter, in the best of health and the worst of tempers. And the reason for his anger had been his lack of success in realising a long-held ambition.

The mill-pond was deep and dark, with a bed made of thick mud and the rotting of a million leaves dropped into it over many autumns. Big fish lived in it, tench and carp and pike; and of these last there was one absolute monster, so otter-lore had it, a pike half as long as a man, as fierce as a wolf, and twice as cunning. Often in his travels between the sea and the hills, this particular otter had spent some time by the mill-pond with one idea in mind, to find this monster and kill him and eat him. And on that particular night he had come close to doing it.

Searching the deepest darkest corner of the thickest

304

tangle of weeds, the otter had suddenly seen, motionless beneath him, a long barred shape with narrow wolf-jaws and cold hard eyes, a shape even longer than himself and he was thirty inches from the end of his nose to the tip of his rudder.

He twirled that rudder now and threw himself over and down in a wonderful display of underwater aquabatics, and drove hard with all four webs. But, quick as he was, the long barred shape was quicker, leaving behind it a swirling fog of rotten leaves and a cloud of soupy water and strings of gas-bubbles and an angry otter.

"I-zaak!" the otter had cried in his fury as he hauled himself out by the black oak sluice-gates all slimy with mosses, "I-zaak!"

The otter spent several days by the mill-pond, enjoying some easy fishing but without further sight of the monster pike, and then, on the day after Daggie and Felicity had had their race, decided to move on downstream. He felt like a trip to the sea, and some salty dabs and crabs to eat as a change from dull-fleshed pond-fish.

He slipped down with the last of the night, past the farm buildings, under Felicity asleep on her alder branch, past the finishing line of the race, and into the reach which led to the pool beneath the high bank. Sometimes he swam on the surface, sometimes only a string of bubbles showed his progress.

But suddenly he saw something which not only made him lift his round tom-cat's head right up out of the water, but actually land and stand up in the grass on his hindlegs, peering and sniffing and moving his head from side to side as though he simply could not believe his eyes. In the pool ahead, swimming rapidly from side to side with a racing turn at either bank, was a pig! It wasn't a very big pig by the look of it, no longer than the otter's body without its rudder, but it was, undoubtedly, a white pig with black spots. And it was, undoubtedly, swimming.

Now otters have a tremendous, if rather twisted, sense of humour, and they love jokes, especially bad jokes. One of the jokes that this otter enjoyed very much was giving people sudden awful frights. As everyone knows, a good way to give someone a sudden awful fright is to appear, from nowhere, when you're least expected, and better still, to make a fearful noise at the same time. A big grin came over the otter's face, and he dropped down and slid into and under the water.

Daggie was exactly in the middle of the pool, swimming along without a care in the world in the peaceful silence of the early morning, when suddenly, right beside him, a grinning whiskery face popped up, opened a wide mouth to show a battery of sharp white teeth, and shouted, right in his ear, "I-ZAAK!"

Daggie felt three sorts of feelings, all at the same

time. Startled, because of the sudden noise, afraid, because of the rows of teeth, and angry, because he was startled and afraid. Of the three he quickly decided that he was mostly angry, and he trod water and said in a shrill breathless voice, "I don't know who you are but this is my pool and you've got no manners frightening people like that and I'll tell my Mammie and Felicity and they'll sort you out and anyway your breath stinks of fish."

Now otters make all sorts of noises, from loud ones when they are angry or want to frighten someone, through chitterings and chatterings, to lovely fluty whistles when they are playing or calling to one another from afar. But when they think something is really very funny, they laugh quite silently.

To Daggie's astonishment, this is what the creature in front of him proceeded to do, splitting his hairy face wide open, and rocking to and fro in the water with his webbed forepaws clasped against his chest. He laughed so much and rocked about so wildly that eventually he sank below the water and swallowed some mouthfuls. Spitting and puffing, he came back to the surface, and, at last, calmed himself enough to speak to the piglet.

"Sorry, old pig," he spluttered, still grinning broadly, "sorry if I scared you."

By now Daggie had got his breath back, and he said with a sort of quiet dignity, "I'm not an old pig,

307

I'm a young pig. And I'm not just a pig, I'm a pedigree Gloucester Old Spots. And my name is Daggie Dogfoot, son of Champion Imperial Challenger III of Ploughbarrow."

The otter's mouth fell wider and wider open during this recital; but whether in astonishment or in preparation for another round of silent laughter Daggie never knew, for at that instant there was a whistle of wings and Felicity splashed down between them.

So busy had she been with Daggie's training that she had quite forgotten to mention the subject of otters to him, as she had realised with horror when this one's shout had woken her. Now she faced the danger bravely, determined to protect her little friend. There was a moment's pause, and then all three animals spoke at the same time.

"Are you all right, Daggie?" said Felicity. "Who in

the water is he?" said Daggie. And "Hullo, old duck," said the otter, and dived beneath the surface.

As the friends swam rather rapidly to the Resthaven bank, they answered each other's questions.

"Yes, I'm all right," said Daggie. "Why shouldn't I be?"

"Because that's an otter," said Felicity. "Great hunter. Kills anything and everything that swims—fish, frogs, eels, ducklings. Never heard of it bothering piglets, but then piglets don't usually swim. Best keep well away from him."

"Well, he didn't hurt me," said Daggie. "He just seemed to find me rather funny. I can't think why."

As they talked, they could see strings of bubbles bobbing up as the otter searched the pool, and after a moment more he surfaced, smooth as oil, and walked out on to the sandy shallow below them.

"No fish in there, old pig," said the otter cheerfully, "and don't say there are 'cos there ain't. Must have driven them away with all that swimming practice of yours. What's a pig doing swimming anyway, old duck?"

"I taught him," said Felicity shortly. "What's your name, if I might ask?"

"Izaak," said the otter. "And don't think it ain't 'cos it is."

Felicity's eyes began to twinkle. "Izaak?" she said. "After Izaak Walton?"

"Who's he, old duck?" said the otter.

"Oh, another famous fisherman," said Felicity and she made her quot-quot-quotting noise.

"Never heard of him," said the otter, "and I know all the otters hereabouts and don't say I don't 'cos I do. No, mother called me that when I was a cub. On account of the noise I make when I'm a bit niggled. Or," and he grinned, "when I'm giving someone a sudden awful fright. Silly name. My friends call me Ike, and don't say they don't 'cos they do."

There was something very nice about the otter, despite his fearful fishy breath. Perhaps it was his cheeriness. Perhaps it was his odd way of speaking. Or maybe it was the growing certainty that he was not in fact an enemy to them, that made the two friends suddenly warm to him.

"Sorry I spoke so rudely to you, Mr Izaak," said Daggie, "but you did give me a sudden awful fright."

"That's all right, old pig," said the otter. "I'm fond of a good laugh and don't say I ain't 'cos I am." He turned to Felicity. "Going back to this business of him"—he nodded at Daggie—"swimming. From what I could see, he's pretty good on the surface. I never expected to see a pig swim, old duck, let alone swim as well as that, and don't say I did 'cos I didn't."

"Yes, he is good," said Felicity. "But then he's lucky enough to have been born specially equipped," and she pointed with her bill at Daggie's forefeet.

"Let's have a look, old pig," said the otter, and after a close examination he sat back with a long low whistle, and looked consideringly at the piglet.

"Tell you what," he said. "I was going to the seaside for a break, but I'm not in a hurry. Now am I right in thinking you haven't done much underwater work?"

"Not much," said Daggie. "Just the odd surface dive."

"It's nearly all been surface work," said Felicity. "I'm afraid I'm not much good down below."

"No, but I am," said the otter.

"And don't say you aren't . . ." said Daggie quickly.

". . . because you are," finished Felicity, and they all laughed in their different ways, the otter silently, the duck quot-quotting, the piglet giving little squeals.

"Seriously," said the otter, "I could teach you a lot, old pig, if you'd like. You've got no webs, and no rudder worth speaking of, so you'll be a bit slow on the turn. But I could teach you a lot about breath control and use of currents and manoeuvrability and general aquabatics. We'd have you taking big fish in no time."

"Well," said Daggie doubtfully. "I'd love to have lessons from you, Mr Izaak, but I don't actually eat fish."

"Rubbish," said Felicity sharply. "You mean you haven't eaten fish—yet. Just think, if this gentleman

311

is kind enough to teach you . . . after all, pigs are omnivorous."

"What's that mean, old duck?" said the otter.

"Means they can eat anything and everything."

"She's clever, she is, ain't she, old pig?" said the otter. "Mind you, they say eating fish is good for your brains, so you might get as clever as her. Though it doesn't seem to have done me much good," and he rocked about in another fit of silent laughter.

So it came about that Daggie Dogfoot acquired a second teacher, and straightaway began another lot of lessons; so that by the time Mrs Barleylove, who had slept through everything, rolled down to the brook for her morning drink, she found that Daggie was more under the water than on it. And often when his head popped up there was a round brown whiskery one beside it and sometimes his squeaks of delight mingled with the stranger's lovely fluty whistles. Felicity explained everything to her, and because it was all right with Felicity, it was all right with her.

Together they went to the top of the high bank and looked down. And in the clear waters of the pool they saw the wonderful submerged aquabatics of the otter as he rolled and curled and twisted and tied himself into a dozen different beautiful fluid knots; and close behind him, following and copying as best he could, was a fast-improving piglet.

All that day Daggie played with and learned from his new tutor, occasionally coming to the bank to see if his old tutor approved and was not upset; and she did and she wasn't; and his mother beamed her usual fatuous smile of pride.

In the afternoon swimmers and spectators moved upstream a little, and the otter caught a big trout, taking it in a lightning upward swirl too fast for the eye to follow. He pulled it out on to the bank and

offered Daggie first bite ("From the shoulder; the flesh is sweetest there, old pig"). Daggie was too polite to refuse, and afterwards glad that he hadn't, for it was delicious. Between them they ate most of the best of it, as they were hungry from their exertions and when they had returned to the brook, Mrs Barleylove ate the rest, head, tail, bones and all, till not a scale was left.

When the light began to fade, the otter said he must be going.

"See you tomorrow, old pig," he said. "You're learning fast."

"Oh, I did enjoy that," said Daggie. "The underwater training, and the trout, and of course meeting you. Thank you so much, Mr Izaak."

"Good-night, old pig," said the otter. "But I told you before, and don't say I didn't 'cos I did—my friends call me Ike."

"Thanks, Ike," said Daggie happily.

CHAPTER II

The Flood

Daggie did not in fact see his new friend Ike on the morrow, because overnight the weather, which controls everything in the countryside, changed completely. As Felicity had said before the race, they hadn't had rain for a long time. But not an hour after the otter had slipped away upstream, the heavens opened and proceeded to make up for their stinginess by such a display of generosity as none of the animals had ever known before. It rained very heavily all that night, and went on without stopping for two further days and nights.

The sows in their sties kept to their inner compartments, only venturing into their soaking outer runs for food. The Squire of course was dry under his verandah roof, but the constant stream of water flowing across the yard from higher ground worried him. He was not concerned for himself, but he couldn't help thinking about the strange son of whose existence he had only just heard. He hoped very much that that existence would not be ended in an untimely way, for he knew that boys will be boys, and this one sounded particularly adventurous. The brook will be

315

very swollen, thought the Squire. I hope the little chap has the savvy to stay on dry land.

He spoke to the servant about it, but the pigman, more hideous than ever in yellow oilskins and sou'wester, was too stupid to understand his master.

At Number One and Number Two Mrs Troughlicker and Mrs Boltapple stood upright at their front doors and looked anxiously over the yard. It was covered with a stream of fast-running water, as indeed were the outer runs of all the sties. Only inside, where each sow had a raised wooden platform six inches high, was there still a dry space for them and their piglets. Mrs Troughlicker spoke first.

"I don't like it, Mrs B," she said in a worried voice. "Never seed rain like this afore. Much more, and the young 'uns will be led in the wet."

"Just what I was saying to Mrs Swedechopper next door," replied Mrs Boltapple. "Then they'll get chilled, and then . . .," she shuddered at her own thoughts.

"What can us do?" asked Mrs Troughlicker.

"I'll be butchered if I know," swore Mrs Boltapple. "If only the rain 'ud stop."

But the rain did not stop. On the contrary, even as they spoke it began to come on heavily again, and the ladies hastily retreated indoors.

The pigman stood at the door of his meal-shed and looked down at the water, now almost over the lower of the two concrete steps. Behind him he heard rats squeaking among the bins and his red face grew redder at the sound of his enemies' voices. But even as he turned to reach up for his hardwood club and do battle, a big buck rat came running out of the gloom of the shed and scampered right over his Wellington boots and out of the door. It fell into the water and swam rapidly away down the yard. And as the pigman watched it open-mouthed, half a dozen more rats of all sizes dashed past him and into the water and away. Something he had heard long ago, at school perhaps, came into his mind. A sinking ship, he thought. Rats leaving a sinking ship.

At that instant the westerly wind, which had been blowing hard from the sea far down at the foot of the valley, dropped for a moment and in the ensuing lull the pigman heard a sound from the other direction, from the upper eastern end. It was a muttering that grew to a grumbling that grew to a mighty rumbling and straining his eyes through the driving rain, he stared back up the line of the brook to where it curved into view round some trees two fields away.

Suddenly, to his horror, he saw a great wall of brown water coming around this bend and he knew in a flash what must have happened. The sluice-gates have gone, thought the pigman, the mill-pond's burst; and for once in his slow lumbering life he acted quickly.

Grabbing up a sack of pig-nuts, he jumped off the

317

steps of the meal-house into the six-inch-deep water, and splashed his way to the sties. Door after door he flung open; Mrs Troughlicker's, Boltapple's, Swede-chopper's, Swiller's, missing the empty Number Five, then Mrs Gobblespud's, Maizemunch's, Graze-grass's, Grubguzzle's. As the sows and litters ran out into the yard, he blundered across it to the store pens and fattening pens, throwing wide door after door till a hundred and fifty spotted shapes of all sizes were stampeding about in the rushing flood. Only when he had opened the last door of all, the Squire's, did he allow himself one fearful glance over his shoulder. The wall of water was halfway across the last field before the buildings, and coming at the speed of a galloping horse.

The pigman, like all his kind, knew that pigs are the most awkward animals in the world to drive, so he did the only thing he could. Handicapped as he was by his bulk and his boots and his long yellow oilskins and the sack of pig-nuts, still he ran as hard as he could for the gate that led to Resthaven, shouting at the top of his voice the pig-keeper's universal feeding-call.

"PIG-pig-pig-pig-PIG-pig-pig-pig-PIG!" he yelled amidst the noise of the rain and the renewed wind and the thundering of the watery threat behind them; and he pounded desperately towards the high ground at the top of the little triangular field.

And behind him rose two waves. One was white, spotted with black, and one was brown. One squealed with fear, and one roared with menace. One was moving as fast as it possibly could, but a pig cannot gallop half as speedily as a horse, and the other wave gained and gained upon the first. As the last and slowest piglet struck the rising ground, the first and fastest breaker of the flood was less than a sow's length from his curly little tail.

Then the flood turned before the steep, and swept across the lower slopes of the field, smashing down the old oak tree from the place where it had stood for three hundred years and carrying it away like a matchstick. Twenty feet above Daggie's take-off place on the high bank went the oak, twisting and turning and thrashing its old arms in agony on its road to the windswept sea.

But the pigs were safe, not just all one hundred and fifty-one of them, but all one hundred and fifty-three. For the first thing the pigman saw, when his pounding heart and bursting lungs had quieted a little, was a group of three figures standing at the very topmost point of Resthaven and staring at the great army of pigs covering the high slope. Old sow from Number Five's all right then, he thought. And that 'orrible little dag. Though the Lord knows what one of my ducks's doing with them.

There was noise all around them, as they stood and panted on their hilltop refuge. The blustering shout of the wind competed with the menacing roar of the brook that had become a great river. On the waters of that river hissed the lash of the never-ending rain. At one moment Daggie fancied he heard, far out on the flood, an excited fluty whistle, as though someone was actually enjoying the storm. But suddenly, clear above the other noises, was heard a sharp cracking sound, and from the hill a hundred and fifty-five heads turned and three hundred and ten eyes looked back towards the homes they had left behind, to see the beginning of the first voyage of a strange craft.

The rats had been right to go, for the cracking noise proclaimed the launching of the pigman's meal–shed, as the floods lifted it bodily from its foundations. Past the drowned sties it came, over the submerged field-gate, and out into the centre of the great expanse of dark sliding eddying water that now stretched before the watchers. Its door hung open, as the pigman had left it when he ran to rescue them and as the shed spun slowly in the current they could see within it the great bins of barley meal and middlings and flaked maize and the piled sacks of pig-nuts, all sailing swiftly away to be food for the fish in the sea.

Another story came into the pigman's slow mind from distant days in the village schoolroom. Looks like the Ark, he thought. Trouble is, we ain't on it. And all the food I got for 'em is this here half hundredweight of nuts. Still they won't be short of a drink.

He went to the topmost point of Resthaven, and, opening the sack, threw the pig-nuts far and wide over the small triangle of field that was left high and

321

dry. Within half a minute everything was eaten, and the multitude was squealing for more, while far in the distance the meal–shed sailed on downriver.

The pigman folded the empty sack, placed it on top of an ant heap, and sat carefully down upon it. He sat motionless, his head in his hands, while the pigs jostled and grumbled below him. Had there been anyone on any of the other hilltops nearby, it would have seemed a strange sight: above, the bright yellow spot of the man's oilskins and sou'wester; below that, the spotted throng; and below them, the chocolate-coloured flood, darkening from milk to plain as the daylight faded. Mrs Barleylove and Daggie and Felicity still stood together.

"Poor old Duckman," said Felicity, "he looks all in."

"Duckman?" said Daggie absently. "Oh, you mean Pigman. Yes, he does. Still, he's a good and faithful servant, you know. He did his duty." Felicity had also been thinking of the story of the Flood, as the arklike meal-shed had drifted by, but, being better educated than the man, remembered more of it. She began to make the quot-quot-quotting noise which Daggie now knew well was her way of giggling.

"What's the joke?" said Daggie.

"I was thinking of a story," said Felicity. "In a book. Called the Bible. About a man called Noah."

"Why?" said Daggie. "Is Pigman like Noah?"

"No," said Felicity. "More like one of his sons."

"What was he called?" asked Daggie.

"Ham," said Felicity happily.

CHAPTER 12

Going for Help

In the early light of the following morning the scene was quite different. To begin with, the flood was not quite as high, for the burst pond was empty now and it had not rained in the night. The water had receded far enough to show the gaping hole where the old oak used to stand, but it was still running very wide and very strong, and there was no sign of the outline of the brook.

The other difference was one of colour. The hill-tops around showed brilliantly green in the light of the early morning sun, but what there was to see of Resthaven was blacky-brown, and moving and milling upon it were blacky-brown creatures. Pedigree Gloucester Old Spots they might be, but no one would have known, for the herd had rooted and routed over every square inch, looking for something, anything, to eat, and they were plastered in dirt.

As the pigman had said, there was no problem about drinking, for millions and millions of gallons of water flowed by them. It was food they were think-

ing about, and the first thing they had done was to
graze off every blade of grass and gobble up every
dock and nettle, every thistle even; every leaf and
shoot which they could reach through the boundary
pig-wire they had torn off, and where a hedgerow
tree was close enough, had chewed its bark. Then
they had turned up the whole top triangle of the field
and ferreted out the roots of every blade of grass,
every patch of clover, every weed. Anything they
came across went down them—worms, slugs,
beetles, even some families of fieldmice, babies and
all; and of all the hundreds of ant heaps which had

325

dotted the upper slopes of Resthaven only one remained, and on it, yellow against the blacky-brown
background, the pigman still sat, head hanging,
shoulders bowed, stomach rumbling with hunger.

Mrs Barleylove and Daggie were just as black and
filthy as the rest, for they too had been rootling
everywhere for food. Only Felicity was spotlessly
clean, not a black nor a white feather out of place, for
she of course had flown out on to the flood for a
thorough wash and brush-up. She stood now on Mrs
Barleylove's broad back, to be out of the way of the
pushing, shoving, squealing multitude of earth-
covered pigs, and spoke into the big droopy ear,
softly so as not to be overheard.

"Look, missus," she said. "We've got to do something, you know as well as I do. This lot's so hungry
they're eating anything now. It only needs a little piglet to get trodden on and they'll gobble him up. And
then they'll start on one another. I'm right, aren't I?"

Mrs Barleylove shuddered. She knew how every
pig worships food, and she was well aware, though
she didn't know the word, that pigs are omnivorous,
eating everything that is remotely edible. She
remembered stories that her mother had told her of
swill-feeding in the old days, when rats, and sometimes cats, would fall into the swill tubs and get
cooked; the pigs would champ them up quite happily,
her mother said.

"Course you'm right, my dear," she said quietly. "We got to get help. We got to get food. But how? It don't look like the servant can swim or he'd have bin gone. And tidn't much good you going, if you'll excuse me; people wouldn't connect a Muscovy duck with a herd of pigs. The only one that can swim, after all, is. . ." and she stopped, and her mouth fell open.

"Oh no!" cried Mrs Barleylove. "Oh no! Not him!"

"It's got to be your Daggie," said Felicity. "If nobody goes, and no one comes to find you all, and the floods don't go down, for a week say, there's going to be all Hell let loose here."

"But he may be drowned!" wailed Mrs Barleylove.

"I don't think so," said Felicity, "though I grant that it's a possibility. As against the probability," she said very slowly and clearly, "that if he stays here, he'll be . . . eaten."

There was a small silence between them, in the middle of the uproar of empty-bellied pigs.

"All right," grunted Mrs Barleylove at last. "If he's willin', bless his little heart," and she blinked her white-lashed eyes very quickly. "But you'll go with him, my dear, won't you? Please?"

"Of course," said Felicity. "Try not to worry, missus. I'm sure it'll all have a happy ending. If we can find some other servants like Duckman, er, Pigman, I mean, somewhere downstream, they'll see

327

Daggie's spots and they'll know where he's from. After all, there's only this one herd of Gloucester Old Spots in the district, isn't there?"

"Far as I know," said Mrs Barleylove.

"Well then," said the duck, "they'll know something's wrong. And they'll get food up somehow, by boat, or helicopter."

The sow had no notion what a helicopter was, but she had a lot of faith in Felicity, and she called loudly for her son.

Daggie came running up, black as the ace of spades. He was very hungry, for his mother's milk had dried up now, and he had been pushed and shoved away from anything that looked like food by his stronger brethren. But his eyes were bright and his courage was high, and as soon as the plan was told to him, he was wild to go.

Felicity flew down to the water's edge, and Mrs Barleylove followed, barging her way through the press of pigs with Daggie at her heels. "Make way! Make way!" she shouted, and the other sows, hearing her voice, pushed forward to see what was happening.

They were all asking questions at once when sharp squeals from above made them look round, and they saw the Squire come rolling down towards them, his tusks showing white in his muddy face as he tossed the stores and fatteners out of his way.

"What's going on?" he asked in his deep voice

when he reached the sows. "Mrs Barleylove, dear lady, what's going on, what?"

"'Tis my son, Squire," replied Mrs Barleylove proudly. "He's going for help. He's going to swim for help, to find someone to bring us food."

Those nearest to her heard her words, and as the news spread the herd fell silent, and every head was turned to listen.

"Your son?" said the Squire loudly. "Your son?"

"Our son, Squire," said Mrs Barleylove softly, feeling her white parts turn pink, and thankful for the mud that hid them.

"That's better," said the Squire, and turning to the little piglet he looked curiously at him. Little shrimp, he thought, he's not much bigger than a rat. And those front feet. . .

He spoke quietly now, so that the pigs at the edge of the press raised their heads to hear the better, as the great boar looked down upon the little dag.

"So you're Daggie Dogfoot, what?" said the Squire.

"Yes, sir," said Daggie politely.

"And you're going for help, are ye, boy?"

"Yes, sir."

"Current's strong, ye know. Water's deep. Understand you can, er, swim pretty well, but it'll be damned dangerous, doncherknow. What?"

"Oh, I'll be all right," said Daggie. "Thank you,

329

Father," he added daringly. The boar cleared his throat as though there were some kind of lump in it.

"Well, good luck, my son," he said in a loud strained voice. "By St Anthony, I wish you the very best of good luck."

And all around the mob of pigs echoed him. "Good luck! Good luck!" they cried, and the pigman got up off his ant heap at the noise, and lumbered down to find out what it was all about.

He was just in time to see Daggie walk out into the shallows, the mud dissolving as the edge of the current began to wash him clean. Soon he was swimming, once again a white piglet with black spots, and then he was in midstream and the full force of the floodwater took him and whirled him away.

But every pig could see how beautifully he swam, and most of them could hear his farewell cry, and one of them stood alone, belly-deep in the shallows while a great tear ran down each of her fat cheeks and plopped into the stream. Come back safely, my Daggie, said Mrs Barleylove to herself.

Just then Felicity came flying back, low over the heads of the herd. The pigman had taken off his hat, the better to scratch his head in his utter bewilderment at the sight of a swimming pig, and Felicity dived down, caught it in her clawed feet and tore it from him.

"I'll take this with me," she shouted to Mrs Barleylove, as she wheeled to follow Daggie. "Maybe someone will know who this belongs to," and she flew rapidly away, the sou'wester dangling below her, while the pigman danced in anger.

"Dratyer!" he cried, and "Dangyer!" and "Blast-yer!", shaking his huge fist at the two fast dis-appearing figures.

"Stupid iggerant duck!" he shouted. "You and that 'orrible little dag, you make a fine pair. Never be no use to no one, not neither of you, nohow!"

And as the pigs ran to the topmost part of Rest-

haven, they caught a final glimpse of Daggie Dog-foot, far down on the flood. They could see Felicity for a little longer as she flew low, directly above the swimmer. And then there was nothing to be seen but a great waste of waters.

CHAPTER 13

Man on a Raft

Jumping about in anger had woken the pigman's brain from the daze of hopelessness into which it had fallen, and he began to think what he could do about the situation. It occurred to him, as it had to the duck much earlier, that there would be trouble with a capital T if the pigs remained unfed. His meal-shed, he knew, was gone, and help, if it ever came, might be a long time arriving; but after much head-scratching, a simple idea came to him. Resthaven after all was only one side of the little conical hill on which they were marooned, so that there must be grass, and bushes, and trees round the back of this island in the floods. All he had to do was to take down the pig-netting that confined his herd, and then they could at any rate find something to keep them going.

To do this was not at all easy, since the fence had been well made in the first place, tightly stretched, and nailed to stout posts or sapling trees. Wirecutters would have done the job in a minute but of course he had none with him. As he stood and looked at the fence, the Squire rolled up and stood beside him. They conversed in their separate languages.

"If only you had the brains, old fellow," said the pigman, "you'd get your great head under the wire and lift it up."

"If you had any sense at all, Pigman," said the Squire, "you'd use that branch that's lying there as a lever to get the bottom of this wire up far enough for me to put my head under it."

"If I had something for a lever," said the pigman, "I might be able to lift the bottom of it a bit. Then perhaps this daft old boar might see what I'm at."

"Man's a fool," said the Squire.

"Oh, there's a branch," said the pigman. "That might do."

"Feller's tumbled to it at last," said the Squire with a sigh, as the pigman slid the branch under the lowest-but-one strand of the pig-wire, stuck the far end into the ground beyond, and began to heave upwards. With great effort he managed to lift the bottom strand six inches above the ground.

"Ladies!" shouted the Squire. "I want you all on parade, please. Chop-chop!" and when the nine sows came galloping up, he said more quietly, "spread out please. Four to one side of me, five to the other. Snouts down. Wait for my word." And from the corner of his mouth he snarled at the servant, "Come on, man. Put your back into it, what?"

Almost as though he could understand, the pigman redoubled his efforts; the bottom of the wire rose a fraction higher, the boar got his head under the lowest strand, then the sow on either side of him, and so on, until all ten heads were under and all ten great bodies tensed.

"Ready! Steady! Heave!" shouted the Squire, and

with a twanging tearing noise a twenty-foot stretch of pig-wire rose up, up, up, till the retaining fence-posts popped out of the ground.

"Forward!" bawled the Squire, and before the advancing weight of more than four thousand pounds of pig the fence burst like a rotten tennis-net, and the rest of the herd poured through. Off round the back of the hill they went, snatching at the fresh grass like mad things, and the pigman was left alone.

The sight of his animals eating again reminded him painfully how empty his own stomach was. If only I had a boat, he thought, and he strained his little piggy eyes upstream as though wishing would make one appear. He did not see one, of course, but he did see something, two things in fact. They were about ten feet apart, halfway between him and his drowned buildings, and he suddenly realised that they were the tops of the gate-posts at the entrance to Resthaven.

Gate-posts, he thought. Water must have gone down a little bit, couldn't see them before. Gate-posts, he thought. There's a gate between 'em. Gate, he thought. Made of wood. Wood, he thought. Floats. Floats, he thought. Like a boat, well, like a raft.

He went down to the water's edge, and began to wade back towards the gate-posts. The current was strong but the pigman was powerful, and he fought his way along, deeper and deeper as he went down the slope. He was shoulder deep when at last he stood between the posts, and feeling underwater, found nothing. For a moment he felt only disappointment and anger, thinking that the flood had carried the gate away. Then he realised that of course it had been open when the waters had first burst upon it, hard on the heels of the fleeing herd; so that now it would be pointing downstream, as a flag streams out before the wind. He felt to one side and found it.

Now was the moment of decision for the pigman. As Mrs Barleylove had guessed, he could not swim. Moreover, he was frightened of the very water. As a child, he had once been taken to the seaside on a school outing, but nothing would persuade him to go beyond the ripples. What he was doing now was, for him, an act of great bravery. But more was needed. In order to grip the heavy gate and clear it from the hanging-post, he would need, at this depth, actually to put his head under the dreaded water!

And if he lifted it free, would it bear him? And if it bore him, where to? To food, and shelter, and help? Or out to the endless sea? Desperate men do desperate things, and the pigman closed his eyes, settled his feet firmly, and took a good grip and a deep deep breath.

There followed a scene which would have seemed pure comedy, had there been a human watcher unaware of the underlying drama; but for the pigman it could so easily have been one of tragedy.

To begin with, the hinges were jammed upon the hanging-pins, and it took three increasingly breathless dips below the surface before his utmost efforts could lift the gate free. And when it was free, the current immediately dragged it away, so that the pigman had to make a wild, belly-flopping leap at it as it went. He caught the back end of it, whereupon it tipped up like a live thing, threatening to throw him off into deeper water. Somehow, gasping, spluttering, panic-stricken, he managed to scramble further on to it, expecting all the time that it would submerge beneath him.

But it bore him, just, though the weight of the heavy man and his waterlogged clothes pushed it below the surface; so that he would have appeared, had there been a watcher, to be floating motionless upon the flood, like a bright yellow hippopotamus.

This was what he looked like to the first eyes that did see him. Most of the herd were on the reverse side of the hill, rooting and tearing at anything they could find, but the Squire and Mrs Barleylove had not moved far from the break in the fence, and it was they who witnessed the pigman's progress.

"By St Anthony!" the Squire burst out. "It's the damned servant! Seems to be lyin' on top of the water. Extraordinary! Feller can't be as stupid as I thought."

Mrs Barleylove watched as the current bore the

pigman steadily away. Daggie, she thought, where are you, my love?

"Going to have a look myself," said the Squire, reading her thoughts. "When the level drops a bit more. So I can see the line of the hedges or fences. Should be easy to bust 'em."

"Easier with two, Squire," said Mrs Barleylove.

Champion Imperial Challenger III of Plough-barrow raised his heavy head and gazed at this wife of his with approval and affection. "Couldn't wish for a better partner," he said. "And try not to worry too much about the lad. We'll find him. You'll see."

CHAPTER 14

On the Dam

Not long after Daggie and Felicity had disappeared
from the sight of the watching herd, the course of the
flood took a turn in a new direction and the course of
their fortunes a turn for the better. A mile or so from
Resthaven the old brook had rounded the foot of a
high spur plunged, south-west and seawards, into
quite a deep steep valley, and though now swollen
to many times its usual width, was nonetheless
narrower at this point than the broad waters on
which Daggie had begun his swim. Consequently the
speed of the current increased dramatically, so that
Felicity needed to fly at her fastest to keep up with the
swimmer.

Daggie of course was too excited to be frightened.
"Weeeeeee!" he yelled as the racing water swept him
along, but the Muscovy, ten feet above him, suddenly
saw trouble ahead.

Something was blocking the way, a kind of rough
dam, it seemed, though she could not yet see what it
was made of; but she could see that the rushing flood
parted before it, swirled away to either side, and fell

340

from sight in a boiling swirl. Felicity knew something about waterfalls and the terrible down-currents beneath them, and she instantly realised the awful danger for Daggie should he be swept over.

Flying her hardest, she dropped low over the piglet, the strings of the yellow sou'wester held tight in her claws, the bonnet hanging low.

"Grab it in your teeth, Daggie!" she shouted, "Quick! Don't argue!", and as soon as she felt his weight she turned and faced upstream, beating her wings with all her strength.

Try as she might she could still feel herself being dragged backwards but at least she was cutting down Daggie's breakneck speed and keeping him dead centre, on line for the obstruction; and when a hasty glance over her shoulder told her the moment was ripe, she turned and dropped down on to a branch that stuck out at water level. Pulling as hard as she could while walking backwards along this, she landed Daggie as an angler lands a fish. They were safe on the dam, and behind and below them they could hear the thunder of falling water.

Its purpose served, the yellow sou'wester slipped over the falls on the start of a journey that was to bring help, for someone spotted it far downstream and fished it out and inside it they could still just read the pigman's name and address in his horrible scrawl.

"Gosh, that thing tasted nasty," panted Daggie,

wrinkling his snout. "What was that all about, Felicity?"

Felicity looked at him and made her quot-quot-quotting noise.

"Oh, nothing," she said. "I just thought we'd have a breather. Let's take a look round."

Curiously, perhaps because he was so breathless, sight was the last of Daggie's five senses to send messages to his brain. With the roar of the falls in his ears and the sour taste of oilskin in his mouth, the next thing he realised, through his sensitive forefeet, was that the bark of the big branch on which he was standing was familiarly rough, as though he had met, not just that *kind* of tree, but this *particular* tree before. Then suddenly, lifting his snout to the wind, he smelt food! And not just food, but pig-food! And not just pig-food somewhere miles away, but pig-food near, very near, here, right on this jumble of objects in the middle of the stream! Then at last—and all this happened in a matter of seconds—he used his eyes. What he suddenly saw excited him so much that he nearly lost his perch and fell off into the water again.

"Look, Felicity!" he shouted. "Look—behind you!"

And there, jammed among the branches, was the meal-shed. It was still upright, its door still hung open, and out of the door came the wonderful smells. Like shipwrecked mariners stumbling upon treasure, they scrambled madly towards it.

Inside, the great bins of barley meal and middlings and flaked maize still stood, their wooden lids tight shut and far too heavy to be lifted by piglet or duck. But that did not matter, for on the floor was a great stack of sacks of pig-nuts and about the edge of the stack were bags that had fallen as the meal-shed had tossed on the flood. Some of these had broken open so that a part of the floor was covered in a rich dark-brown carpet of nuts which Daggie rushed upon and

some of this carpet had been wetted into a beautiful mush by water seeping through the floorboards, so that Felicity could suck up a kind of lovely pig-nut porridge. For a long time there was nothing to be heard in the meal-shed but the sounds of eating.

Felicity stopped eating first, because her crop was full; she went out to the edge of the dam for a drink, and when her thirst was satisfied, flew round to take a look at the far side of the obstruction. She found, as she had suspected, that the jam of timber had caused a wicked waterfall down which Daggie would surely have plunged to a horrid death.

When she came back into the meal-shed, he was still eating. At last he staggered out and picked his way to the water and drank deeply. Returning, he let out a huge belch followed by a long sigh of contentment, flopped upon his side on the floor, and fell fast asleep, his little spotted balloon of a tummy rising and falling. Not a bad idea, thought the Muscovy, closing her eyes.

An hour or so later Daggie woke suddenly with a shout of "Mammie!" A series of muddled dreams had turned into a nightmare, something to do with his babyhood; and sure enough, the very first thing he focused upon was the hardwood club, still hanging on its rusty nail. Then he saw the kind face of his friend Felicity looking down at him from the top of a meal bin, and remembered what had happened.

Looking out of the door he saw a big branch which stuck up in the air; and on the branch were familiar crinkly-edged leaves; and among the leaves were some acorns.

"It's the oak, isn't it, Felicity?" he said. "It's the old oak from Resthaven."

"Yes," said the duck. "It jammed across this narrow place, against some rocks probably, and then caught everything else that came down, including, thank goodness, this shed."

"Gosh, yes," said Daggie. "What a bit of luck. What super grub. I feel a new piglet."

"You look a new piglet," said Felicity. "Your mother wouldn't recognise you."

Daggie's mood changed instantly. "Mammie!" he cried, jumping to his feet. "Oh, Mammie! Oh, how selfish I am! Here I am, making a pig of myself, and all the time Mammie's hungry, starving perhaps. And Father. And my aunties. And my brothers and sisters. And all the others. Oh, what a selfish pig I am!"

"Don't be silly," said Felicity shortly. "It's only sensible that as we've been lucky enough to find all this food, we should eat our fill. We must keep up our strength, you know. There's an awful lot to do."

"Yes, I suppose so," said Daggie, a little less miserably. "But what can we do? How can we get this food back to the others? We can't carry it."

"I don't know," said Felicity. "I honestly don't

know. But I've got a feeling that something will turn up." And she began to preen herself and to rearrange her feathers, while Daggie lay down again on his distended stomach and gazed out of the door.

And as he gazed, something did turn up. At first Daggie could not see clearly what it was, for the sun was in his eyes: all he noticed was a yellowish lump in the distance, coming down towards them; a dead tree perhaps, he thought. But as it came nearer he could see that it was not vegetable but animal, that it was not dead but alive, for it had a staring white face and wide flaring nostrils and its teeth were bared in a grin of fear, while its tongue licked nervously over its thick lips; its body, he could now see, was bright yellow, and it seemed to ride effortlessly upon the surface.

"Felicity!" yelled Daggie in an agony of terror. "A monster! A monster! He's coming straight for us!"

Felicity waddled to the door.

"I hope he is," she said. "We need him. It's Duckman."

CHAPTER 15

Breakfast and Bed

The pigman, low in the water, did not realise the danger ahead. Even if he had, it is doubtful that he could have done much about it, so paralysed was he with terror. All he was concerned with was hanging on to his gate like grim death. This in fact was the saving of him, for when the current took hold and whirled him off to one side of the dam and over the falls, he held tight; had he let go then, he would probably have been sucked under by the down-currents in the pool below and drowned.

Felicity, flying round to the other side of the dam, saw the man and his raft plunge down beneath the boiling surface; but then the heavy wooden gate rose again, its rider still clinging to it, water cascading off the soaking yellow oilskins. Once he's clear of the pool down there and out in midstream again, he'll be gone, with nothing to stop him between here and the sea, thought Felicity. But at that moment a freakish current dragged the gate back towards the dam, towards a point indeed where a strong branch of the old oak stuck out invitingly.

347

"If only he'd let go of the gate and grab that branch," shouted the Muscovy over the noise of the falls to Daggie who was standing above watching, "otherwise he'll be gone in a minute."

Inspiration came to Daggie.

"Scratch his hands, Felicity," he yelled. "Fly down and scratch his hands. That'll make him let go!"

As the piglet looked on, she flew down, pitched on the end of the gate, and deliberately dragged her sharp claws across the backs of the pigman's tightly-gripping hands. Then everything happened at once. The pigman loosed his hold with a yell of pain and anger, and grabbed frantically at the branch. The gate shot from under him, caught the force of the stream again, and sailed steadily away. The duck flew back up on to the dam and perched beside Daggie.

Side by side, the friends watched anxiously as the pigman struggled to pull himself along the branch to safety. His clothes were soaked, his boots full of water, his tired limbs cramped, his hungry body chilled. But he was strong and he was desperate, and at last, somehow, he scrambled on to the dam.

For a while he lay in the tangle of timber, gasping for breath. When at last he sat up and looked about him, he saw the two watchers, and some colour came back into his wet white face.

"Dratyer!" he cried, shaking his bleeding fists at them, and "Dangyer!" and "Blastyer!"

Then, suddenly, he lurched to his feet. His mouth, open from the last shout, gaped wider still, his piggy eyes glinted, and in a kind of mad blundering stumble he began to clamber over the mess of timber in the direction of the two animals.

349

Hurriedly the stupid iggerant duck and the 'orrible little dag moved out of the way, but they soon realised the reason for the servant's excitement. Pigman had seen the back of the meal-shed.

Above everything else, the pigman was hungry, excruciatingly, ravenously hungry. For most of the thirty odd hours which had passed since he ran from this shed in the face of the approaching flood, he had thought of food in general, and in particular of a packet of sandwiches left in the pocket of his old coat (the very pocket which had once carried Daggie) which hung from a second rusty nail beside the hardwood club. Ham sandwiches they were, his favourites, and the spittle ran down over his three chins as he fought his way round to the door.

He clambered in, and there was the coat. He plunged his great hand in the pocket, and there were the sandwiches. He tore off the paper in which they were wrapped and crammed them into his mouth. By the time Daggie and Felicity had summoned up courage to peep round the door, the sandwiches were gone, for there were only two of them, meant for a mid-morning snack. As they watched, the pigman broke open a sack of pig-nuts, picked out a handful, and began to chew them. A considering look came over his face, then something like a smile, and then he sat down and began to stuff himself.

"Gosh, he must be full," said Daggie after a while.

"What d'you think he'll do next?"

"Don't know what to think," said Felicity. "First he comes floating down the river like a duck. . ."

". . . and then he makes a pig of himself!" laughed Daggie. "Extraordinary feller, doncherknow!" he said in a passable falsetto imitation of his father, and they both giggled in a chorus of little grunts and quot-quot-quotting noises.

The pigman had in fact decided what to do next. He had never had a deep thought in his whole life, but when certain simple ideas occurred to him he acted upon them without further ado.

Just at the moment his stomach was full, but the rest of his body was wet and cold and tired. His brain therefore received three messages. Get dry. Get warm. Get sleep.

The two heads looking round the door again saw the pigman move slowly into action. First he took off his yellow oilskins and hung them on a third rusty nail beside the old coat and the hardwood club. Then he opened the three great wooden meal-bins one after the other, and looked into each long and earnestly, scratching his head like mad. At the last, the flaked maize bin, he took off his gum-boots, emptied the water out of them on to the floor, and then solemnly filled them full of the crackly golden stuff.

Next he went to the middlings bin. He took off his trousers, his pullover, his shirt, and his socks, and carefully buried them all deep in the brown sawdusty stuff.

Lastly the pigman went to the barley meal bin, a strange sight now clothed only in enormous thick woolly greyish combinations. Laboriously, with much grunting, he climbed into the bin and began to work himself down into the thick white powdery stuff like some giant lugworm burying itself in soft sand. When he was waist deep in it, he reached up to a shelf above for a bundle of old copies of *The Pig Breeder's Gazette*. He wriggled on down till he was shoulder deep. Then he slipped the magazines under his head, plunged his arms under the barley blanket, and lay back with a sigh.

"By St Anthony," said Daggie mischievously as the pigman closed his eyes, "feller's actually goin' to sleep, what, what?" and they both burst out into another fit of the giggles.

CHAPTER 16

Dreams

"Water's actually goin' down a bit, what, what?" said the Squire at precisely the same moment. "Take a look at those young porkers over there, Mrs Barleylove. They're grazin' grass that was under water a couple of hours ago."

By now the hungry herd had eaten everything growing on the little hill of which Resthaven formed a part so that the whole of it was now a blacky-brown hump; but at its edges a fresh green rim kept appearing as the flood level gradually dropped and as fast as it appeared the herd ate it off. The vegetable matter kept them going, but such a diet was rather like humans living on nothing but soggy lettuce, and they longed for solid substantial food.

"Couldn't us try to get downstream now, Squire?" said Mrs Barleylove. Her belly ached for a square meal and her heart ached for Daggie. The Squire heard the note of pleading in her voice, and nodded his heavy head.

"Not long now, dear lady," he said. "Don't fancy either of us as swimmers, doncherknow, so we must

353

be able to keep in our depth. But you can see the line of the willows that mark the brook's edge pretty clearly now. And the tops of some fences."

He thought for a moment. Then he gave his deep coughing grunt, and shouted "Ladies! This way, please. Chop-chop!", and when the other eight sows had joined Mrs Barleylove, and all were standing round him in a respectful circle, he addressed them thus.

"Listen carefully please, ladies. Don't want to have to repeat myself. Now, it doesn't look as though help is coming. On the other trotter, water's dropping. Not enough yet to get the youngsters downstream, but Mrs Barleylove and I are going to take a little stroll and see what we can find." He paused. "Any objections?" he barked, but the sows noticed the fierceness of his look and said nothing.

"Right then," said the Squire. "Look after the herd. And ladies, one last thing. Do not attempt to follow us," and he waded off, breast-deep, Mrs Barleylove in his wake.

Back at the meal-shed, everyone was now asleep and dreaming. Felicity dreamed her usual simple happy kind of dream, all peace and warm sunlight and dancing water.

The pigman's dream was more complex, and, like his waking thoughts, concerned food. In it he was collecting together all the things in the shed which he needed—matches, paper sacks and boxes to start a fire, a big square tin for a container, the bottle of vegetable oil which he used to shine his show pigs. A dream-smell of roast sucking-pig ran up his flaring nostrils, and he stirred restlessly in the barley meal bin, his white-lashed eyelids fluttering.

Daggie was having a nightmare. He lay in a pool of sunlight by the door, but in his mind he was back in Resthaven, before the flood, playing King of the Castle, jumping on Mammie's big stomach. Outside the meal-shed, the real sun disappeared behind a cloud bank, and the pool of sunlight was no more. And in his dream, too, the day turned grey, and his Mammie vanished, and something horrible was coming towards him, something huge, and fat, and white.

The pigman had settled so low in the barley meal that eventually he snored some of the floury stuff right up his nose. He woke up and rubbed at his face with his mealy hands, so that he was white from top to toe. His brain received a message. I am thirsty. He levered himself out of the bin.

Then everything happened at once. Daggie woke and squealed with terror as his nightmare became reality. Felicity woke, and thinking her friend to be in danger, flew at the pigman's head. The pigman put up his hands to ward her off, tripped as the piglet dashed between his legs, stubbed his toes in the door-

355

way, caught his foot in a branch outside, and like a great tree falling, crashed into the water and sank below the surface.

As Daggie and Felicity watched horrified, they saw on the far bank two great spotted figures galloping down towards the pool, and they heard in the distance a strange clattering noise.

The pigman's head broke water. "Heeeelp!" he roared. "Heee-gurgle-glug!" and down he went again.

CHAPTER 17

The Great Strange Bird

Back at Resthaven, things were looking up. To be more exact, pigs were looking up, at a great strange bird in the sky.

They had heard the bird before they had seen it, for it had a loud rattling voice, and they raised their heads and watched it appear over the eastern hills. It flew down the valley towards them, pausing over the mill with its ruined pond, and again over the farm buildings, now almost empty of water. Its glassy eyes twinkled in the bright sunlight and its wings whirled above its body at great speed.

Suddenly it saw the herd in Resthaven, and it darted sideways towards the pigs and hovered above the little hill like some huge hawk, so low that they could feel the terrible wind of it. None of the pigs had ever seen a helicopter before and they galloped about in panic. But the bird came no lower, so they gathered in a nervous huddle and watched as a hole appeared in its side and a brown object fell out of it.

"It's layin' eggs on us!" shouted Mrs Grubguzzle in alarm, but before the words were out of her mouth

357

the brown object hit the ground and burst open. A familiar smell came wafting to the snouts of the herd, growing stronger by the minute as two, four, eight more sacks of pig-nuts were tipped from the door of the helicopter. Then it turned and slid away westwards down the line of the brook.

When the helicopter reached the dam, the strangest scene met its glassy eyes. If it had really been a bird, it would have had the tallest of tall stories to tell to its children. As it was of course, there were three men in it, the pilot, the observer, and the winchman. And in later years, when they had children of their own, old enough for story-telling, they all told the same tale to their goggle-eyed families.

It was during the Great Summer Flood, they said, when people and animals in that part of the country had been cut off from supplies. Alerted by the discovery of the yellow sou'wester, they had been sent to an isolated pig-farm, and had found a herd of pigs, and dropped food for them. Then—"And you'll never believe this," each said—they had come to a place where a big jumble of uprooted trees and other rubbish, including what looked like a shed, had dammed the stream and formed a big pool.

On one side of this pool stood two great spotted pigs. And flying above the pool was a black-and-white duck. And in the middle of the pool was a man, a huge fat man from what they could see of him,

358

struggling madly in the water; they could hear nothing because of the noise of the rotors, but they could see his mouth open in a shout for help before he went down again.

Then—"It's true, I promise you," each said—a little spotty piglet—"odd looking thing with a head too big for its body and funny feet"—dived off the dam into the pool, swam—"yes, *swam*"—across it at tremendous speed, and seemed to say something to the two big pigs. They in turn put their heads down and tipped a stout piece of wood into the pool—"a fencing stake it was"—and the piglet lined it up so the sharp end was pointing at the struggling man ("cross my heart"); then it swam round and pressed its snout to the blunt end ("Scout's honour"); the duck landed on top of the stake and flapped its wings like mad ("honest Injun"); and the piglet swam like billy-o, and the stake went whizzing across the pool like a torpedo, and they got to the man just as he was going down for the third time, and he managed to grab the stake and hang on to it, and so the duck and the amazing swimming piglet saved his life ("see this wet, see this dry").

"But is all that really true, Dad?" said each of the families.

"Of course it is," said each father.

And of course it was.

As soon as the pigman had hit the water, Daggie

and Felicity knew that they must try to save him. They could not simply let the servant drown.

"Shout to Father and Mammie to help!" yelled Daggie, doing a racing dive into the pool.

"Quick!" cried Felicity, flying out towards the two big pigs. "Find a heavyish bit of wood and get it into the water."

"Here's a big old stake," panted Mrs Barleylove, and, "How about this, what?" grunted the Squire as they levered it out of the bankside rubbish.

"Let her go!" squeaked Daggie, and when he had lined up the stake, and Felicity had perched on its sharp end, he squealed, "Full speed ahead!" and away they went.

The pool was smaller, the current less strong, and the waterfalls less menacing than they had been; but nonetheless the pigman, though now safe from drowning, was not safe from being swept down and away.

Then the miracle happened, to the amazement of the four animals who had been so intent that they had not noticed the hovering helicopter. Suddenly and dramatically its shadow fell across them, and its clatter burst upon their ears, and the water of the pool blossomed into a thousand catspaws under the down-draught of the rotors as the pilot dropped the craft to treetop height.

Leaning from the hatch, the observer directed him, while at the end of the rescue cable the winchman hung suspended over the pigman's head.

"Up a bit, on a bit, back a bit, down a bit!" and then "Hold it!" as the winchman slipped a rope beneath the pigman's arms and held up his hand to the watchers above.

Then the great strange bird lifted the big fat servant as easily as you would lift a spider on its thread, and drew him up into itself. Thoughtfully, it laid one more brown egg on the bank near the Squire and his wife, and then it turned and flew away.

The pool was quiet and its surface smooth again. The lifesaving fencing stake had gone down the waterfall, the bristles on the big pigs' backs lay flat again, and Daggie was beginning to control the shivering fit brought on by the excitement and terror of it all. Everybody reacted in a different way.

"It gobbled him up!" said Daggie with horror.

"Don't matter so long as you're all right," said Mrs Barleylove with relief.

"In the name of St Anthony, what the devil was that thing?" said the Squire angrily.

"It was a helicopter," said Felicity with amusement.

There was a pause while they all tucked into the pig-nuts.

"Extraordinary," said the Squire with his mouth full. "Damn feller's got no right to go flyin' off like that you know. Think we'll go home, when we've finished eatin'. Like to give the feller a piece of my mind. After all, said and done, you saved his life, my son, you and your friend here, what?"

"Saved my life, saved my life," babbled the pigman as he lay on the floor of the clattering machine. "And to think I called 'em stupid, and iggerant, and 'orrible. And now see what they done for me. I'll make it up to 'em, I'll make it up to 'em. You see if I don't."

"Yes, yes, old chap," said the helicopter crew soothingly. "Just you relax and don't worry. We'll soon have you in hospital."

"Hospital?" said the pigman loudly, struggling to his wet feet. "I don't want to go to no hospital. You get me back to the farm. I got a job to do. I got to get everything ready for 'em. When they come home."

CHAPTER 18

Missing

By evening the herd was comfortably full of food and the pigman once again ragingly hungry. He stood beside the helicopter which had landed in the yard, and stared at the concrete foundations where the meal-shed had stood. He was shocked and soaked, and his sluggish brain was hardly working at all. What thoughts he had were all of eating. But not pig-meat, not ever again, he said slowly to himself. Not ever again. Nor duck. Not after what they done for me. Not nohow.

And almost as though he were a mind-reader, the helicopter pilot said, "I say, you must be pretty hungry, old chap. I mean, we had a jolly good break-fast of bacon and eggs"—the pigman shuddered—"but you probably haven't eaten for days. Have my sandwiches. They're Spam."

"I couldn't," said the pigman in a low voice, and, thinking that he was nervous of accepting their hospitality, the observer said in a very friendly tone, "Well I can offer you something better than Spam, old fellow. Have mine. They're duck paste."

363

"Oh, I couldn't," said the pigman, more miserably still.

"You're welcome to mine," said the winchman, holding out a large packet of thick sandwiches, "but they're nothing very special."

"What are they?" asked the pigman in a tremulous voice.

"Marmite," said the winchman, and then leapt back in surprise as, with a great grunt of delight, the pigman snatched the packet from his hands, tore off the wrapping, and stuffed the whole wad in his mouth.

The crew of the helicopter watched silently as the pigman chomped and chawed with his strong yellow tusks, his big nostrils flaring, his little eyes tight shut in ecstasy.

"No wonder he's fat as a pig," thought the pilot.

"Talk about greedy as a pig," thought the observer.

"Blowed if he doesn't look like a pig," thought the winchman, as with a last snort of pleasure the pigman finished the Marmite sandwiches and ran his tongue over his three chins in search of crumbs.

And almost as though he were reading the crew's thoughts, the pigman suddenly shouted, "Pigs!"

"What d'you mean?" cried the crew, jumping back nervously.

"Pigs. My pigs. Out there." The pigman gestured towards Resthaven.

"They must be fair starved. Got to get grub to 'em. Got to get my meal-shed back somehow."

They explained to him that they had dropped food, enough to be going on with, they thought, and then the pilot said, "That hut thing we sighted—where we pulled you out of the water—is that your meal-shed?"

"That's her," said the pigman.

"How did it get there?"

"She floated."

"Well," said the pilot. "How about us towing the thing back for you? If it floated down, it might float back. No use to you down there."

So they left the pigman with dry clothing, and lifted away downstream. On their way to the dam, they passed the black-and-white duck flying towards the farm.

Felicity landed on her perch in the alder tree and looked about her. In the distance she could see the herd in Resthaven. They were lying about in the sunshine, apparently contented. Way beyond them she could just make out the figures of the Squire and Mrs Barleylove sploshing homewards. Near to her, the pigman was hard at work sweeping the last of the water from the sties, and bringing dry bedding straw from the top of the barn where the flood had not reached it. He was a picture in navy blue overalls and flying boots. Everything's returning to normal, she

365

thought to herself. Except for the meal-shed, but that's asking a bit much.

But it wasn't, for before long she heard the rattly voice of the great strange bird, and there beneath and behind it was the meal-shed, stately as a galleon, coming slowly upstream on the end of a long tow-rope.

At the dam, both winchman and observer had gone down the cable while the pilot hovered, and had

fastened ropes both around and under the shed as though tying up a giant parcel. Now, close by Felicity's alder tree, the winchman released the tow-rope, re-fastened the cable to the top of the parcel, and raised his hand.

Gradually the meal-shed rose out of the stream, timbers creaking, open door swinging, sailed over the buildings, and was lowered, gently, exactly, on to its foundations. The ropes were released and drawn up, and once again the flying machine dropped down into the yard.

"OK?" shouted the pilot to the pigman. "All right now? All your pigs back?"

"I'll just check," yelled the pigman, and he walked out into Resthaven.

Five minutes later he was back at a run, his big face white and his fat cheeks wobbling.

"My dag! My little dag!" he shouted. "He's not come home!"

"Dag?" cried the pilot.

"Yes! The one who saved my life!" roared the pigman, and a couple of tears came out of his piggy eyes and ran down his cheeks and over the hills and valleys of his three chins.

"Oh, is that what he's called?" yelled the pilot. "Well, don't you worry, old chap. We'll nip back and see where he's got to. He's probably swimming home," and away they went downstream again.

CHAPTER 19

A Sudden Awful Fright

When the Squire and Mrs Barleylove had started home from the dam, they had given Daggie permission to go on ahead of them. They did not believe he could come to any harm on the fast-drying bank. He's a big boy now, and sensible, they said to each other.

But like any adventurous youngster, Daggie decided not to do what he had been told, but something much more exciting instead.

"Let them go home by land," he said loudly, as soon as he was out of earshot, "I'm a swimming pig, and I'm going to swim home."

He hid himself until he saw the meal-shed sailing by, and until his mother and father had passed him and disappeared. Then he slipped into the water.

The current was still fairly strong but he was confident he could swim against it; still he thought he would start in a quietish place, a deep inlet that was out of the main run of water. He glided out from the bank, but instead of going straight into his usual racing crawl, he decided to have a splash and a play.

368

He put his head under, and found himself staring into a pair of cold hard eyes, set behind narrow wolf-jaws, and backed by a long barred body.

Before he could move, there was an explosion in the depths beneath him, he felt a violent blow which almost lifted him out of the water, and the pike had clamped its jaws on the end of his snout.

In an agony of fear, Daggie pulled back with all his strength, thrashing and flailing in the water as he strove to get free. But the pike was bigger than he,

and stronger than he, and its cruel teeth were tight in his tender nose, and he could not breathe. Gradually he grew weaker, and gradually the fierce fish pulled him deeper, and his mind began to spin, and a whole series of faces flashed across it, all in a split second. His Mammie's face, and the faces of his father the Squire, and his kind aunts, and the servant, and Felicity. And before his whirling senses became a blank black emptiness, there sounded in his ear a thin hard cry.

"I-zaak!" it seemed to say. "I-zaak!"

When Daggie Dogfoot came to himself, there was still a face in front of him. But this time it was a real face, a live face, a round whiskery face wearing a look of deep anxiety. And out of it came a worried voice.

"Old pig! Old pig!" the voice said. 'You're all right, aren't you? You're all right? Now don't say you ain't 'cos you are."

Daggie looked about him and found that he was lying in the grass by the brookside. He sicked up a lot of water and lay panting, his whole body shaking with shock.

"Ike!" he croaked. "Oh, Ike! What happened? What was it? Oh, my nose! And the back of my neck!"

"What happened, old pig," said Ike, "was that you came pretty close to being drowned and eaten, and don't say you didn't 'cos you did. Your nose is sore because you've had a couple of dozen razor-sharp teeth stuck in it, and your neck's sore because I had to haul you out by the scruff."

"But what was it, Ike? What was that dreadful fish?"

"Pike," said Ike. "That was a pike, old pig."

"But it was so huge," said Daggie. "I never knew they were as big as that. Felicity never warned me."

"She never knew either, old pig," said Ike. "That's the biggest ever. Lived in the mill-pond and got washed out when the sluice-gates burst. Dying to meet him, I've been, and now I've met him, *he's* dying!" and the otter threw back his head and shook with silent laughter.

Daggie staggered to his feet and looked down into the water. Floating there on its side was the long barred shape of the monster pike of the mill-pond, the wolf-jaws split wide in the gape of agony caused by the otter's death-bite. Between the dorsal fin and the tail was a terrible scooped-out gash.

"I broke his back, old pig," said Ike, standing beside the gazing piglet. "And don't say I didn't 'cos I did. Now I'll fetch him out and we'll eat the best of him. I'll be laughing all the way to the bank!"

CHAPTER 20

"Tidden 'Might', 'Tis 'Can'!"

Daggie was very very full. He was also, suddenly, very tired, from the strain of all his adventures, and particularly the shock of the last of them. He flopped down on the bank and rolled over into a slight hollow, so that he lay upon his back, all four legs stuck up in the air. Immediately, he fell into the deepest of deep sleeps.

Minutes passed, and in the bright evening sunshine bees buzzed and a big fat bluebottle landed neatly on the staring eye of the dead pike.

Suddenly there came a wailing mewing noise from the blue sky above, and Ike, looking up from the bushes where he was dozing, saw a solitary buzzard circling on wide wings over the sleeping piglet. It had come down from the high moors, feeding on the carcasses of drowned sheep.

The otter knew that buzzards were carrion-eating cowards, and he had no fears for Daggie's safety. If his friend did not wake, he thought, he would give it a sudden awful fright. He grinned happily.

The big hawk dropped lower. It could see below what appeared to be a very dead animal, whose belly was blown up like a drum and whose legs stuck out stiffly. Moreover, its nose was caked with dried blood.

The scavenger prepared to land, but at that moment it heard a loud noise in the distance, and a great strange bird with twinkling glassy eyes and wings that whirled above its body came clattering downstream. The buzzard flew away with a cry of alarm, and even the bold Ike slid out of the bushes and into the water, where he lay with only his mask showing and watched. The helicopter checked and the crew peered down.

"There he is!" shouted the observer. "But dead as a button by the look of him. Something's got the poor little chap. Look at the blood on his snout."

"We'd better pick him up," the pilot said.

"Death of a Hero," said the winchman.

All of a sudden the same thought occurred to the three men of the Fleet Air Arm, as they hovered above the still-broad river in their blue machine with the proud letters "R.N." upon its side. They remembered the story of Nelson's last voyage, his coffin carried upon a barge up the Thames to the Admiralty.

"Tell you what," said the pilot. "We can't float him home in state, but we can fly him. After all he was quite unique, the one and only swimming pig. Let's give him the grandest possible return to his last resting-place."

"On the end of the rescue cable, eh?" said the observer. "So that the mourning multitudes can pay their respects?"

"That's it," said the pilot. "Remember the old saying—'pigs might fly!'" and the three young men grinned at each other.

"Well, let's make a proper job of it," said the winchman. "I'll go down and strap him on—I can adjust the harness—and then I'll wait here on the river bank and you can pick me up later when you've delivered him home."

So down went the cable with the winchman, and he fitted the straps around the small spotty body, thinking as he did so that the piglet could not have been dead long, he was so warm. He raised his hand, and the helicopter lifted gently away with Daggie Dogfoot dangling thirty feet below it.

Until that moment—and only St Anthony knows how—Daggie had remained in his deepest of sleeps. Through the cries of the buzzard, and the rattling and down-draught of the flying machine, and even the harnessing of his body, he had slept on relentlessly. Indeed he had just begun to dream his old dream, of flying with his mother and father through a warm and milky sky, when the tightening of the straps and the rush of air at last wakened him to reality.

Twisting in the harness so that his little legs hung down, he saw below him, fast growing smaller, a

man on the ground and an otter in the water, staring up at him. His ears flapped and his tail whirled, and in terrified surprise he kicked like mad with all four legs, his mouth wide open as he squealed with horror. The watchers, two above him, two below, could of course hear nothing of it, but they could see that the gallant hero was in fact very much alive. Three of them grinned their relief and pleasure, and the fourth one laughed so much and rocked about so wildly that eventually he sank below the water and swallowed some mouthfuls.

But once he had come to his senses and understood that he was safely anchored to the great bird above, Daggie stopped feeling so panic stricken and began to look around. Below him, as they gained height for the homeward run, the river became a stream and the stream a trickle. Great trees shrank to the size of thistles, and far below him the swallows flew in ignorance of the miracle above. He opened wide his mouth again, but this time the unheard squeal was of excitement, of happiness, of triumph!

"Pigs might fly!" shouted Daggie, his accent growing broader as the thrill grew more keen. "Thass wot thee said, A'ntie Gobblespud, theesknow! Tidden 'might', 'tis 'can'! Theseyer pig be flyin'! So look out, A'ntie, look out the rest of ee, look out Father, look out Mammie! WEEEEEEEEEEEEEEEE! Yur Oi come!"

CHAPTER 21

Home and Dry

Meanwhile back at the farm they were indeed looking out, every one of them. The Squire had brought the herd down into the yard and called the roll, and now everyone knew that Daggie was missing, Daggie who had somehow saved them all by going for help, summoning the great clattering bird, bringing back the servant and his meal-shed. They did not doubt that it was he who had now caused the waters to go down. Probably he could not just swim in them, but walk upon them too. But would he? Would they ever see him again?

At the distant sound of the approaching helicopter every head was raised. At first they could only make out the machine itself, coming up the line of the brook, a black dot in the eye of the westering sun. But as it drew nearer they could see below it a small figure and knew themselves to be looking at yet another miracle.

And now what rejoicing broke out among the Ploughbarrow herd! How the weaners waltzed and the store pigs sported and the fatteners frolicked!

"Love him!" shouted the eight aunts, shaking their floppy ears, "if he ain't the cleverest ever!"

"Oh Squire!" cried Mrs Barleylove. "Whatever's happening? Surely Daggie can't really be flying?"

The great boar looked at her and then up at this amazing son of theirs kicking and flapping and twirling away above them.

"By St Anthony!" bawled the Squire. "He's doing better than that, m'dear. Must be something wrong with that damned thing doncherknow, and the boy's towing it in, butchered if he ain't!"

Once above the buildings, the pilot made his machine describe a couple of tight circles so that Daggie was whirled around in much larger circles, just as a boy whirls a conker on the end of its string. Felicity flew up to greet him, but he was travelling so fast that she could only catch his squeals of excitement each time he flashed by her on this most marvellous of roundabouts.

Now the helicopter was hovering steady, directly above the yard, directly above the figure of the pigman in his new navy overalls waiting anxiously below. Gradually Daggie's circles grew smaller and slower, until at last he hung still like a plumb-bob. Gently, very gently, the pilot lowered the piglet. Gently, very gently, the piglet touched down. Gently, very gently, the pigman came forward to release the straps of the harness. To do so he needed to kneel down, and the herd of course was duly impressed that at long last the servant was showing a proper degree of respect.

"Hey you, Pigman. Scratch my back," said Daggie Dogfoot. And the servant of course obeyed.

Above them all the pilot and the observer waved

their final farewells before clattering away into the sunset to pick up the winchman and set course for their base. And as they went down the stream a string of bubbles came up it, and as their racket died away a shrill clear whistle pierced the evening air, and a long low creature with a grinning whiskery face and a battery of sharp white teeth hauled out of the water by Felicity's alder and came to join the pigs.

Now everybody looked at the returned adventurer. And everybody saw his bloody nose, which only one of them knew the reason for. And everybody saw his curious puppy-like forefeet, which some of them knew about. But what everybody saw and everybody knew was that here in front of them was a Brave Hero, the only dag ever to be taken away and yet come back, who had risked his life on the swollen waters to swim for help. And that help had come, precious food from out of the skies, manna from heaven. Thanks to Daggie Dogfoot they were all home and dry.

Then the herd turned and moved contentedly away to the familiar comfort of their sties and pens and the pleasant anticipation of a good supper to come. The otter slipped back into the brook and the duck followed him. Only Mrs Barleylove and the servant still stood by the hero. The pigman brushed a great hand across his face and sniffed a bit.

"Drat me!" he said softly, and "Dang me!" and

"Blast me!" And he too turned away and went to prepare the meal.

"Happy, my baby?" said Mrs Barleylove gently.

"Oh yes," said Daggie, "but Mammie, there's just one thing I'd like to do before bedtime. Can I have a swim?"

"Of course," said his mother, and together they walked down through Resthaven to the old pool below the high bank, where the water was almost back to its usual level. The kingfisher sat once again upon his perching root, brilliant in the last light of the setting sun, and the moorhens murmured happily in the reeds. Two bathers were already in the pool.

"Coming in, Daggie?" called Felicity as she twirled and splashed in a shower of golden drops, but he was already gone, running to the top of the slope to prepare for the downhill take-off. "What about you, missus?" said the duck mischievously. "Going to have a go?"

"Blimey, old duck," said Ike softly, "that'd be a sight to see, and don't say it wouldn't 'cos it would!" and he opened his mouth very wide and rocked to and fro.

But Mrs Barleylove wasn't listening. She gave an absent-minded grunt and moved away up the field to the spot where the old oak had stood, her eyes upon her son.

And now Daggie Dogfoot turned and began to run

381

downhill at great speed, faster, faster, faster, till at last he leaped out over the high bank of the stream, and disappeared from her sight. What clever things her brilliant baby was doing in his favourite element she could not see, but she could hear the joyful squeals and the fluty whistles and the soft quot–quot–quotting noises, as he dived and splashed and raced with his friends.

And high above she could hear the cries of the homecoming rooks, as they circled in the warm air and marvelled at the miraculous skills of the amazing swimming pig.

"Cor!" they shouted to one another in awestruck admiration. "Cor! Cor! Cor!"

Also available in Puffin by

DICK KING-SMITH

CLEVER DUCK

Another hilarious farmyard tale from the master of animal stories, Dick King-Smith.

Damaris the duck has had enough of the farmyard pigs with their insults and pompous behaviour. Teaming up with her sheepdog friend Rory, the clever duck helps the pigs make a break for freedom, and sends them on a voyage of bruises, bellyaches and pignapping, to teach them a lesson they'll never forget.

Also available in Puffin by

DICK KING-SMITH

DODOS ARE FOREVER

Beatrice and Bertie, two dodos in love, are
quietly planning their future on the island
paradise that is their home, and watch the
ship approach with no thought of danger. But
Bertie is alarmed to realize that the newly
arrived giant sea-monkeys are the enemy, and
the rats they bring with them are worse still.
Does this mean the end of dodos for ever? Or
can a few brave birds among them pull off a
daring escape?

Also available in Puffin by

DICK KING-SMITH

THE FOX BUSTERS

Ransome, Sims and Jefferies were three
astonishing chickens. So exceptional were
they, that they were to become a legend to
future generations at Foxearth Farm. Not only
could they fly out of the reach of foxes, but
they found a way of defeating even the most
crafty of attacks. Their deeds would be told in
years to come by every hen to every brood of
chicks, and by every vixen to every litter of
foxcubs. For these three sisters were
the Fox Busters.

Also available in Puffin by

DICK KING-SMITH

HARRY'S MAD

**'Great Uncle George has left you what appears to have been his most cherished possession,' said Harry's father.
'What's that?' said Harry.
'His parrot.'**

Having a parrot foisted upon him, all the way from America, isn't Harry's idea of a decent legacy. He'd been dreaming of untold riches! But soon Harry discovers that his parrot has hidden talents. He's an ace at board games and crosswords, a fund of useful information and a natural mimic – something which leads to some hair-raising adventures!

'His very name guarantees quality' – *Guardian*